AGAINST
THE
CURRENT

BARRY COLE

GoodDog Publishing, LLC

DEC 1 5 2015

For information, address:

GoodDog Publishing, LLC
P.O. Box 410
Mancelona MI 49659
gooddogpublishing.net

GoodDog Publishing, LLC

ISBN: 978-0-578-16401-4

Library of Congress Control Number: 2015907550

PRINTED IN THE UNITED STATES OF AMERICA

This book is dedicated to my wife and daughters for their oceans of love, faith, and inspiration.

Other books by Barry Cole:

THE COMPANY

Contents

"One day man will connect his apparatus to the very wheelwork of the universe ... and the very forces that motivate the planets in their orbits and cause them to rotate will rotate his own machinery."

—Nicola Tesla—

Prologue

The explosion would have been big enough to engulf our entire solar system and hot enough to forge the heavier substances listed on our periodic table of elements. It was a supernova—the final act of a very old and very large star.

This particular supernova occurred somewhere nearby in our galaxy over four billion years ago, and fortunately for us, like a pollinating flower, the explosion sent forth a shower of particles toward what would eventually become planet Earth. These particles were elements, and these elements, along with other interstellar debris, coalesced into this beautiful, blue planet—our home.

Only the largest stars resolve as supernovae, and only a supernova could have produced the nucleosynthesis energy required to create the heavier elements such as iron, nickel, copper, zinc, silver, cadmium, platinum, gold, mercury, and neodymium. Neodymium is a rare-earth element first isolated in 1885. It was subsequently discovered to have a unique property of concentrating electromagnetic energy, commonly known as magnets.

Supernovae occur only after stars are billions of years old. They are rare and occur with vast amounts of space and time between these explosions. It would seem to be very lucky indeed, therefore, to be the recipient of any pollen from these rare flowers.

In addition to being fortunate enough to be in the path of these particles, the timing had to be equally fortuitous. Earth had to have been formed and molded enough to have a significant gravitational field capable of attracting and trapping the particles, but still be molten enough to concentrate these elements into deposits large enough to be later retrieved and used. So many elements arrived in the same very small window of time to a primordial planet located in the perfect proximity to a perfect star—the sun. All of this happened to not only sustain life, but also to provide that life with all of the elements required to evolve technologically and, thereby, socially and morally.

Whether it was serendipitous or by design, our planet was blessed with these various elements, which are the necessary building blocks of everything. Some elements make up our bodies, others keep our bodies alive, and still others make up the environment in which we live.

We have learned to use some of the elements, but we have not yet found a use for many of them. If experience is any indicator, unimaginable technological wonders will be revealed when we unlock the remaining secrets held by the unused elements.

Iron was an element found in ore and, once understood, used to usher in the Iron Age. This ushering brought about the Industrial Revolution and meaningful technological advancement that then resulted in the discovery of new elements— some of which are as important as iron in shaping our world and allowing our civilization to evolve.

It is possible that the next age ushered in by the elements will be the "Electromagnetic Age," or EM Age. The Iron Age was identified by having its structure or matrix founded in solids, while the EM Age will be characterized by electromagnetic waves replacing solids for structure. The discovery of properties and uses for one or more currently unused or undiscovered elements will make such EM technology possible. This technology will include energy harvested from the energy contained in the EM spectrum.

During the Iron Age, energy was primarily harvested by releasing or converting energy found in fossil fuels. In the EM Age, energy will be initially harvested from magnetic fields. The energy found within such fields is limitless and clean. Currently, science cannot explain how it got there, or how it works, but we know it exists. Just because we can't explain it doesn't mean we should ignore what it can do—but we are.

We know that two magnets can be used to create movement. Set one magnet down and slide the other magnet toward it. Depending upon the orientation of the poles, as one magnet approaches the other magnet, the fields will cause them to jump together or push apart. This is natural movement; that is, it is movement created by nature, which is free energy.

Our atmosphere results in moving air that we call wind. We use the natural movement of wind to power windmills and generate electricity. Gravity results in moving water that we call a river. We use the natural movement of rivers to power turbines that are used to generate electricity.

We readily understood the beginnings of the natural movements of air and water; therefore, creating mechanisms to harvest those energies was obvious. We do not understand the origin of the natural movement exhibited by multiple magnetic fields, so harvesting this energy is less intuitive.

In the words of President John Fitzgerald Kennedy:

We realize now that progress in technology depends on progress in theory; that the most abstract investigations can lead to the most concrete results; and that the vitality of a scientific community springs from its passion to answer science's most fundamental questions.

The EM energy that runs the universe is clean and limitless. It is everywhere—manifesting itself as magnetism, gravity, and lightning. Creating a mechanism to harvest this energy has eluded us until now. Its untapped effect will be profound, completely eliminating the need for our current forms of energy, notably fossil fuels.

Those who own and control contemporary energy sources will stop at nothing to prevent this from happening. Their shortsighted greed could stop this new technology long enough to cause the end of our civilization.

Fortunately, there are some among us willing to risk their lives and create what the world needs in spite of this evil.

We have everything we need to create a new energy source, and it would change everything—eventually taking us back to the Garden. We need to make this a global priority.

Chapter 1

2000

It is the year 2000. The new millennium was barely six months old and the world was being offered a second chance. A critical, new technology that had been discovered and then systematically suppressed for nearly a century was about to be revealed. But, unfortunately, the forces that buried the invention and its creator all those years ago were at the apex of their power and would do anything to stop it again!

Tom Craft bent down and removed the small, dusty, wooden box from between the floor joists. While bent over, the beads of sweat on his forehead coalesced into a small drop that ran off the end of his nose and exploded onto the dust covered floor. The box was heavy for its size, well crafted, and clearly designed to fit in its hiding place.

"Remodeling grandmother's house may turn out to be a good idea after all," he whispered to himself. His hands began to shake slightly as he excitedly wiped off a layer of dust while pulling back the small, brass latch that held the box shut.

Tom was standing in the middle of the beautifully appointed library of the house his older brother, Dave, and he had inherited. They were remodeling the grand old home, and Tom was there that morning following a hunch that had come to him in an extremely vivid dream he'd had last night. In the dream, he had been working on the same loose floorboard in the library when suddenly, instead of the cool stale smell of an old, empty house, the aroma of bacon and freshly baked bread permeated the air. Tom heard footsteps and turned to see a tall, dignified man who appeared to be in his late twenties or early thirties whom he knew was his grandfather coming toward him.

Tom was caught off guard and a tad scared by this "specter," because his grandfather had mysteriously disappeared back in 1913 and was declared dead long before Tom and his brother had been born. Tom had seen a few old pictures—turn of the century, posed representations—but he knew who that was standing there in living color, dressed in a morning coat. It was his mother's father, Thomas Cunningham.

Tom thought, *He looks a lot like me thirty years ago—right down to the red hair!*

Tom stood up to say something, but his thoughts outpaced his ability to speak, and before he could gather himself, his grandfather looked at him, pointed to the floor where Tom was working, and said, "You know, Tom, as far as the world is concerned, what's under that board is the *only* thing that matters."

And with that, his grandfather turned and walked away toward the kitchen.

Tom managed to spit out, "But, wait," as he looked back at the loose board and suddenly sensed that the delicious smell of breakfast had been replaced by the dusty, stale air he was accustomed to breathing in the old house. He turned back, and his grandfather was gone, along with the lived-in feel of a home. This sudden change of environment had woken him up with a start. Tom's wife, Jane, was propped up on her elbow, staring at him.

"Are you alright, Honey?" asked Jane. "Looked like you were having quite a dream."

Tom looked lovingly at her, thinking how beautiful she looked in the glow of the morning light and about how well she knew him. "You sure got that right, Sweetheart! I've never had a dream like this one before. I was with my mom's dad, Grandfather Thomas, in the old house ... . It was so real, so detailed that I could smell bacon frying! I'm gonna have to go to the house right away to check something out. You know that damn loose floorboard I need to fix in the library that creaks every time someone steps on it? My dream told me to check it out or, rather, under it! It's probably just last night's pepperoni pizza talking, but I have to go see if there's anything there."

Tom slammed down a protein drink, grabbed some tools, jumped into the car, and headed for his grandmother's old house. He was like that; if something needed to be done, it had to be done *now*. It was about a twenty minute drive in good traffic. On this brown, hazy, and hot midsummer Saturday morning, most people were home enjoying a relaxing day in the predominately white-collar part of town, so once Tom was on the expressway, it would be any easy trip north to the house.

The house was the oldest home in what was still an afflu-ent neighborhood. The surrounding landscape, together with the placement of the home and its stature, made it clear that the adjacent homes were mere interlopers—added long after the neighborhood's glory days were over. These intermeddlers were certainly worth a great deal of money and of beautiful and modern design. But it was plain to see which home was the dominant one here.

Constructed for the matriarch of one of the wealthiest families in the Midwest, the house was a three-story Victorian of intricate and magnificent design. The stately home was most certainly the result of an attention to detail found only in the best construction by the best craftsmen, with no expense spared. Each gabled peak even sported its own unique, delicately hand-carved insert. The top floor housed two gigantic bedrooms—each with a spacious porch on the front of the house that joined and acted as a roof over the front door. The second story housed four bedrooms, each with small, walkout decks on the east and west sides of the house, while the ground floor was surrounded on three sides with a wide, majestic veranda.

The oak tree-lined drive curved through a gate in a tall iron fence. The drive continued on to a huge, one-story garage that was connected to and ran most of the full length of the manor's west side. A circle of the main drive passed a brick sidewalk leading to the edge of the front porch that ushered visitors to the front door.

The house and attached garage sat on the top of a small, grass covered hill that gently rose to about ten feet above street level. The hand-forged, iron fence was stretched one hundred feet on each side of the gate and eventually terminated into a two-foot thick cedar hedge. The carefully tended front yard was strategically dotted with splendid blue spruces that made a clear view of the house impossible. The east side contained a large, stone patio replete with fireplace, barbeque, entertainment area, and shuffleboard court.

Construction of the manor house and a much smaller version of the garage were completed on the ten-acre site in 1908.

It was located close to the city, yet because of hilly geography and clever planning of streets, few even knew the secluded neighborhood with its impressive crowning jewel of a home existed. It had survived world wars, a depression, and decades of elements, but unfortunate neglect and inevitable age had brought this grand dame of a home to her knees. However, she wasn't done yet. The brothers, Dave and Tom, inherited the house upon the condition that they restore her to a reasonable facsimile of her prior glory. They took up this challenge, and using designated funds from the estate and three years of their lives, the exterior was completely refurbished, and the work on the interior was nearly completed.

Neither Tom nor Dave were carpenters, so most of the remodeling was being done by a builder they had hired. Tom would soon be sixty and had recently retired from thirty-plus years as the local high school's physics teacher and boy's junior varsity basketball coach. Dave had just sold the financial advisory business he'd created and, therefore, was also recently retired. Remodeling the house they so fondly remembered from their frequent visits to grandmother's house when they were young boys was a labor of love for them.

Tom was a tall, slightly overweight, affable gentleman of obvious sincerity and intelligence. He had bright red hair and a round, lightly freckled face with a comforting smile and warm, blue eyes that gave him an aura of goodness. As a young college student, he had earned a degree in electrical engineering, but realized soon after graduation that teaching was his true calling. So, he went back to school to become a science teacher. Tom was always interested in science - particularly physics - and his passion to understand it sparked a desire to help others to also understand it. He deeply believed that science was the only way to make the future possible; therefore, teaching it was a sacred duty to him.

Mr. C.'s students loved him, because he truly loved teaching. Teaching is one of the most unselfish acts anyone can do. As such, a love of teaching tells a lot about a person. Such a passion cannot be faked, because it is revealed in everything a dedicated teacher does. Tom was such a teacher, and so was his beloved spouse, Jane.

She was a blue-eyed enchantress with naturally curly, brunette hair and an athletic build. Jane loved the sun, the water, and all living things—save some insects. Generous of spirit and kind of heart, she was a true nature's child.

Jane and Tom met in college when Tom went back for his teaching degree. She was an art major and an extremely talented artist. An unspoken connection existed between them from the moment they set eyes upon each other. Their personalities complimented one another in a way that seldom happened with couples. It was like their souls already knew each other. Their love became deep and transcendent.

The couple were inseparable, eventually married, and had two daughters, Brooke and Chelsea. Brooke followed in her dad's footsteps, pursued an engineering degree, and taught physics at a community college in Boulder, Colorado. Chelsea, like her mother, pursued an art degree and became an accomplished artist and author, spending the bulk of her time in New York City.

Tom and Jane worked in the same school district until they retired together last year. Jane, too, was loved by all due to her love of teaching and her students. Jane and Tom were two of the best teachers the district had ever had, and their effect on at least two generations of the town's young people was profound and immeasurable.

Suddenly, though, that part of their lives was over. They came home from the retirement party to new lives. Routines, colleagues, and responsibilities changed virtually overnight. Their daughters' lives were mournfully distant—both were happy, busy, and usually seen only on special occasions. Jane focused on her art while Tom immersed himself in the remodeling of Grandma's house. With his brother Dave now recently retired, the two of them worked together on the house project, rekindling a connection their busy lives had weakened.

When Dave and Tom were young, they were very close as brothers go, so when Dave went off to college, it was an adjustment for Tom. He immersed himself in his studies, got accepted to Caltech, and the brothers pursued their separate lives—as it should be. Dave married Sally Davenport, a sweet, highly intelligent, dainty woman with the soul of an Amazon.

Sally and Dave were business majors—sharp, articulate, and result-driven. Each reached the pinnacle of their respective careers—hers corporate, his financial. Hard-working and devoted to high performance, they might never have retired if Tom's and Jane's retirements had not reminded them that it was past time. While they always kept their house in Michigan, they lived most of their lives on the East Coast as was required by their careers. When they retired, they moved back home. The brothers' lives had come full circle, and life was good. They were healthy, happy, and enjoying working on the house together.

Work was finishing on their final "punch list" of odds and

ends to finally complete remodeling the villa. Installing new kitchen appliances was all that remained, except for that pesky board in the wood flooring of the library. The floor was made of exquisite, wide, red oak boards with one—dead center in the middle of the room—that *"squeeeeked"* when stepped on. Tom resolved weeks ago to fix that damn board and planned to get at it on Saturday. It was the Friday night before that, after eating nearly an entire pizza on his own, when he'd had the extraordinary dream.

Tom having dreams about the house was not that unusual, but *this* dream was different—so real, so clear, almost like it was in high definition. He got to the house as soon as he could, removed the floorboard, and found the hidden box! He was sweating profusely in anticipation, the hair on the back of his neck stood up, and he could almost smell the bacon again. Tom quickly removed the box from its resting place and opened it.

Inside the box was a file folder that was thick and heavy with papers. It also contained a meticulously sealed postal package with a note glued to it: *DO NOT OPEN!* Tom pulled back the cover of the file folder, and a handwritten note fell to the floor. As he leaned over to pick it up, he could see his grandfather's name at the end of the writing, which read:

*"To whomever finds this file, you are now a target, and your life is in danger. The fact that you have found this box means that I have died unexpectedly, and that the **device** has been lost — until now. The contents of this file can change the world, and knowing this means that your life has now changed. Be*

wise, be careful, and you may survive! Good luck, Godspeed, and may you be more successful than me!"

Thomas Cunningham - November 24, 1913

Tom shuddered, staggered back a step, and dropped the box. He looked like he hadn't just *seen* a ghost—he looked more as if a ghost had just slapped his face! Tom, remembering the family stories, knew what this box contained and was frozen by a combination of fear, disbelief, and excitement.

"So, the old family story really *is* true," he said in a trembling voice, loud enough to startle himself. It was at this point that he realized the gravity of what this discovery meant and how his life would likely never be the same again.

The sturdy box was not damaged by the drop. In fact, it was clearly handmade in such a fashion so as to survive almost any calamity. The box was a fitting repose for the treasure that it held - if the old family story was accurate. Turning over the note, Tom noticed a sentence toward the bottom that read:

"P.S. Originally, it was my choice not to put the good of all ahead of myself. I did try to change that, but whatever happened to me was fair." T.C.

Tom felt another shudder ripple through him, as if his long-dead grandfather's hand was on his shoulder. He immediately gathered up the box and note and headed toward the back door with a quick step. Panic set in as Tom grabbed the door handle.

He thought, *Who is watching? After all of these years, is it possible someone could still be watching?* Aloud, he muttered, "If they find out I have this ... I'm screwed."

"If who finds out you have *what?*" came a voice from the shadows in the next room.

Tom immediately recognized his big brother Dave's voice and was comforted. "What's up, Fat Boy? I just stopped by to see how it was going," Dave said.

Tom's mind raced for a plausible explanation for the box, but could find none. If he told Dave, then Dave, too, could be in jeopardy, but Dave knew the old family story and had probably already guessed what the box might contain.

Dave Craft was four years the elder. This meant that the entire time Tom was growing up, Dave was already doing things *he* couldn't wait to do. Everything—from running and climbing when they were kids to little league and band when they were a bit older to high school sports and then driving! Oh, that blessed feeling of freedom that came with the ability to operate a motorized vehicle on the road; there was nothing like it. The times Dave took Tom for a ride would never be forgotten. It was a magical time, and Tom admired his older brother immensely. Dave was the first person he turned to for help when needed. And that was *now* more than ever.

Dave was everything a younger brother could look up to: popular, an excellent student, athletic, and an all-around remarkable person. He was the family and class clown who could always be counted upon to recite a topic-appropriate quote, quip, or joke. His quick wit was a useful business tool that served him well on his way to the top of the financial advisory market. Tom always sought his brother's counsel.

"Hello, Jackass. Your timing is amazing, as always," Tom said appreciatively. They had called each other "Fat Boy" and "Jackass" ever since he could remember. "This is exactly what you are surmising—it's a file from Grandpa. I just found it in the floor of the library!"

"Holy shit! Are you sure? The box does look pretty old, but, holy shit!" The magnitude of the moment hit Dave like a ton of bricks and, in turn, reminded Tom of the danger they might already be in. Tom handed Dave the note, which he read.

Dave gathered his senses. "I can't believe it's real, which means it's still a secret, which means it's still dangerous, and that really scares the crap out of me. Doesn't it scare you?"

"Down to my toes! So, maybe it falls upon us to attempt what our grandfather apparently died trying to do. Especially now, a hundred years later, this invention—if it's what I think it is—is *exactly* what our world needs. We have no real choice but to try and make this happen."

Tom stepped away from the door, slid up next to the wall, leaned over, and looked out the window. The old, affluent neighborhood was quiet and peaceful—status quo in this neck of the woods. Dave ran to the living room window to look searchingly out at the street. Between the tall spruces, a dark green minivan caught his eye. It was parked across the street and down at the neighbors. Everything was suspect now, as if the whole world was watching the house.

"We have to get it out of here," Dave said in a hushed voice. "This house would be well known to them, and our refurbishing it might have caught their attention. Every second counts! First things first—take the file folder out of its box, and I'll put it under my raincoat when we leave, which means you're driving. Leave the sealed package in the box for now. Second, put the box back where you found it and replace the board so it won't be seen by anyone snooping around the house. Now, we have to decide where to take the file. We can't take it to our homes."

Tom again looked nervously out of the window as if he expected to see someone looking in. "I know," he said, "that would put the girls in too much danger. It has to be put where no one can break into, and it can't have anyone around who could be harmed. A safety deposit box at a bank is perfect for now. I have one, so let's go to my house and get its key. The bank is open until noon."

Tom grabbed the file out of the box and handed it to Dave, replaced the box in the library floor, and carefully laid and partially nailed the floorboard back into place. They left through the back door and headed out to the driveway where Tom's car was parked.

As they headed toward Tom's house, neither of them knew what to say. They thought of the stories their mom and grandma would occasionally tell them about an invention Tom and Dave's grandfather Thomas created that had something to do with energy and how it had ruined his life and made them rich, but was believed to be the reason he disappeared. The story was a cautionary tale—a *"be careful what you wish for ..."* anecdote—laced with prideful family history. It had never been a buried treasure story. Everyone assumed the invention had disappeared with Grandpa, because no information of any kind was ever found. Now, nearly a century later, here it was.

"So, now what, Dave?" Tom asked. His voice quivered with both fear and excitement.

Dave tightened his coat around the file. "First of all, we have to hide it; then, we figure out what it is. After that, all of us have to decide whether we bury it with a shovel and then bury the shovel or take the same chances Grandpa did. Your background in physics and mine in finance will help us decide what to do, and then the girls will tell us if we're right and how to do it."

Dave had attended Yale and retired from a successful career as a financial advisor and venture capitalist. The brothers had benefitted greatly from trusts created by their grandmother, Joanna. She'd made a great deal of money from shrewd investing of the money she got from life insurance on Grandpa Thomas. However, most of the family fortune came from money and stock received from the sale of the rights to the invention.

All they were told was that the invention was so huge that it would have revolutionized the energy business and put many very large corporations out of business. One company's CEO learned of its potential and vehemently went after ownership of the invention before it could be completed and made public. Their tactics were ruthless and well organized. Eventually, the brothers' grandfather succumbed to the pressure and was paid a ton of money to sell them his rights to it so that company could keep the invention a secret. They knew that if this technology became public, their company's days were over.

Grandma Joanna didn't like to talk much about any of that with her grandsons, Dave and Tom, so most of what they knew was from their mother, Dorothy, or "Dot" as everyone had lovingly called her. Dot was the youngest of two children whom Joanna and Thomas had before *it* had come into their lives. Dot's older sister, Ethel (or "Aunt Toot," as Tom and Dave called her), married badly, got divorced, and moved back into the house. Joanna welcomed the company even though she was often away tending to her many charities or participating in "a cause," usually involving equal rights.

In 1935, when Dot was twenty-nine, she married Dave and Tom's father, Henry Craft, an engineer. They'd met at a wedding, danced all night, and stayed by each other's side ever since—it was love at first sight for them both. Tom and Dave had great parents, attended all the best schools, and had led relatively blessed lives—until now.

Grandma Joanna blamed the invention for untold misery and was always afraid that one day the curse would return. She passed in 1962 at age eighty-three and left the house to her daughters, Dot and Toot.

"Aunt Toot" was a junior high school English and math teacher at a nearby private school. While she did not have to work, she looked at it as being productive, adding to society, making a contribution to the whole—nurturing the soul.

"Aunt Toot used to spoil the hell out of us," said Dave. "Grandma Joanna was a tad 'old school,' expecting proper behavior and eating habits. Aunt Toot always had candy stashed away for us that we kept secret. She was also the one we'd tell first when we screwed up, so she could help break the news to Grandma. Aunt Toot was great!

"I think it's a really good thing this wasn't found until after they all died," he continued. "Its return would have made Mom miserable. Maybe it was supposed to be this way. Remember after Mom died, Aunt Toot said she was leaving the house to us *only* if we agreed to remodel it, which is what led to you finding it."

They pulled into Tom's garage and went into the house. Jane, Tom's wife of nearly thirty-five years, was in the kitchen. "Oh, I didn't expect you home this early ... ." She turned from the sink toward the brothers. "Oh, hi, Dave ... . What's wrong?"

"I found something at the old house, just like my dream said I would," Tom said. Dave opened his coat to reveal the file.

"What dream?" Dave asked.

"Later," answered Tom.

"Oh, God, Tom, is that ... is that ... what I think it ...?" Jane stammered.

"Yes, we think so. I need the safety deposit box key so we can hide it in a secure place, for now."

"I'll get the key for you. We can talk about it when you two get back from the bank." She quickly left the room. Tom went to the window to survey the street.

Dave rebuttoned the file into his coat. "Take a check to cash or something so our going to the bank looks normal."

"Cool," said Tom. Jane handed him the key and admonished them to "*Go, go, go!*"

On the way to the bank, curiosity got the best of Dave. He started to pull the file out of his coat.

"Are you crazy? Put that away," cried Tom. "If the successors of whomever disposed of Grandpa are still around—and I'm sure they are—we know they will stop at nothing to keep this thing from happening for as long as they can."

"Well, I'm not into disappearing. I'll feel better when it's locked up in the bank." Dave tucked the file deeper into his coat.

Fortunately, the bank was not busy. Only a few customers were around, so the brothers felt comfortable that no one was watching or had followed them. They got access to the safety deposit box and quickly put the file inside. Tom then cashed a check at a teller's window while Dave went back to the car looking for anything that seemed unusual.

On the way back to Tom's house, Dave called his wife, Sally. "Meet me at Tom and Jane's as soon as possible."

"Why? What's the matter?"

"Everybody's fine. They invited us for lunch, that's all." He didn't want to say anything over the phone that others might hear.

Sally made it to Tom and Jane's in short order and had even managed to pick up a macaroni salad on the way.

Dave looked at her flatly. "Nice salad, but we're not really having lunch. Tom found something at the old house that we need to talk about."

"Hold up, dude. That doesn't mean we can't have some lunch!" Tom retorted. Tom loved food almost as much as he loved Jane, and she felt the same.

"No lunch? Are you insane?" quipped Jane. The two considered themselves "foodies," and self-proclaimed hedonists. They loved food, dance, and drink and not necessarily in that order. "Sit," she insisted. "We can munch while we talk."

Chapter 2

1900

A disgruntled horse pulling the milkman's delivery wagon voiced its opinion outside Thomas Cunningham's window, waking him. Thomas pulled back the lace curtain his fiancee had recently hung there in an attempt to add some "womanly touches" to his drab apartment. It was dawn, and the southern Michigan city was waking to a cool but sunny midsummer's day. Already, at this early hour, the smell of horse urine, kerosine, wood, coal, and fuel oil smoke blended into a nauseating yet familiar fragrance.

The year was 1900— a new century that heralded the end of the "Gilded Age." The Spanish-American War had elevated the United States to world-power status, and the Civil War gave rise to an industrial complex with unparalleled capacity. Its industrial prowess was being unleashed as it became the world's leading steel producing nation. President McKinley ran for a second term, and many social reforms had begun to take shape. The entire nation was changing in every way possible.

Cities were growing due to the availability of electricity and transportation. Telephones were widely used, and moving pictures were another sign of progressing technology. Edison, Ford, Tesla, and many others were changing the world. It was a time when progress was constant and expected. There was a shared optimism that vibrated through the entire country. It was a society on the verge of greatness.

The Industrial Revolution shifted into high gear, and Detroit poised itself as the center for the manufacture of all things involving transportation. The abundance of natural resources, the shipping capabilities of the Great Lakes, and Detroit's proximity to many major cities made it a likely location to become a manufacturing Mecca, but it was men like Henry Ford, Thomas Edison, William H. Murphy, Alexander Malcomson, John and Horace Dodge, and William Besancon who made it happen.

Detroit's exponential growth meant that all of southern Michigan became industrialized virtually overnight. Sleepy little rural villages changed into industrial centers by the rapid erection of factories and the infrastructure to support them. This expansion brought opportunity to those with talent and drive. The middle class began to emerge, which ushered in social changes—some welcomed by those in power, and some not.

A progressive movement gained traction with proposals that included women's suffrage, minimum wage, work standards, and regulatory rates. The government was seen by some as a mechanism for controlling, reforming, and regulating the corporations in ways not done before. This was met with great resistance by the business community, men who vowed to kill any regulation of their activities. As such, this was a time of great economic and political change that naturally brought the owners and workers into conflict.

Capitalism was being defined, and battle lines were being drawn by those intimately affected by the shape it would take. Those who created the Industrial Revolution were not going to be told that there were rules they must follow, while those who worked for them demanded that the government take an active role in protecting them. Unsafe working conditions, slave hours, and slave wages were killing them.

In 1878 Thomas Cunningham was born and then raised in such a place. He saw the tiny town of his youth turned into a city of tens of thousands. Industry brought immigrants from other states and from other countries around the world. Many of these were skilled tradesmen who opened businesses of their own. Inter-urban rail lines allowed communities to flourish, spread, and engage in commerce outside of their boundaries.

A product of the Midwestern work ethic of "doing more than what was expected and then doing a little bit more than that," Thomas was accustomed to hard work. He spent his last two summers before college working in a sawmill near Grayling. "Red" they'd called him due to his red hair that he wore in a longer than usual style for the day. He stood 6'4", weighed about 250 pounds, and was the quintessential gentle giant. Even-tempered with a quick and kind smile, Red was liked by all. His bright, blue eyes were framed by his big, pink cheeks and bushy, red eyebrows. One could say that he was slightly overweight, but one probably would not want to say that to his face. After obtaining an engineering degree, Thomas went to work for a local tool and die shop.

Thomas looked out the window and thought about the recurring dream he had just had again. He asked himself if a sane person would actually commence a difficult and speculative project based mainly upon dreams. But he already knew the answer, because last night's dream was different from the other dreams. It was crystal clear and more vivid than any dream he'd had before. It all seemed to come together in his head at once; he knew the concept behind a new kind of motor would work and that it must be built, even if it took years. If it could be made, its potential was limitless and included the practically free and nonpolluting production of electricity.

Thomas thought to himself, *I don't understand why me, but I can no longer dismiss these dreams as nothing unusual. The dream last night was like no dream I've ever had. It seems like it was a sign—a sign that this project is real and must be pursued. Given what such a device would do to those invested in the fossil fuel industry, this could get a bit dicey. Is it really possible that I've been given a chance to change the world? Me? I have to see!*

The recurring dreams started a few months ago as an unarticulated goal or task that Thomas couldn't seem to accomplish or even define. It was essentially just feelings of frustration and bewilderment flowing from an inability to do something or make something. As a talented mechanical engineer—some called him an artist—Thomas was accustomed to analyzing and designing solutions to fulfill a customer's goals, needs, and requirements. He always awoke from the frustrating, repetitive dreams bathed in a cold sweat due to feelings of failure and inadequacy. The dreams had even assaulted his self-confidence, affecting Thomas's mental and physical well-being. As a graduate of MIT's metallurgy program, he was familiar with challenge, but this was becoming an obsession.

Recently, the dreams had become more focused. Two weeks ago, he dreamt that the world's oil supplies were dangerously low. His best customer had come into the shop and asked Thomas to create a new energy source—one that could generate electricity without using fossil fuels. Then, he'd dreamt that he couldn't get electricity to run his shop, so he'd hooked up a windmill to run a generator.

Thomas began to realize that he needed to create a better way to generate electricity. That was the unarticulated goal of the dreams, and his task was to design and manufacture a motor that could operate an electric generator without using the typical forms of fuel—gasoline, wood, coal, fuel oil ... . The mechanism began to take shape in his mind's eye, revealing itself to be a type of reciprocating piston design, not unlike the steam engine and older designs of the internal combustion engine. The problem was how to make the motor operate from an energy that naturally existed and did not deplete. Thomas needed a new way to force a piston to move back and forth that did not use fossil fuels. His cogent dream last night provided the answer he knew had to be right: magnets!

In this dream, Thomas watched the wind turn the blades of a windmill and felt that same wind blow him backward. He was then standing in a shallow stream watching the water turn a paddle wheel and felt that same water push against his legs. Next, he held two large magnets and felt the push or pull on his hands as he inverted one of them. All three of these sensations of movement were natural, but only wind and water had mechanisms to harvest the energy. The natural movement created by two opposite magnetic fields had never been used to produce work.

He then saw a piston made from a magnet and the inspiration filled him so completely that it woke him up. "I can use the push and pull of magnetic fields to force a piston to move back and forth!" he cried out loud.

He finally knew it could be done. Now, he had to figure out the design to make it happen.

Coincidentally, the previous month a new customer had hired Thomas to design a part of a machine for his factory that would use electromagnets to lift a small steel part and then release it at the appropriate moment. The problem was that due to the part's light weight, it would become magnetized and "stick" to the steel core of the electromagnet after it was turned off. At some point afterward, it would release, once gravity overcame the degrading magnetic field briefly acquired by the part. As this customer's manufacturing process required precise timing of the release of the part, a solution was needed to accomplish this goal.

Thomas's solution was to install an electromagnet that could reverse its polarity from positive to negative. Switching the electromagnet to "negative" immediately negated the residual magnetism in the part and caused it to release when desired. Subsequent discussions with a company that designed and manufactured electromagnets revealed that such a design was not difficult to produce.

Certainly, this project had resulted in last night's vivid dream where Thomas "saw" a piston made of a permanent magnet being driven by alternating electromagnetic fields at the top end of the piston's stroke.

The electromagnet was set to pull, and when turned on, it pulled the magnetic piston toward it. When the piston reached the top of its stroke, the electromagnet was reversed, and it repelled the magnetic piston, causing it to move in the other direction.

The basic design was now reasonably in focus, and Thomas

knew he had to build it. His thoughts turned to how it worked and what he would have to build to test the theory. He started sketching various designs, all the while thinking, *I have to capture the natural movement created by the permanent magnet in the piston and cause it to do most, if not nearly all, of the work. The electromagnet must use less energy than can be harvested from the permanent magnet, which means that the magnet has to be the strongest permanent magnet that can be made.* He knew this would take time and effort. Little did Thomas realize that his decision to pursue this invention would drastically alter his life.

Thomas was twenty-two years old and engaged to a very smart and beautiful woman he had known for most of his life. Her name was Joanna Swanson, and she taught at the school. Joanna's parents owned the local hardware store and were highly respected. Thomas's parents were friends with Joanna's parents, so the two young people first met when they were babies. While they didn't know it until they were older, they were soul mates who had luckily found each other early in their lives.

After a quick *knock*, the door to Thomas's apartment swung open. "Breakfast is ready," Joanna said as she placed a picnic basket on the table and hastily produced coffee, scrambled eggs, bacon, biscuits with honey, and more bacon. The aroma filled the tiny apartment.

Thomas grinned and kissed her good morning. "You amaze me more every day. How could you possibly know I had a craving for bacon?"

"I just know. Better eat it while it's still hot." The meal was unexpected and wonderful.

Joanna was a shapely, dark-haired beauty of extremely

high intelligence. A classic beauty-n-brains bombshell—classy, finely educated, polished, and sophisticated. Thomas was a very lucky man, and he knew it.

"I had another dream last night, Joanna."

"The electricity thing again?"

"Yeah, but this time I think I've figured it out—magnetic fields. I need a way to force a piston back and forth, and I can do that with magnetic fields or, more precisely, the effect magnetic fields have on other magnetic fields. If I'm right, magnets can be used to do it."

"To do what?"

"Create movement. As you know, there are natural forces from which we harvest energy and then use that energy to generate electricity. Movement is a form of energy, and wind is a type of naturally occurring movement. A windmill harvests wind energy to turn a shaft that is used to operate an electric generator. We capture; harness; and, thereby, harvest the energy contained within moving air. In the same fashion, we harvest the energy of moving water to operate generators large enough to provide electricity to power entire cities.

"Wind and moving water are sources of natural energy, and we have created effective mechanisms that harvest that energy to produce the electricity we need. The problem is that wind or water is not present in sufficient amounts in all places and at all times. There is a solution to this problem that must be related to how we harvest energy from wind and water. That's how nature works. One solution or discovery leads to another, and I believe we have been given everything we need to solve this problem. We just have to figure it out."

"Do you mean that everything we need, in this case

energy, exists in nature and is at our disposal, and we just have to figure out how to use it?"

"Yes, I believe that."

"Is that belief of yours faith-driven or science-driven?"

The question was very astute. Joanna could sense that Thomas was beginning to become immersed in this project that came to him in his sleep. Given the enormity of the benefit to mankind and the seemingly divine inspiration of the dreams, Thomas believed that he was on a mission from God.

"I'm not sure," Thomas admitted. "But I know somehow that the concept has to be true. Wind and water show us that natural energy exists. We just have to find a better source of natural energy that can be used anytime, anywhere. Natural movement, like wind and moving water, is what we must look for, and in my dream last night, I realized that magnetic fields also have natural movement. Now that I have found another form of natural movement, I have to come up with an effective mechanism to harvest that energy. That's where the reciprocating piston motor comes into the picture. Instead of steam or an explosion of gases to force the piston to move, I can use the natural movement from the push and pull of magnetic fields to force the piston to move."

Joanna showed a thoughtful face. "If you use electricity to operate the electromagnet, won't the motor use more electricity to operate than it can generate by operating a generator? I studied physics, and Newton's *First Law of Conservation of Energy* essentially says that you cannot create energy, and that is exactly what it sounds like you're trying to do. Simply put, a generator always uses more energy to operate than it can generate."

"True, but I believe this motor will harvest the energy contained within the permanent magnet in the piston, thereby increasing its power while reducing the electricity needed for the electromagnet. The question is: can *enough* such energy be harvested to make it worthwhile? There are a lot of uncertainties and 'bugs' yet, but I truly believe this is the right path. Maybe that makes it more faith than science."

"Yes, I think it does," said Joanna as she kissed him on the forehead.

"But it doesn't really matter," he said with a stern and determined look. "I have to try, because if I'm right, it would mean that for the first time in human history, we'll have discovered an inexhaustible energy source that will allow our civilization to endure and flourish."

Thomas went to work at the factory, all the while thinking he might be ready to open his own business. He had always known it was just a matter of time, and doing it now would give him some time to get established before their wedding next summer. Also, he could work on the invention and not have to explain to anybody what he was doing. Thomas resolved that now was the time to make his move.

On the way back to his apartment, Thomas stopped by his parents' home to talk with them about a loan to open his own business. His parents did very well in the timber business in Michigan at a time when wood generated more money here than gold ever did in California.

Thomas walked in the front door of his parents' home. "Mom? Dad? It's me. Thomas. Anybody home?" he yelled.

"I'm in the kitchen," his mother yelled back. "Your dad is

in the garage." Thomas kissed his mom on her cheek and went out to the garage to run his proposal past his father.

"I knew this day was going to happen sooner or later, that you'd want to go out on your own," his father replied after hearing his son's proposal. "I've got a building in mind. Put together a list of equipment you'll be needing. Can you stay for dinner? It's steak."

"Oh, yes, sir. I'd love to. Thank you, Father. I'll pay you back every cent as soon as I can."

"I know, son. You're welcome. It'll take some time to put it all together. You should talk to your boss in the near future. They've been good to you, and you don't want to burn any bridges. Go wash up for dinner now."

Thomas was relieved to know that his father would be helping him put his new shop together. They purchased the building and ordered equipment they could not find locally. Remodeling the building to meet new building codes took awhile. Six months later, he opened for business and started to acquire customers.

Dealing with the details of opening his new shop left precious little time to work on the design of the motor, but he could not stop thinking about it.

"You seem unusually preoccupied tonight, Thomas," said Joanna. They were seated across the table from each other in their favorite booth at their favorite diner. Even though the eatery had only recently opened, Thomas liked the place, and it soon became their restaurant of choice.

"If I could put an electromagnet at each end of the piston, the motor would be much stronger, possibly doubled. I've been trying to create a design for the piston and for the connection of the piston to the crankshaft. I just can't seem to come up with it. Sorry, Sweetheart, didn't mean to be distracted, but I thought I would be working on constructing the prototype by now and not still stuck in the design phase."

Even though he was relatively young, Thomas's reputation for being exceptional was well-known throughout the city, and he was soon expanding his facilities. This left even less time to work on the design of the motor, but Thomas constantly thought about various designs and how to make the magnets the motor would require. Time was slipping away, and no significant progress had been made.

Joanna and Thomas married in the summer of 1901, and they fell deeper in love with every passing day. Thomas's parents gave them a very special wedding present. Due to their lumber business, Thomas's parents visited Harbor Springs on Little Traverse Bay. It was a lumber boom town then, thanks to its vast surrounding woods and the Grand Rapids & Indiana Railroad Company that delivered the wood directly to the growing cities in the south.

As the timber resources began to dwindle, the railroad company saw an opportunity—the natural beauty of the area was beginning to attract tourists seeking to avoid the stifling heat and humidity of summer in the cities. The railroad began to advertise the fresh air and healing, clear, cool waters as a way to escape the sweltering heat in the congested south. Within twenty-five years, it turned the area into a large tourist destination with trains delivering nearly a thousand travelers a day during the hot summer months.

Harbor Springs became the destination for large ships, such as the *Manitou* transporting passengers from Chicago and all points in between. Trains were then used to take these tourists from Harbor Springs to Petoskey and other destinations of interest. On the weekends, these trains ferried as many as six thousand passengers a day to the many resorts and the hotel-lined streets of Petoskey.

The disembarking passengers found themselves in an unspoiled, natural paradise—crystal clear water and air surrounded by emerald hills with lakes teaming with fish. In addition to the wilderness, they could enjoy world-class accommodations at large hotels built to spoil their guests.

Thomas's parents knew that a week there was the perfect wedding present. They purchased a package that included travel and a week at a smaller (but luxurious) hotel just built in Petoskey. It was a splendid honeymoon. The day after their wedding, they took a train to Muskegon where they boarded the *Manitou* bound for Harbor Springs.

The natural harbor upon which the village of Harbor Springs is located is like no other harbor on Lake Michigan. Situated just inside the mouth of Little Traverse Bay on its northern shore, the harbor is perfectly shielded from the fury that the big lake is famous for unleashing. Many ships have met their ill-fated sinking just a few miles to the west where storm winds reconverge after circumnavigating Beaver Island. Making it to this tiny harbor—for those who knew how to find it—was all too often a matter of life and death.

The harbor was formed by a hook of land that protruded south and then east into the bay from the north shore like a crooked index finger that curled back toward the land. This natural feature creates an opening to the east that is reasonably wide and sixty feet deep right up to the shore—large enough to house any Great Lakes freighter when the gales blow. Its white sand beach and calm, pristine waters are always a welcome sight for mariners and sportsmen alike.

Upon arrival they could hardly believe their eyes or their other senses. The smell of unspoiled air had a sweetness to it that they had never before experienced; more than just clean, it was wholesome and invigorating. The water was the area's crown jewel because of its clarity and color—turquoise blue-green gave way to green, which turned to royal blue as the bay opened up into Lake Michigan.

There were as yet no improved roads to this paradise—only commuter trains that they took from the dock at Harbor Springs to their hotel in Petoskey on the other side of the bay. Upon arriving at the hotel, they discovered it was just completed. The hotel registry was still on its first page when Thomas eagerly signed their names—*Mr. & Mrs. Thomas Cunningham*—and the date: August 16, 1901.

The hotel clerk, with a very pleasant smile, added Room 1 to the signature and said, "Welcome, Mr. and Mrs. Cunningham. You'll be staying in one of our two presidential suites. The bellhop will show you the way, and your luggage will be brought up shortly."

Their week on the bay flew by and was filled with five-star meals, including Maine lobsters and French pastries. They attended plays, listened to orchestras, swam in the cool waters, and took daily excursion trains to neighboring communities. It was a trip they would never forget, and it was worthy of the celebration of the union of two soul mates.

On their last day, they were having ice cream in a parlor toward the middle of town. They were discussing what had occurred after the play, "Hiawatha," performed by Native Americans that they had attended the night before. Joanna had always been fascinated by the indigenous cultures and equally saddened by these first Americans' second-class treatment in their own home. After the play, while buying quill boxes and black ash baskets, Joanna and Thomas were approached by a very old and distinguished Indian fellow who walked directly up to Thomas and said, "The Great Spirit has put you on a path, and you must not fail. If you fail, the Earth and all her inhabitants will suffer for a hundred years!" Suddenly, the old man's retinue appeared out of nowhere and quickly engulfed him. He disappeared into the crowd before they could speak with him.

"The elderly Indian gentleman who spoke to you after the play last night seemed very dignified and had an aura of weathered wisdom. I can't stop thinking about what he said. What do you think he meant by that reference to the Great Spirit and a hundred years of suffering?" asked Joanna.

"I can't be sure, but it seemed apparent to me that he was talking about the motor. But how could that be?"

"Native peoples have deep spirituality. He may know more than we could guess."

As they were leaving the parlor, they saw a photograph of the Indian man who had spoken so cryptically to Thomas the previous night. Under the picture was written the name, "Andrew J. Blackbird. Tribal leader and area's first postmaster." Joanna and Thomas looked at each other in utter amazement and could not stop thinking about him during their trip home.

Soon, they were back to their routines, but the encounter

with the old man never left them. It caused Thomas to re-double his efforts to create the design of the motor.

Growing the business and enjoying their lives together took all of their time. Joanna decided to retire from teaching. The only thing missing was a product of their love, and she was born in January 1904. Her name was Ethel, and her sister, Dorothy, was born in August of the following year. The family moved into a comfortable home, and life was wonderful.

In his spare time, often late at night, Thomas went to the shop and worked on the motor. His primary material was aluminum, because of its nonmagnetic properties; however, it was very expensive. Not very long before, it was more costly per ounce than gold, but new production methods fortunately reduced its cost. Also, stainless steel was pricey and difficult to craft. Given the cost of the materials, Thomas spent almost another year designing the motor in an effort to avoid an expensive failure. Finally, after being unable to create a working design, he abandoned the idea of having an electromagnet at each end of the piston's stroke as unworkable.

The motor he designed had a single piston of similar shape to a conventional internal combustion engine piston—round, with a flat top and hollow bottom. Protruding from the bottom, connected to the piston with a wrist pin, was a rod connected at its other end to a crankshaft, again, in similar fashion to existing reciprocating piston designs.

Once the design was completed, Thomas ordered an electromagnet akin to the one he'd previously designed for his customer. This time, he asked the magnet company to build it not only to reverse polarity, but to do it as quickly as possible. Thomas also ordered the most powerful permanent magnet made in the size specifications he required. Lastly, he ordered the aluminum and stainless steel he'd need to construct the body of the motor and the piston. It took over six months to get the materials and nearly a year to get prototype magnets.

In total, nearly three years passed since Thomas first dreamed of using magnets and, finally, the assembly of his first prototype motor was happening. An aluminum block with a hole drilled through its middle created a cylinder that held the piston. The top of the piston contained the permanent magnet, and the bottom had the rod connecting the piston to a crankshaft. The crankshaft assembly was supported by a housing connected to the bottom of the aluminum block. At the other end of the aluminum block was the electromagnet, positioned just above where the piston's upward stroke ended. The electromagnet was operated by a six-volt battery and controlled by a hand-operated three-position toggle switch— left was "pull," middle was "off," and right was "repel."

Finally, all the parts were together, the battery was hooked up, and the switch thrown. The piston lethargically moved downward, stopped at the bottom of its stroke, and refused to go up unless helped by manually turning the crankshaft. Once it got close to the pulling electromagnet, the piston was pulled the rest of the way to the top and pushed down when the electromagnet was switched to repel. But no matter what Thomas did, the piston stopped and stayed at the bottom of its stroke!

Over the next two years, he redesigned the piston and the crankshaft, added a flywheel, and changed the stroke without success. It became clear to Thomas that this design wasn't going to work. The piston had to be pushed and pulled simultaneously from each end of the piston cylinder. Also, the electromagnet did not work fast enough, and the permanent magnet wasn't strong enough. He felt like giving up. At the same time, the demands of his business were overwhelming.

Before he knew it, the fifth anniversary of the day the business opened was upon him. Joanna asked Thomas if they should have a celebration of some kind.

"Hadn't thought much about it," he said.

"Well, you should. It's time to show your gratitude to all the people who helped with your success." Joanna was a bit aggravated, and Thomas noticed her tone. She was not a woman to be trifled with, especially when she was right.

"You're absolutely correct. I'll start putting together an invitation list right away."

The party was a huge success and was attended by his customers, employees, managers, executives, a few politicians, and many of the city's prominent citizens. The Cunninghams were certainly on their way up the social ladder, but then something happened that changed everything. That night, Thomas had another strikingly vivid dream about the motor.

In this dream, Thomas was standing next to the Indian chief he had seen in Petoskey. The chief removed a blanket covering the motor. Immediately, Thomas saw that the permanent magnet was contained within a housing that was supported by, and moved along rods connected at each end to a housing that contained the electromagnets. Also, he saw that the piston housing had a wishbone-connecting rod attaching it to the crankshaft. The wishbone rod attached on either side of the piston housing, allowing the piston to travel freely between electromagnets. When he awoke, he immediately sketched the design.

This was the design he had been trying to develop for years and, suddenly, there it was! Thomas knew he could build this design, but when could he find the time? And how could he get the magnets he needed to make it work?

Over the next five years, he sporadically designed, built, redesigned, and rebuilt the moving parts for the motor and experimented with the magnets that were being designed and built for him. The magnets had many difficulties: first, there were the electromagnets that had to be capable of quickly reversing polarity with the flip of a switch. Then, there was the permanent magnet in the piston housing; it had to be as strong as current technology allowed and extend a positive field from each open face of the housing. In the summer of 1911, word finally came from the magnet company that all of the prototype magnets for the most recent design were ready.

Hugh Simmons, the president of United Oil Company, finished reading the report and sat back in his chair. Then, he stood and walked to the oversized window with its commanding view of the city below. "This is huge," he said to his assistant. "Put together a meeting of the Board of Directors for tonight in my office at 7:00."

The assistant trotted out of the room, creating a mental list of the very powerful people she had to contact with the news that their evening plans had just changed.

Simmons thought about how he was going to present this information to the Board.

Hubert Andrew "Hugh" Simmons was a sly, old fox who had been with United Oil for decades. He led the company through its transition years and was feared by all of his competitors. The Board trusted him implicitly. And that made him very powerful.

"I had to cancel our dinner reservation at Ivan's, and my family is not pleased," the Board chairman said to Hugh when they all arrived at the company's headquarters for the meeting. "This had better be good."

"It is—or could be—if we're careful. Please, everyone take a seat, so we can get started. As you all know, we have been funding research to see if it is possible to make a more powerful permanent magnet. Our R & D men feel that we could use such a magnet in a variety of applications—from drilling to transporting oil and gas. Recently, one of these facilities found that the element, neodymium, has shown great promise. They believe that when combined with iron and other elements, it will result in a new type of permanent magnet many, many times stronger than anything we have now.

"Coincidentally, last month, I had the opportunity to learn of an unpatented invention that is attempting to harvest energy from a permanent magnet. So, I sent our 'reconnaissance' people to investigate its potential because of our related research and because of the possible effect such an invention could have on our business.

"I've just finished reading their report, and I believe that it is reasonably possible that this invention, if enhanced by the theoretical neodymium magnet that only we know about, could result in a magnetically fueled motor that could replace the combustion engine and make fossil fuels obsolete. Our R & D men agree with this assessment.

"If we get out ahead of this, we can control and suppress this technology, hopefully, long enough into the future to use up the oil supplies that we've already purchased. If we do this right, we can keep control over it and prevent it from happening, at least until we want it to happen. However, if we don't act now, sooner or later, we will be out of business and bankrupt."

An uncomfortable silence fell on the room as everyone digested the importance of what was just revealed to them. Simmons had an uncanny ability to be at the head of the line when it came to developing trends. The company was one of the first to know about Henry Ford's plans to construct large assembly line plants to build his new "Model T." This gasoline-powered automobile was affordable, reliable, abundant, and soon to be copied by many others; all this combined to rapidly increase the demand for gasoline. And gasoline required great amounts of oil to produce.

The company's primary product in the past, kerosine, had seen a dramatic drop in sales due to the increasing use of natural gas and electricity. Simultaneously, they saw an increase in the demand for gasoline (a previously less than desirable by-product from the manufacture of kerosine) due to the increasing use of internal combustion engines in a variety of applications, especially automobiles.

Simmons believed the only way for the company to survive was to adapt to changes in demand before their competitors did. "Get out ahead of them, and then use that advantage to take them down," he advised the Board. The automobile created a huge demand for gasoline, and acquiring most of the rights to the newly discovered oil in Texas would insure the company's dominance in the commodity. Hugh Simmons talked the Board into betting everything on it.

It was ten years ago that the company leveraged all the assets they owned to lease all of the mineral rights they could get. Their efforts made the company the largest owner, by far, of such leases in the U.S. They had bet everything on gasoline being the fuel of the future, and their bet was beginning to pay off—big time. They gobbled up most of their competitors and were poised to become the most powerful company on the planet. The possibility of a motor that could cheaply produce electricity without fossil fuels was the last thing they wanted to hear. "Every effort has to be made to stop this technology in its tracks. We control the neodymium research and can probably suppress any further advances toward the creation of such a magnet for a long time to come, but that still leaves the motor that would use it. We need to launch a campaign to force the inventor to sign over all rights to us, including an airtight confidentiality agreement preventing him from telling anyone about it. He can't fight in a burning house, so we must light his life on fire. We must break him and sign him before this gets out of hand," Simmons said.

Thomas looked over the piston housing he'd just finished by inserting into it the new permanent magnet. Next, he slid the housing onto the housing support rods. The piston housing now contained the largest, most powerful permanent magnet that he could afford to have made. Thomas then finished connecting the two, new electromagnets to the battery.

That should do it; this design has to work, he thought. Thomas connected the toggle switch to the housing and aligned it with the trip bars he had just attached.

"Ready ... . Ready to see if it works," he whispered. He flipped the switch controlling the electricity to the electromagnets and *bam, bam, bam*, the piston came to life, reciprocating back and forth between the two electromagnets at each end of the piston. "Yes, yes, it works! It works!" Thomas cried as he danced a jig he called his *happy dance* around the prototype. He was looking at the world's first functioning magnetic, reciprocating piston motor. "It *really, really* works!"

He thought, *Now, if it will turn a crankshaft and if I can get a strong enough magnet in the piston, it might even be able to harvest enough of that energy to run itself and something else —like an electric motor in a car.*

This would make it possible to generate electricity anywhere without having to constantly add fuel and without creating the pollution caused by fossil fuels. A game-changer, indeed, he reasoned.

Thomas decided that his next step was to talk with a lawyer about patenting his invention. Certainly, oil companies would want to steal it or do what they could to prevent it from becoming a reality. The lawyer had to be someone he trusted, and the only patent lawyer he'd ever met he didn't trust. Thomas had the occasion to build a part for a customer who was in the process of getting a patent on that part. This brought him into contact with the customer's patent attorney whom Thomas found to be a little shady and very expensive.

Thomas happened to be building this customer's part at the same time he was working on the design of the electromagnet for his magnetic motor. After discussing his concept in very vague terms with that patent attorney, Thomas decided to hire a partial patent search regarding the electromagnets to see what similar designs might exist. While expensive, the search was very useful and revealed that no similar design had been patented and that the existing designs attempting to operate off the same forces were worthless.

Given the magnitude of what this invention could do, coupled with the results of the brief patent search, Thomas decided that maybe he didn't need to hire a patent attorney to do a full search. This invention would change the world and, therefore, would be well-known by now if it had already been invented by someone else and, besides, he could never afford the cost. Thomas was left with the obvious choice.

I'll call Bob, he thought.

"Bob" was Robert Connors, Esquire, and Thomas's business and family attorney. Ever since Thomas had gone into business, he'd hired the consistently competent counselor to do anything and everything he needed. Hiring a patent lawyer to do a search and then write a patent application was something only the very rich could afford.

"I bet Bob could write the patent application, and he might do it in return for owning some of it. I'll go see him tomorrow."

At the close of the board meeting, Mr. Simmons looked at those sitting around the meeting table. "We found out about this invention through someone who had access to information in a patent attorney's office. Our information is that this office is not pursuing a patent at this time. Hire that firm immediately; find something for them to do—anything. We just want to create a conflict of interest, so they can't represent the inventor against us. Do the same thing with every decent patent attorney in the area.

"Regarding the inventor, this project should assume first priority. Devote all of our resources to it. Hold nothing back. It should be just like our takeover of Abacus Oil Company. Remember? Use the same people and strategy. Drain the inventor's resources by suing him in every way possible. Attack his personal life, his family ... and when he's completely demoralized, prove to him that it's not worth the fight.

"Toward that end, we need to bring all of our science people to bear to create an argument that the invention will never be useful. We need to present proof that this thing cannot work!" he yelled, red-faced, pounding his fist on the table. "The last thing we need is a new energy source!"

Chapter 3

Disclosure

The rapid, measured *clop, clop, clop* of the horse-drawn ice wagon was heard as it hurried down the cobblestone street. It was a beautiful fall morning, and the trees, especially the sugar maples, were putting on their much-anticipated annual color show. The dew was getting heavier with each passing day, and the air had a brisk feel about it that was a subtle reminder of the winter cold that was to come.

But not today, thought Bob Connors as he walked from his home to his law office a few blocks away. *Not today.*

Today was autumn in all its spectacular, visual glory—red, orange, burgundy, yellow, and green—set against a deep blue sky. The smell of fallen leaves drifted on the dew-laden air, and the robins warbled their farewell song. Everyone seemed to acknowledge with a smile and a spring in their step the gift from Mother Nature of this incredible day.

"Hello, Bob. Another beautiful day," the postman said. He handed Bob his mail and then strode off on his familiar route.

Bob went into his office through the back door and heard his secretary, Cynthia, talking with someone in the reception area. He knew he did not have any appointments scheduled this morning, so he stayed in his office to avoid getting caught up in an unscheduled office call. Bob needed to finish an answer to a complaint and get it filed before the approaching deadline; however, Cynthia soon poked her head in his doorway.

"Thought I heard you. Thomas Cunningham would like to see you as soon as possible," she said sheepishly and in a hushed voice. "I know you're busy, but he really wants—needs—to speak with you." Cynthia knew that if her boss had a deadline to meet, he could be brusque and, initially, Bob was aggravated, but then he smiled.

"Alright. I am busy, but I'll be right out," he said.

After forty years of practicing law, Bob knew the value of taking time to talk with people who came to his office unannounced or without an appointment—no matter how busy he was at that moment—especially people for whom he had done work in the past. His practice had grown with the town that had grown alongside the neighboring city.

Despite increasing demands, Bob remained a solo practitioner of the law and resisted the trend to grow his business as large as he could. *A handful of good clients is better than a room full of bad ones,* was his motto. Good clients were hard to come by, and Thomas was just such a client. Drafting the answer to that complaint could wait an hour or two. Bob entered the reception area and warmly reached out his hand.

"Hello, Thomas. I hope you are well?"

The two men heartily shook hands.

"Good morning, Bob. I need your advice to possibly help me change the world. Got a minute?"

"I think I'd better find one from the sound of *that.* Come in, come in, and let's talk." Bob was always the type of lawyer who listened. He really cared about helping people and that meant that retirement was not on his agenda. His wife, Carol, enjoyed helping with their grandchildren and great-grandchildren. Fly-fishing, family, and the law filled his life, and he was fulfilled.

The two men walked back to Bob's office.

"What's going on?" Bob asked as they both sat down.

Thomas explained the purpose of his invention and its potential in relatively short order. He was careful to reveal very little about its construction. Thomas expounded that his invention was a motor that used the kinetic energy contained in a magnet to force a piston to move. His current prototype worked in that it used this energy to cause a piston to reciprocate. Further, it empirically demonstrated that it took very little electricity to move the piston and that the piston moved with a great deal of force.

"I believe this prototype proves that the concept works," he exclaimed. "To be testable, it must turn a crankshaft so that torque, or horsepower, can be measured. Then, and only then, can I conclusively prove that the invention harvests energy—like a windmill, Bob."

"If it was most anybody else but *you* telling me this, I'd have thought they were crazy. You know I'm not a patent lawyer, so why come to me?"

"First, I trust you, and second, I need advice from an experienced lawyer with good judgment. This invention will hurt oil companies and others, so it cannot be trusted to any law firm that could be influenced by large corporations, which is all the big firms. I believe that's doubly true for patent law firms. Almost all of their business is from big companies, and this invention could completely change the fortunes of many of their clients. Nothing like this has ever happened before, so no one has any experience with how to handle it. I need smart, intuitive people helping me that I can trust, so I decided to start with you."

Since he was young, and having grown up in the town, Thomas had always known of Bob Connors. The lawyer's reputation for being very good at what he did was well-known locally and by some in the larger legal profession. A past president of the Michigan Bar Association described Bob as "A shark in a pond full of goldfish."

"Oh, my. Thanks for your confidence in me, Thomas, but you're talking about taking on very powerful people—people with resources beyond our knowledge or imagination and our ability to defend against. If your invention does what you believe it can do, it's nothing less than a new energy source. This is *historic*! Free, clean, and endless electricity would create an economic earthquake that would seismically and completely change the current financial landscape. Those who like things the way they *are* will come at you with everything they've got. Who else have you disclosed this to?"

"No one, not even my wife knows that I have a partially working prototype. Maybe I'm just getting oversuspicious, but for about the last four months now, I've had this feeling that I'm being watched, or at the very least, followed. It just seems like there's always someone behind me wherever I go, and every time I look at them, they seem to walk away. Sound crazy?"

"Who knows? I think anything is possible, Thomas. Has anyone been questioning people or suppliers that you deal with?"

"Not that I'm aware of, but there's no way of knowing. I've had a lot of time to think about the ramifications of this invention, and this has led to a healthy respect for the danger I may be putting myself and others in. Once the magnets were nearing completion, I decided to stop telling Joanna about my progress and, in fact, I told her I'd stopped working on it for awhile. I figured the less she knows about it, the safer she'd probably be. I'm not sure what else I can do to keep the girls and her safe. The same is true for you, Bob, so I won't be telling you any more than I have about how it works."

Thomas had decided that the knowledge of the final design—the only one that worked—was where the *real* danger lay. While it was a relatively simple design, it had eluded him for years. He had to keep it secret to avoid putting anyone else in danger. This secrecy, however, came at a cost, the dearest of which was the gulf that opened between Joanna and him due to his quiet preoccupation and mysterious absences into the early morning hours.

If he wasn't working on the motor, what was it? she wondered. Her question would haunt him later.

"Bob, you're the only other person who knows that I have a partially completed prototype and that the concept of using magnetic fields to move a piston actually works. Now, I'm trying to hook it to a crankshaft so that I can test its power and prove that this motor harvests more energy than it takes to operate it. Once that's completed, I intend to attach the motor to a generator that will, in turn, run the motor and a set of lights.

"If the motor can run itself and have power left over, it would prove—by simple observation—that it is, in fact, a new source of energy. That may be a long way off, so I'm wondering if I should file a patent application on what I've done so far, but I'm sure I don't want to talk with a patent lawyer about it. What do you think?" Thomas was out of breath.

"My, my, this *is* astounding. I thought I'd seen, or at the very least, heard it all. You're trying to change, hell, save the world, and you've come to me for help. I'm flattered, but as I said, way overmatched. Nonetheless, I'll do what I can. Few people have the opportunity to make a difference for all, and such an opportunity should never be forsaken. So—I'm in! Now, let's discuss a patent." Bob was fired up and determined to help. "While I'm not a patent attorney, I know a little bit about them and the process to obtain one.

"The idea of a patent is to provide the public with knowledge of an invention or process, while protecting the proprietary rights of the inventor. It allows the knowledge to be shared with the world while reserving the right to make money off of it to the patent holder. This helps promote the process of improving or creating inventions using the prior work of other people. Getting a patent requires that the subject matter be unique and useful. The application process for this type of invention is complex, and it would definitely require a patent lawyer.

"Unfortunately, the patent system can also be used to prevent the use of technology if that is the desire of the patent holder. Also, the patent laws can be used to question who is entitled to the patent. As such, challenging the ownership of patents is a very common way of tying up the use of the technology for years, with eventual victory usually going to the litigant with the deepest pockets. Because we know the fossil fuel industry will do this, applying for a patent would tell them all of your design secrets and provide them with a forum to tie you up in court for years!

"Nope ... no. I suggest you document all of your work and

once it's written down, put it in a package as if you were mailing it to yourself. Be sure to completely seal the package, and place stamps on all the packing seams. Take it to the post office and have it postmarked. Don't *ever* open it. The postmark will prove the date of the package's contents for future use, if needed. This could be crucial if the fight is over who invented it first.

"The longer we can keep them in the dark—no pun intended—the better. Once they *do* find out, they still won't have enough information to file a patent application themselves, so they'd have to come after you in our local circuit court, instead of federal court. This distinction is very important. Patent controversies are handled by the federal district court, which would give them the home field advantage. Their lawyers appear in federal court constantly, and their lobby in Washington has some influence over the selection of federal judges. No, we don't want to fight them *there*—if we seek a patent, that would open the door for them to go after you on their home turf.

"Not seeking a patent at this time forces them to use Judge Stanley, our locally elected circuit court judge, in our courthouse, in our town. They have to come and fight us on *our* field and, Thomas, that'll make it more of a fair fight!

"Next, given that litigation will develop, I suggest we set up a corporation that'll own the invention and to help protect your personal assets from any such lawsuits. I'll get started on that right away and have a courier deliver the documents to your shop tomorrow."

"That sounds good. Thank you," said Thomas. "Meanwhile, I'll keep working on the motor and working on keeping it secret. I'll be in touch. By the way, if all that litigation gets really expensive, would you be interested in taking some share of stock in the new corporation as payment?"

"Hmm, maybe … . We'll talk later about that. What I'll be doing at this point won't be that much. You just worry about you and staying safe. I'll contact you in a few days."

Thomas left Bob's office feeling much better about what he was doing and that he finally had some real help. As he rode the inter-urban train back into the city, he again felt like he was being watched. Two men got on the train car after he did, and they seemed to eye him suspiciously. Thomas was relieved to see that they stayed on the train when he got off.

Thomas opened the door to his home, and the smell of Joanna's tomato soup dominated the air. His mouth watered, and suddenly he realized how hungry he was. Their girls, Ethel and Dorothy, rambunctiously ran out of the living room to greet him. Once again, Thomas was reminded that he was the luckiest man on the planet. "Daddy, Daddy, you're home!" the girls cried gleefully.

"Hello, my lovelies!" Thomas endearingly said as each daughter grabbed a leg and squeezed tightly. Joanna stepped around the corner.

"I decided to come home for lunch today, Sweetheart. I hope that's alright?"

"From the looks and sounds of that greeting, I'd say it was *more* than *alright*. I made tomato soup and toasted cheese sandwiches. How does that sound?" asked Joanna.

Thomas scooped up each child in his arms. "Perfect." And it was. It really was.

Thomas loved his family more than life itself. They *were* his life, his source of unspeakable joys, and the centerpiece of his being. Thomas would do anything to see that they remained healthy and happy. He came home for lunch as often as he could just to spend more time with them. Every moment like this was what made his life worth living. Running his business and working on the motor were his passions, but nothing made him happier than being with "his girls." *That* was the stuff of life. The three of them were what made Thomas complete. Lunch was wonderful.

"I'm going to bake an apple pie for dessert tonight. Does that sound good?"

"You know how I feel about pie, my love ... anywhere, anytime is the right time for pie!" he exclaimed. Thomas had a zest for life, and eating was a large part of that. Joanna and he shared a love for food that was second only to their love for each other and their daughters. Pie was their special delight.

"We stopped by the shop this morning, but you were gone. Nobody seemed to know where you'd gone. Where were you?" Joanna asked. It was out of character for her to ask after her husband's comings and goings.

"Oh, I had some errands to run. Speaking of which, I should be getting back as soon as I can." He could not tell her that he had been at Bob's office, because he could not explain why, and he did not want to lie to her.

Just then someone knocked loudly on the front door. Thomas opened it, and a man in a dapper suit stood there. "Are you Thomas Cunningham?" inquired the man.

"Yes."

"Then, this is for you. Good day." Before Thomas could react, the man handed him a large envelope with the name

"Thomas Cunningham" typed on it. With that, the man abruptly turned and walked away.

"That was strange," remarked Thomas. He closed the door and opened the envelope.

"What is it?" asked Joanna.

"It looks like papers from a court. I'll take a look at them at work. I love you." He leaned over and kissed Joanna.

"Goodbye, my lovelies!" he shouted toward the living room where their daughters were playing house.

"Bye, bye, Daddy. We love you," they chorused in unison. Thomas thought to himself that their voices were the sweetest music on Earth.

Once back at the shop, Thomas went into his office to read the contents of the envelope. It was from a downtown law firm that was one of the largest in the state. He saw his name as "Defendant," but did not recognize the name of the company that was suing him. Once he began reading the complaint, he discovered that the plaintiff was the assignee of a company that he did some work for a number of years ago. It was the company that had hired Thomas to fix an assembly machine that wouldn't properly release small, metal parts. He had the magnet company create a reversing electromagnet to release the part when switched to repel. This magnet company now produced the reversing electromagnets Thomas used in the motor.

Accompanying the complaint was an *exparte* motion for a temporary restraining order and an order stating that he, "... immediately cease and desist from any use of any electromagnet capable of reversing polarity, until further order of this Court."

"What the hell? I'd better get this to Bob right away," Thomas said aloud. He grabbed the documents, stuffed them in the envelope, and left for his attorney's office.

Once again, Thomas noticed two men who got on the same train as he did and stayed with him until he got off at Bob's office location. And again, the two men stayed on the train, but this time Thomas noticed that a *different* man standing next to them got off at this stop with him. Thomas quickly walked to Bob's office and darted in the door while looking behind him.

Cynthia, Bob's good-natured and very experienced secretary, was at her desk. "Good to see you again, Mr. Cunningham. Hmm, twice in one day. Mr. Connor's in court this afternoon, but what can we do for you?"

Thomas handed her the envelope. "I received this today, and from the look of it, I thought I'd get it to Bob right away." Cynthia opened the envelope, removed the contents, and briefly flipped through the documents.

"Yes. Better get you in here as soon as possible." Cynthia reached for her appointment book and pen. "How's tomorrow at 11:00 a.m.? Does that work for you?"

"That'll work. I'll see you then. Thank you." Once again, Thomas sensed that someone followed him all the way back to his shop.

❧

Simmons looked out his window at the fantastic fall sunset. The United Oil Company building had a commanding view of the city and the valley to the west, and the president's office had *the* best vista in the building. The golden light shining from the sunset ignited the red, orange, and yellow autumn leaves—setting them ablaze. He walked over to his desk and pushed a button on the newfangled inter-office communication system or intercom recently installed.

"Can you hear me?" Simmons quizzically asked the box. Nothing happened, so he pushed another button. "Can you hear me?" Again, nothing. "Mrs. Francis!" he finally shouted in exasperation.

Simmons's office door flew open and in rushed his secretary. "Yessir?"

"This damn box doesn't work!"

Mrs. Francis kept a frozen, professional smile painted on her face. "Use this button to talk with me, sir," she explained and pushed the proper button.

"Thanks. Send in Mr. Dawson." Simmons appeared annoyed that she, a lowly office employee, understood the new communications contraption. But then again, in general, when *wasn't* he annoyed?

After showing Mr. Dawson in, Mrs. Francis returned to her desk and noticed that the intercom switch must have been left on, because she could plainly hear both men talking. While she did not mean to eavesdrop, she could not *believe* what she was hearing! She was not about to turn the "damn box" off. As Mrs. Francis sat back down at her desk, the first thing she heard her boss say to this Mr. Dawson was, "You guys did an epic hatchet job on those people over at Abacus Oil. I hope you do as well on this job."

"Yessir. He will be miserable. We found out who he's using to manufacture his magnets, and in addition to learning about the magnets he purchased, we got some bonus information. It seems he used similar electromagnets before in a job to build a parts assembly machine for one of his customers. It occurred to me that this could provide us with yet another avenue of pressure, so I met with the owner of the company. I told him that I represented a buyer interested in that assembly machine and offered to buy it together with the company's proprietary interest in the machine and its design. After acquiring their ownership, I had our lawyers draft a lawsuit alleging that Mr. Cunningham is illegally using our electromagnet design, and we got a temporary restraining order to stop him from using it. That lawsuit was served on Cunningham today, sir," said Dawson.

"Is that all?"

"Hardly," Dawson snottily answered. "We purchased the property next to his shop, and our lawyers are filing suit against him for encroachment and asking for quiet-title to a good portion of his property. Essentially, we are attacking his title or his ownership of his shop based upon its use in the past. And further, he'll soon be getting a little visit from our friends at the building department and drain commission. Also, we have a list of his current and regular customers and are now in the process of combing through our contacts to see who we can 'persuade' to do business elsewhere. Finally, we hired a lady-of-the-evening to file a paternity action against him."

"Ouch. My, my, my, you guys *are* nasty! I sure hope you never come after *me*," said Simmons as he peered at Dawson through his thick, bushy eyebrows. That look sent a chill down Dawson's spine. "I'll have our R & D boys' report that trashes his design on my desk by the end of the week. I'll let you know when and where we'll want to use that; in the meantime, full speed ahead. Keep me informed."

"Yessir, of course." As Dawson left, he noticed Mrs. Francis turning off the intercom.

That next week, Thomas was served with the complaint for encroachment and seeking quiet-title from the new owners of the adjoining property. Before he could get that complaint to his attorney, the building inspector barged in and ordered that the building's electricity be shut off until a laundry list of violations and repairs were completed to the city's satisfaction.

Little did Thomas know that the worst was yet to come.

Chapter 4

Defense

Thomas sat across from his lawyer's humongous desk while Bob reviewed the latest complaint alleging encroachment and seeking quiet-title that had been filed by his new neighbor at the shop. Next, Bob reviewed the Notice of Violation of Building Code that shut off the electricity to Thomas's shop.

"Two lawsuits *and* an administrative action in less than two weeks," Bob muttered. "I'd say you've made some extremely powerful people extremely nervous, and I'm betting it's an oil company or two. Regardless, this kind of effort tells me that someone believes your invention is a real threat to them. They are turning up the heat to make you as uncomfortable and as desperate as possible to take the fight out of you. I think we can expect a low-ball offer in the not- too-distant future. The question becomes, just how 'low' are they willing to get? And, by low, I mean nasty!

"Regarding the magnet lawsuit, we have a hearing next week on the temporary restraining order, or TRO, as they're known in my world. Essentially, if we are successful, the TRO will be dissolved, and you can resume work on that part of the motor. If we lose, the restraining order becomes a prelimi-nary injunction until further order of the court. That would mean you must discontinue work with the reversing electro-magnet for now."

Bob continued. "To win this motion, the plaintiff must

convince the court that they will suffer irreparable harm if you are allowed to continue using the electromagnet while this lawsuit is pending. I don't think they will be able to do that because 'irreparable harm' means that they'd have to show that money is inadequate to recompense any such harm. In a nutshell, they can't even point to any harm, let alone show that money damages could not compensate them for any harm they might show.

"In other words, we should be able to get the restraining order lifted, so you can continue your work for now. However, you would have to stop if we ultimately lose the lawsuit and the court rules that they *do* have proprietary rights over this design of electromagnet. We'll worry about that later. In the meantime, we can expect extensive discovery."

Thomas looked puzzled. "What does that mean?"

"It means a lot of time and annoyance answering and objecting to questions about everything! First, in written form called 'interrogatories.' Then, face to face in testimony called a 'deposition' taken before a court stenographer. It takes a lot of time and, therefore, costs a lot of money. Plus, it'll happen in both suits to make it as expensive as possible for you."

Thomas said that he understood and explained that he didn't have a lot of extra money due to the high cost of materials and parts. "I would like to trade stock in the new corporation to cover your services, if you're willing. How about ten percent"

"I think ten percent is more than fair as long as you cover all of my out-of-pocket expenses, which will mainly be the cost of a private investigator. We need to know as much as possible about who these people are and what they have done to manufacture these lawsuits against you. I know just the guy! He's a former detective in the Chicago Police Department who now lives here. His name is Matthew Springer—Matt. He's very good and will help us figure out what is really going on here. He's a bulldog of a PI."

Thomas left Bob's office feeling a little better about his ability to cover the costs of everything. Paying attorney fees might cost more than he could afford, what with the cost of the materials and parts for the motor, and those *lawsuits* ... . Having to explain these expenditures to Joanna without her suspecting anything was weighing on his mind. Thomas's top priority was protecting the girls, so he simply could not tell Joanna any of this.

The worry over the lawsuits and keeping the girls safe was more than Thomas could handle. To stay sane, he had to keep his mind off it as much as possible. He immersed himself completely into hooking up a crankcase to the piston. Drawing after drawing were crumpled and tossed aside. Then, in the middle of the night, Thomas began sketching a cylinder on each side of a crankshaft—one pushing, while the other one pulled.

"That's it!" he cried, "That's the key to causing and keeping continual rotation—one on each side, a two-cylinder motor using four electromagnets and two permanent magnets, with the crankshaft in the middle!"

The next few weeks brought promise and new hope. Thomas finished the multi-cylinder design, and Bob was sounding confident about being successful in getting the court to dissolve the restraining order. Getting it dissolved would allow Thomas to order the new set of electromagnets needed to build a two-cylinder prototype. This second generation motor would have a cylinder on each side of a crankshaft so that more electromagnets were needed. Thomas was convinced this design would greatly enhance the efficiency and power the motor could produce, but he had to wait until the court hearing to find out if he could continue.

Finally, the day for the court hearing arrived. Thomas was nervous. A lot was at stake, and it was their first courtroom skirmish. He was not quite sure what to expect, and walking up the courthouse steps to the two large doors added to the suspense.

The doors opened into a foyer with a marble floor and two swinging interior doors that opened onto a small flight of stairs. The marble stairs led to a wide hallway that opened to various parts of the building. Straight ahead was a wide, wooden staircase with a landing at the top that serviced stairs on either side leading up to the second floor.

Bob stood on the landing. "Up here, Thomas." The stair steps creaked in protest as he ascended each one to where the barrister was juggling an armful of law books. "We're a bit early, but grab that briefcase for me, please, and we can go into the courtroom to wait our turn. Before we do, any questions?"

"If we have a few minutes, tell me more about what to expect in there." Thomas pointed to the courtroom door with trepidation.

"Sure, sure. In Michigan the circuit court holds the highest trial court jurisdiction. It hears only the more serious matters, such as felonies and civil suits of higher dollar values. It also is the only court that has what's called 'equitable jurisdiction.'

In essence, this means the court can do something because it is *right*, in spite of the fact that the law says differently.

"Over hundreds of years, this concept has resulted in a number of well defined equitable remedies that only the circuit court can enforce. These remedies include the issuance of TROs and injunctions ordering you to stop working with the electromagnets, as it did here."

"But, Bob, I didn't even get a chance to tell the judge *my* side. How can that be fair?"

"The Order the court issued is actually called an '*ex parte* temporary restraining order.' The term '*ex parte*' means that it was issued without the presence of the other party to the lawsuit. The term 'temporary' means it will automatically dissolve in this case within fourteen days or sooner if so ordered by the court. Defense is the name of the game at this stage of the litigation.

"If the plaintiff wants to continue the restraining order past that point in time, they must show the court that another order called a 'preliminary injunctive order' should be entered. That's what today's hearing is about.

"The law requires that they must show to the court that if the act prohibited in the TRO is allowed to recommence while the lawsuit is pending, they'll be damaged in such a way that a mere award of money would be inadequate to compensate them for the damages they'd incur from even a temporary removal of the prohibition.

"It's a very, very difficult thing to do. Their argument is that they own the design, and you experimenting with it may result in your coming up with an invention that uses it before they do. It's quite ludicrous, frankly. I'm surprised the court even granted the TRO. In no way should it now grant a preliminary injunction.

"We should go in now," Bob said as he nodded toward the courtroom doors.

County courthouses are a source of local pride, and each is built to outdo the ones in the adjacent counties. This county's courthouse was no exception. It was the centerpiece of local government, and the circuit courtroom was the cynosure of the courthouse. It was opulent and ornate.

Thomas and Bob walked up to two giant wooden doors that swung open from the middle of the entrance. They appeared to be ten feet tall with the upper halves enclosing large, smoked glass windows. Each door was at least four feet wide with polished wooden inserts occupying the bottom half. Oversized brass plates met in the center about chest high. The door on the right read *CIRCUIT COURT* in gold-plated lettering.

Bob pushed open that door, gestured to the left, and whispered, "Let's have a seat."

They walked over to a row of uncomfortable looking wooden chairs—Joanna would have called them 'marquis de Sade' quality—facing the center of the room and sat down. The court was in session, and the judge was addressing a fellow wearing black-and-white striped jail garb.

The circuit courtroom is used to do the most serious things the state government can do. Everything from sentencing a person to life in prison to awarding a verdict with life-changing consequences. It is where ultimate power is wielded, and it is, therefore, a room designed to intimidate and demand submission.

It begins with the presence of at least one armed police officer and continues with the oversized jet-black robe worn by the judge. Then, the construction of the room takes over with the elevation of the judge's desk—the bench—situated high above everyone else in the room. Oversized State of Michigan and American flags frame the bench and add an air of omnipotence.

In this particular courtroom, the gigantic entry doors were positioned directly across the room from the judge's bench, creating an aisle bordered by chairs facing the bench. A wooden partition, or bannister, about three feet high bifurcated the room and marked the separation between the gallery and the court's area. Two small, swinging doors on the partition—where the aisle ended—were made of the same wood.

Just on the other side of this partition, between it and the judge's bench, were two massive tables separated by about the same distance as the width of the aisle that led to the little doors. Each table had six chairs facing the bench. To the right of the tables and against the wall was a box shaped by the same bannister that enclosed twelve wooden chairs facing the center of the room. It had two rows of six chairs each. The back row was elevated about a foot over the front row of chairs. This was the jury box.

Not far from the jury box was a much smaller witness box, with one chair elevated a step above floor level. It was connected to the side of the judge's bench that was elevated about three feet above floor level.

The judge's bench in a circuit courtroom was usually as ornate as the county could afford. This one appeared to be handmade from local black walnut trees. It was dark and impressive. Connected to the bench on the other side from the witness box was a lesser and lower desk occupied by the court's clerk.

In front of the bench, positioned between the witness box and the judge was a small desk made from the same wood next to an equally small but comfortable looking leather chair. This was where the court stenographer sat with her bizarre looking stenographic machine that looked like a truncated typewriter. It was the stenographer's job to type every single word uttered in court.

Thomas saw the prisoner's striped pant legs shake as he quivered uncontrollably in them. The judge looked down at him and said, "Breaking into a home is a serious offense to this Court. It insults our community's senses of safety and security, and this is the second time you have been caught. It is the sentence of this Court that you be remanded to the Prison Commission for a period of ten to fifteen years in the Jackson State Prison. That is all."

The court clerk stood and said, "The next matter before the Court is *E-M Technologies, Inc. versus Cunningham, case number 11-2107.* The parties shall step forward and be heard."

Bob rose to his feet, and Thomas followed him through the little wooden doors to the table on the left. Behind them, an entourage of six lawyers filed to the chairs at the table on the right. Each produced a briefcase full of files and books that they meticulously spread on the table.

The judge was an older gentleman of obvious intelligence and experience. He had been on the bench for over twenty years and was one of the most respected jurists in the state. He was known for not suffering fools or bullshit. He expected counsel to know the law and accurately state the facts. Judge Archibald M. Stanley reached over and grabbed the file off the top of a rather tall pile of files. He opened the file, quickly thumbed through the top layer, peered over the top of his glasses at each counsel table, and said, "The Court calls the case of *EM Technologies versus Cunningham*. Would counsel please place their appearances on the record beginning with the plaintiff?"

"May it please the Court, your Honor, Christopher A. Brown of Reed Rogers Brown appearing as lead counsel for the plaintiff." All six of them then smugly eyed the defense counsel's table.

"May it please the Court, your Honor, Robert Connors, counsel for the defendant."

"Thank you, gentlemen, the Court has read your briefs and is only interested in hearing anything not contained in your briefs. If you left something out or have something to correct, now is the time. Otherwise, we'll go directly to my ruling. Mr. Brown on behalf of the plaintiff?"

"Thank you, your Honor. My client is the owner, by assignment, of a design of an electromagnet ... ."

"I know. That is what your Complaint alleges, Mr. Brown, and that issue is for another day. Limit your argument to the issuance of a preliminary injunction, please."

"Yessir, your Honor. A preliminary injunction is appropriate in this case, because the facts will clearly show that the defendant is using my client's property illegally, that ... ."

"What damage will your client incur between now and this Court's ruling on who owns it, if any one does," Judge Stanley asked in a commanding tone.

"The defendant may create and then claim ownership of various inventions between now and then using my client's property. His unlawful use of these magnets will likely result in my client losing untold millions of dollars in inventions. His misappropriation of this technology ... ."

"The damage you point to then is that the defendant will likely invent things using what your client alleges it owns. Interesting. Mr. Connors, what response do you have?" the judge asked Bob.

"Thank you, your Honor. My response is twofold. First, the alleged damages their client points to are speculative and if they occur at all, it would be the direct result of their own inability to find applications for what they *claim* is their property. Secondly, using their term, any 'misappropriation' of a proprietary right that results in damages can be easily calculated, resulting in full and complete compensation. In conclusion, damages are unlikely, and at-law damages, if any, would adequately compensate the plaintiff; therefore, it is not entitled to further injunctive relief. And the TRO should be dissolved."

Judge Stanley pursed his lips and stroked his chin. "The law is clear that equitable injunctive relief is only available if at-law remedies are inadequate. The Court finds that plaintiff's likelihood of sustaining damages attributable to the defendant is slim to none. Further, even if such damages do occur, monetary damages would adequately compensate the plaintiff.

"Based upon these findings, the Court denies plaintiff's motion for a preliminary injunction and dismisses the TRO. That is all for today, gentlemen."

"Thank you, your Honor," Bob said respectfully. Turning to Thomas, he said, "Congratulations. Go back to work!"

Thomas immediately ordered the new electromagnets and spent the next four months building the new parts and working almost nonstop at the shop after dinner and on weekends. He made good progress, and things were going well toward the completion of the new two-cylinder prototype.

Bob set up a meeting with Thomas to bring him up to date. He told him that Matt, the private eye, had made good progress figuring out who was ultimately behind all of this. It was United Oil Company, as they had suspected, so it came as no surprise. Matt initially focused on the new neighbor who had filed the suit seeking to quiet-title. The lawsuit was based upon the fact that the building next door to Thomas's shop was much older and used to have a driveway and side lot where part of Thomas's building was subsequently built.

The private eye learned that United Oil Company was behind it all once he discovered that the corporation that purchased the property, and was named as the plaintiff in the lawsuit, was essentially owned by United Oil Company. It seems they'd sent their people to research the title and history of all of the property surrounding Thomas's shop. They uncovered the use of the prior driveway and side lot that had been used to tether horses.

Armed with this information, United Oil set up a corporation controlled by one of its vice-presidents to purchase that property. It then sued Thomas alleging that, as the successor of the prior owners of the building, it had title to that portion of Thomas's property previously used by those prior owners under the legal theory of adverse possession. This legal theory was often referred to as the "squatter's rights" law. It basically stated that if someone openly used land belonging to another, and no one told them to leave, then after fifteen years, they could claim legal title to it.

Once learning that United Oil was behind that lawsuit, it had been relatively easy to find evidence that they were behind the electromagnet lawsuit and the bogus electrical violation that closed Thomas's shop for two weeks. Bob was very successful in and out of court due in large part to the information obtained by Matt.

Thomas was encouraged by how the lawsuits were going, but he had noticed that an alarming number of his customers moved their business to other shops. He wasn't sure why until the private eye discovered a discarded telegram that told one of his customers to move their business or face foreclosure of their mortgage. The mortgage company was, of course, owned by none other than United Oil, so it was clear they were now attacking his shop directly.

Just when I believed we might be winning the battle, they turn the screws by threatening our livelihood, thought Thomas on his way home. *What is next?* he wondered.

When he got home, he opened the door and noticed that the house was mostly dark; no sounds or the familiar smell of dinner cooking.

"Joanna?" Frantically, he thought that something was wrong.

"In here." Her voice came from the kitchen, and she sounded despondent.

Thomas walked in the kitchen. "What is wrong?"

"*This! This* is what is wrong! It came in today's mail." In her

shaking hand, Joanna held out a letter to Thomas. He hastily
read the short but devastating condemnation. It read, in part:

*You cannot ignore me any longer. He is your son, and you
know it. Contact me or I am going to hire a lawyer.*

Sandy

Thomas stood there tightly gripping the letter. "I don't
know who this person is, and I certainly am not the father of
anyone's son. This is not true, Joanna. You must believe me."

Thomas stopped himself from telling her about his success
with the prototype and the resulting harassment. He thought,
*What can I say? Telling her would put her in danger, but not telling
her will put our marriage in jeopardy. I can't tell her no matter what.
The girls must stay safe!*

"You have to trust me," he said. "This is nonsense. I've
had a lot to do at work, and I cannot get it done during regular work hours. You know owning a business is a twenty-four
hour, seven days a week job. Your parents own a business, for
chrissakes."

"I know, I know. I love you and trust you when you say
that it is not true," she cried.

But Joanna knew he was not telling her something. She
knew him far too well to be fooled for a minute, and he knew
that. Thomas was so angry about this latest and most personal
attack that he could hardly contain himself.

"Please believe me." Having lied to her and the sadness of
knowing she didn't believe him, together with the sheer frustration of being unable to tell her the truth and his extreme

anger toward the people who did this, brought Thomas to tears.

His worst fears had come true. For years Thomas thought about the impact this invention would have on those invested in the oil and gas industry. Wars had been fought over control of commodities such as this. The lives of a handful of people meant nothing to them. Anyone with any significant knowledge of the technology was a danger to them. If the girls didn't have any such knowledge, they were no threat and, therefore, were supposedly safe. Thomas simply couldn't tell Joanna the truth, and that broke his heart—and hers.

The next day, Thomas took the letter to Bob to have it investigated. "Look what they've done now," he said, sliding the letter across Bob's smooth, oaken desk.

Bob read the contents. "Wow, I'm so sorry this is happening to you. These people are ruthless. They plan to take over the world, and that's no overstatement. They control the only types of energy used to fuel the industrial revolution currently taking place. Technology will demand energy, and they mean to be the only suppliers. I wonder sometimes if they might just kill us all!

"I'll contact Matt Springer as soon as I can and have him get started on this latest attack. Also, I just got this letter from the company suing you over the electromagnets. It essentially says they are aware of your attempts to build a magnetic motor, and while they believe it won't amount to much, they are willing to purchase the rights from you for $5,000.00. They would also require a confidentiality agreement to prevent you from saying anything about it."

Thomas listened intently. "As predicted, a low-ball offer

to bury the technology. I'm expecting the new magnets next week, and then I can complete the new prototype. If all goes well, I'll have a two-cylinder motor turning a crankshaft that is then capable of producing useable and measurable torque. Then, we'll know if the design actually harvests energy from the permanent magnets. If it does, we're on our way, because it will prove this is, or at least can be, a new energy source. It would be worth millions. Tell them thanks but, NO THANKS!"

The next week, another letter came that read:

Your son and I need you. You said you loved me and that you would leave her so we could be together. You had better do it!

Sandy Meadows

At least Thomas *now* had her last name, and he passed that added information along to the private investigator. Joanna was angry, extremely hurt, and simply did not know what to say—so, she said nothing.

The week after that, Thomas was served with a paternity suit alleging that he was the father of an eight-month old baby boy. The mother's name, address, and place of employment were listed in the pleadings. She lived in an upscale part of town and was the executive secretary to the president of a local steel company. Consequently, it didn't appear she was doing this for the money, which made things seem that much more credible. Also, it referred to an eighteen-month long affair, when and how the child was conceived, together with sworn affidavits from witnesses claiming to have knowledge of the affair. Finally, the suit showed a bank account opened four months ago by Thomas, and in *her* name.

It was all very specific and very professionally done. Dawson's company was the best there was at destroying people's lives, and this was some of their best work. Their documents appeared to create an airtight case capable of fooling even the most cynical observer.

Joanna was so hurt by the very convincing documentation that she wept and wondered if they should separate so that she could consider what to do. Thomas, sensing what she was thinking and knowing the girls would be safer if he lived somewhere else, proposed moving out while he gathered evidence of his innocence.

This was way too much for Joanna. She tearfully agreed that Thomas leave their family and their home. Thomas was a broken man. His heart was torn apart. The love of his life was slipping away, and the only way to protect her was to let it happen. He moved into the shop and out of the life he loved so much. Thomas often visited the children, but Joanna would seldom stay at home when he was there. She loved Thomas so much, but she could not bear the thought of such a betrayal. She ached—inside and out. It simply hurt too much to be around him.

Chapter 5

Destiny

Thomas's depression from even the temporary loss of his love created a compulsion to work. Because his business was substantially reduced by United Oil's efforts, he spent most of his time working on the motor. Ironically, this resulted in virtually a superhuman effort to get it to work and, one night, it did. Thomas flipped the master switch, the motor sprang to life, and Thomas stepped into his *happy dance*. After years of work, there it was in front of him—a twin-cylinder design turning a crankshaft and ready to measure the power it produced. But how to measure it?

During his many hours of trial and error in the design of each of the many crucial parts that combined to make the world's first functioning multi-cylinder magnetic motor, Thomas resolved to finish the motor, prove that it worked (to be out of danger), and win Joanna back.

"Finish it and finish *all* of this!" Thomas said to himself. "The world won't take no for an answer once it sees that a clean and free energy source exists. Maybe it's finish it or finish *me*. Time for bed." He yawned and stretched. His back hurt.

Thomas had an appointment with his lawyer, Bob, the next morning to discuss their private eye's investigation of the lawsuits. Apparently, they had something important to discuss. Thomas hoped to hear that Matt Springer finally had proof that the paternity claim was a lie.

Hugh Simmons of United Oil finished the phone call with the lead attorney on the electromagnet lawsuit and pushed the intercom button. "Send him in, please." In stepped the one man Simmons almost feared, Charles Dawson, the mastermind behind the miseries in Thomas's life. "Good morning." He offered Dawson a seat.

"Thank you. Good morning," said Dawson in a very serious tone. "I wanted to speak to you in person because I have some very important news. It appears he's finished a working two-cylinder prototype and is in the process of trying to measure it to see if it can actually get usable energy from the magnets. Essentially, he may be on the verge of a breakthrough in a direction you do *not* want to go."

Simmons's brows were knitted. "Our scientists tell me it cannot work, and you're telling me it does. How do you know this?"

"You know I can't disclose my sources, but you can be sure that the information is accurate. It works. The only question is whether it can do anything worthwhile."

"Well, I think I'll have a talk with our research and development people nonetheless about all of that. Do you have anything else?"

"Briefly, yes, we can find no indication that they're seeking a patent at this time. And, lastly, it appears the paternity action worked. He moved out of his house and into his shop. Emotionally, he's probably at his most vulnerable."

"Alright. Thank you, Charles."

"You're very welcome, Mr. Simmons. My pleasure."

Dawson had small, sharply pointed teeth, and he smiled wickedly. "Oh, one last thing. His lawyer hired a private eye who is snooping around. I know of this man, and he's good, so be careful." Telling this Big Dog to *be careful* gave Dawson an inexplicable sense of superiority.

Simmons scheduled a Board meeting that evening to inform them of the status of this "project," and suggested they make a more substantial offer to buy the invention. Despite his lawyers' successes, he knew that Thomas Cunningham was nearly out of money and was now emotionally bankrupt.

A patent application had not been filed yet, but that could happen in the near future. Filing such an application would end up making the technology public, and that was exactly contrary to the oil company's plan to suppress the technology. Simmons thought, *If the report is true and the prototype actually works, it could be proven at any moment to be the energy of the future. However, being and proving are two different things, but Cunningham would be feverishly working on proving it.* The risk of this happening was too great. Now was the time to negotiate the best deal they could, and negotiate a deal they would!

If it became public knowledge, by patent or otherwise, that there existed a device capable of capturing, harnessing, and harvesting energy from permanent magnets, the search would be on for more powerful magnets. Inevitably, this would lead others researching neodymium to make a powerful enough magnet to allow the device to harvest a usable amount of energy. If that happened, United Oil, and all fossil fuel-related corporations, were out of business.

Thomas's attorney saw the large envelope on his morning mail pile and opened it before Cynthia could, because he had a feeling about its contents. He read the letter and thought to himself with a sly smile, *I was right! They've upped their offer to $100,000 for the invention. They must've decided to take us seriously. It's about time.*

"See if Thomas can get in here as soon as possible!" he cried to Cynthia.

After researching various ways to test the motor's power, Thomas finally decided upon a method to get some hard numbers to crunch. He decided on and was in the process of finishing a "de Prony brake" that would allow him to get a good estimate of the horsepower created by the motor. Then, he could convert horsepower into watts, and this would allow him to compare the watts used to operate the motor with watts created by the motor. If more watts were coming out than were going in, it proved the motor was harvesting energy. One more weld, and he'd give it a try, but he had to get going if he was to be on time for his appointment with Bob.

Thomas arrived at his attorney's opulent office a bit late. The dark pecan walls added to the room's sense of professionalism. Cynthia immediately ushered him into Bob's office. Standing near the desk was a tall, distinguished, middle-aged gentleman who stepped toward Thomas.

"Hello, Mr. Cunningham. I'm Matthew Springer, your private investigator. Please call me Matt."

The two shook hands. "Nice to meet you. You've done some great work for us," Thomas said.

"Thank you, but you haven't heard anything yet. I've found the witness that will sink these bottom-feeders. I've been checking into a Hugh Simmons, the president of United Oil Company, and I happened to come across an executive secretary of his, a Miss Francis, that he'd recently fired. She's not very happy with him and was eager to tell me what she knew.

"It seems they'd had that new-fangled office intercommunication system installed, and it'd been mistakenly left on during a meeting where she'd overheard Simmons and another man talking about everything they did to you. She can testify it was all fabricated just to pressure you into selling them your invention. It's the end of their lawsuits.

"Also, regarding the paternity suit, I'll be interviewing some folks soon, but it looks like she's a complete fraud. I'll have a report for you as soon as possible. Unfortunately, it'll take more time to untie this one. It's well done."

"And *I've* got more good news," said Bob. "The plaintiff in the electromagnet case has just offered $100,000 for the invention, which means that we're finally getting some respect. Incidentally, they require that no patent application be filed."

Thomas had a smug look. "Well, did you tell them to forget it, Bob?"

"Not yet, but I'm looking forward to that when I tell them about us finding that secretary." Bob had a big smile on his face.

"I have some good news of my *own*," Thomas said to both men. "I'm about to test the prototype and get proof as to whether it is actually harvesting energy. I'll let you know when I know more. Mr. Springer, it was indeed a pleasure to meet you. Bob, I'll be seeing you." He quickly left the office and went back to work on the motor. Getting proof and documenting it were the next steps to getting Joanna and the children back, and nothing stood in the way of that.

Meanwhile, Bob Connors enjoyed dictating the letter to the attorney he had just spanked in the recent circuit court hearing. The letter explained how they'd discovered and had proof that United Oil Company was the *real* party in interest in all of the lawsuits and, further, that they could prove the oil company fabricated this and other lawsuits in an effort to "persuade" his client to sell them his invention. As such, it was likely that a counter-suit for abuse of process would be filed in the near future.

The letter concluded by rejecting the $100,000 offer they'd made for the invention and settlement of the suit and suggested that the real party in interest come forward to negotiate a global settlement for all of the lawsuits. Sale of the invention was not up for negotiation. Bob also sent a copy of the letter to the lawyer suing Thomas on behalf of the company located next to Thomas's shop.

After dictating the letter, he looked up at Cynthia and said, "I'd give anything to be a fly on the wall at the office of the bastard at United Oil who gets handed this letter."

Cynthia giggled. It wasn't the first time she'd heard her boss say that, nor would it be the last.

Within twenty-four hours, Hugh Simmons read that letter and broke out in a cold sweat. *How could they have proof of what we did*, he thought to himself. Out loud he said, "Dawson."

"Excuse me, sir?" asked the secretary who had brought him the letter.

"Get me Dawson on the telephone as soon as possible," Simmons growled to her.

"Yes, sir."

"This has to be resolved soon," he whispered to himself.

Simmons knew that if the press got wind of this scandal regarding the lawsuits and, worse, the paternity farce, they might dig up the real reason for it all—the invention. That goddamned invention. This put the very existence of the company into play. He thought, *I simply have to know what their lawyer knows, and settle accordingly.* But the deal had to include the exclusive rights to the invention. That afternoon, Mr. Dawson appeared as summoned.

"Read this," said Simmons.

"I already have. It's my job to know what is happening in an effort to be proactive. But this time, I couldn't stop it. He found her and got to her before I could," said Dawson.

Hugh Simmons looked puzzled. "Who found what her?"

"Their private eye found your former executive secretary, Miss Francis. You apparently fired her for what she considers to be no good reason, and that makes her an eager witness. Normally, such a witness can be dismissed as someone simply seeking revenge for being fired. Sour grapes, you know. But I believe she did overhear our conversation about our global efforts to break Mr. Cunningham, because I saw her quickly flip off the intercom switch when I left your office. What's worse, I *know* she saw me watch her turn it off. That puts me in a very difficult position by possibly making *me* a witness against *you.* It's high time to get what you're after and settle the lawsuits."

"Well, that's easier said than done. But I have a plan for that, too. Next, I need you to find out how close they may be to blowing the lid off the paternity suit. If they discover who she really is, the whole thing will unwrap and explode in our faces. I want to know if and possibly when that might happen before it does. Also, and more importantly, we need to know if Cunningham has completed any testing on his motor. We have to know the status of his efforts. Get back to me with this information as soon as you can, Dawson."

"Consider it done. You'll be hearing from me shortly."

Simmons yelled out to his secretary. "Get me all the lawyers handling the Cunningham lawsuits right away!"

Within the hour, in his office, Simmons was seated with the two senior partners from each of the law firms suing Thomas. Simmons relayed to the attorneys the information about the witness that he had gotten that day from Charles Dawson. He informed them that negotiations by United Oil's lawyers would soon begin to dismiss the lawsuits.

"I've told you as much as you need to know," Simmons addressed the lawyers. "I want you to contact our attorney in Detroit and follow his instructions." He slid his attorney's business card to them across the vast expanse of desk. They immediately recognized the law firm and the name on the card.

Thomas put the last piece of the de Prony brake together, turned on the motor, and took readings that he then converted into watts. After numerous readings, he came up with a range of fifty to sixty watts of output. At the time, the motor used forty watts to operate. This meant that the motor was harvesting at least ten watts of power off the permanent magnets; therefore, the concept worked!

"It works! It works! Yahoo! It works!," he yelled as he again did his happy dance.

This was a historic moment, and at the moment when he realized it, a thrill coursed through his abdomen like when he was a kid being handed a new toy. Tears flooded his eyes, and for a moment, he openly wept. After all he'd been through, it was a catharsis—a purging—a cleansing.

He wiped his eyes with the thumb and index finger of his left hand while he put his pen down. He thought of all the previous inventors through history and knew how they must have felt at that moment—that singular moment—when it was revealed to them that they were right, that their idea worked. It was then and there he knew for sure that the project really was his destiny.

By harvesting and applying energy from the permanent magnets in the pistons, the motor ran on less energy than it produced. This meant it could operate a fifty-watt generator, use forty watts to operate itself, and have ten watts left over to light a ten-watt bulb—*indefinitely*! It was a scientific milestone like no other!

But ten watts wasn't enough to power anything useful. That was to say, while it did work, it was really just a toy—a curiosity that conclusively demonstrated the point, but harvested too little energy to be useful to industry. Replacing the internal combustion engine would require power, and lots of it.

It was at that time that Thomas realized he had reached the limits of his capabilities. Two insurmountable hurdles stood in his way—the switches and the magnets. Limitations in technology convinced him that he would never be able to make a motor capable of sustained operation. And even if he did, it would not be able to harvest sufficient power to replace fossil fuel-powered motors.

The mechanical switches used to reverse the polarity of the electromagnets always came apart after a few dozen revolutions. No matter how Thomas redesigned the switch, it could not handle the forces. A better switching process was needed for the motor to keep running. Some sort of nonmechanical process was required that could be invented only by the best engineers with unlimited resources.

More important than the switches, he needed a much stronger permanent magnet for the pistons. Thomas had the strongest magnets that local technology could produce, but a stronger magnet meant more energy to harvest. More energy meant more power, and this meant that the motor could then take the place of fossil fuel motors. Someday, technology would create a strong enough magnet, but without that, the motor would remain just a toy. It was time to seek help. *But where,* he thought.

It was Tuesday evening, and that was one of his nights to see Ethel and Dorothy. I'll worry about this stuff later. *Time now to see my little lovelies,* Thomas thought. This prospect made him very happy and extremely sad—all at once. Thomas was reduced to seeing them a couple times a week. And that was killing him. He heard a knock at the shop door. It was a courier with a letter from Bob with an attached letter from an attorney, a Mr. Horvath. The letter read:

Dear Mr. Connors:

Our firm represents United Oil Company who is interested in purchasing your client's magnetic motor prototype(s) and all rights he may have pertaining to the invention, conditioned upon the inclusion of a confidentiality agreement.

Only our client has the resources to determine if the design will ever be of any use. We understand that your client has exhausted his resources and has not filed a patent application to date.

As you know, United Oil Company's subsidiary owns the design rights to the electromagnets that your client is using. Selling your client's alleged interest in the invention to our client would resolve that lawsuit and others. Having us be the owner of the rights to all of the major parts would help a great deal in the motor's development.

Our client does not share your client's high expectations for this technology, but we do agree that the limits of current technology prevent it from being completed by your client. My client, on the other hand, has the resources to possibly overcome the current problems. If Mr. Cunningham really wants to see this invention become a reality, the effort should now be borne by those with the resources to determine if that is possible.

As a way to accommodate our clients' differing views of the invention's potential, in addition to a cash payment, the compensation package could include a generous stock option that your client could exercise at any time. Assuming the rights to the invention have already been transferred to a corporation, this offer would be transferrable to its stockholders in proportion to their stock.
Please consult with your client to ascertain if there is any interest in selling his alleged rights in the invention to our

client. *If so, I would ask that you create a proposed purchase agreement for my client's consideration.*

We look forward to your response, and remain,

> *Sincerely,*
> *Taft Reynolds*
> *Benjamin Horvath*

By: *Benjamin Horvath*
Its: *Senior Partner*
cc: *United Oil Company*

The accompanying enclosure letter from Bob read as follows:

Dear Thomas:

Attached is the letter that just arrived from a very large law firm. I wanted it to get to you immediately so that you could read it before we meet. I have set aside a time to meet with you tomorrow morning at 10:00. Please bring the letter with you.

Very truly yours,
Robert Connors
Robert Connors

Thomas thought, *The timing of this is amazing. Maybe I should sell. After all, I'm stuck where I'm at, and it may stay that way for a long while. This needs to end, so I can get Joanna and my girls back. That's all that really matters to me now.*

Thomas's resolve weakened. He grabbed the letters and headed toward home, or what used to be home. The sadness hit him again like a ton of bricks, but this time he had a glimmer of hope. Thomas hoped Joanna would believe him now that he could tell her some of what had been going on. This letter changed everything—and nothing.

Now that the bad men had been outed, the danger of telling her about the lawsuits was considerably reduced. At least now, he could explain why United Oil would create those lies. Thomas decided he still could not tell Joanna any specifics about the motor, if only to keep her safe. But finally —finally—he could tell her everything else. Thomas prayed that by showing her the letter from the oil company attorney, she'd believe that they had also created the lies in the paternity suit. He anxiously walked up the split fieldstone sidewalk and knocked on the door.

Joanna heard someone at the front door. She was kneading bread and quickly wiped her hands on her apron as she headed to the foyer.

"Hello, Joanna," Thomas said softly after she'd opened the door. She left him standing on the porch. "Can we please talk for just a minute? I just received a letter from my lawyer that I want you to see, because I think it will help show you that I'm telling you the truth."

Joanna frowned and looked him in the eye, seeing his sincerity. "Alright, briefly. And only because I want so desperately to believe you. Come in. Let's go to the kitchen."

After reading the letter, Joanna sat thoughtfully. "It does appear these are people capable of doing such a thing. It also shows they had a motive for doing it. But it still does nothing to refute the overwhelming evidence presented in the paternity suit."

"I know, I know. The private eye hired by my lawyer is working on that as we speak. I know it did not happen, so I also know this fellow will find proof of that. He'd been working on the lawsuits and has just recently turned his attention to investigating the woman they got to lie for them. He'll figure it out, and then we can put all of this behind us."

"Well, this helped a lot. I love you so much, Thomas, but I have to be sure." Her voice cracked with emotion, and she was on the brink of tears. He knew he still could not return home, because that would put them in danger.

"Shh, shh, now. I understand, my love. These people are experts at what they've done, but so are the people I've hired. Soon, I will prove to you that my love has never failed."

The next day as Thomas sat in Bob's office thinking about how well the previous evening had gone with Joanna, Bob came in with two cups of steaming coffee.

"A new café just opened across the street, and their coffee is wonderful," Bob said as he handed a cup to Thomas. "But you didn't come here for the coffee now, did you." It sounded like a question, but it needed no answer. "Looks like we're getting down to it. Finally, they've made your life as miserable as they could to soften you up for this moment. Do you want to sell it to them or not?"

"A year ago, I would have said no, and *hell no*. Today, I feel differently, and it's not because of all the bullshit they put me through. Now, for the first time, I doubt that I can overcome the power and switching issues that my prototype revealed. I can prove that the motor does harvest clean, free energy, and that is monumental, but the amount it can harvest remains too small to run anything worthwhile. If a stronger type of permanent magnet cannot be made, then the motor will always remain a toy.

"I know that if I sell it, they will not allow this technology to ever see the light of day again, and *that* thought weighs heavily on me. But should I ruin my life over something that may never happen? I can't take this anymore. It's been years of my life, and now my marriage ... the price is too high when it may all just be a fool's errand anyway. I'll sell, but only if they dismiss all the suits—especially the paternity suit—and provide a written acknowledgment that they made it all up."

Thomas was defiant, and his face got redder than normal. "I hate these bastards, and I know the kind of world they would make. They treat the planet like it's a garbage dump and would bend society to suffer their endless greed. This invention could have ended the monopoly they have on energy and would have allowed us to undo the damage they have done. I was afraid it was too good to be true, *that one man could possibly save the world and the future of humanity*. I'm a fool with a fool's hope." His defiance soon gave way to quiet exasperation.

"Anyone who's tried as hard and sacrificed as much as you have in an effort to make life better for all is no fool, believe me, but only you can decide if you should continue. No one can place such a burden on another," Bob said softly as he looked deep into Thomas's eyes. "I'll contact this Benjamin Horvath and tell him we are interested in a meeting to settle all of the lawsuits, but that sale of the rights to the invention is *not* up for discussion. We'll meet at his office at the soonest opportunity. I think it will be to our advantage to settle the lawsuits first and then negotiate a sale of the invention—so as not to tie them together."

"Whatever you say, Bob. Just let me know when the meeting is and where to meet up with you to get there," said Thomas.

Chapter 6

Doubt

United Oil Company's bet on gasoline proved to be even better than they could have hoped. The year was 1912. The automobile, and the industry it spawned, pushed demand for fuel through the roof. They greedily and inexorably moved toward their goal of world economic domination. This tremendous influx of capital allowed United Oil to hire the best available talent, including lawyers. Taft Reynolds was the law firm to the rich and famous. Based in New York City, the firm had offices in all of the major cities and had recently opened one in Detroit due to the burgeoning automobile industry. The principal partners at Taft Reynolds foresaw that the region would become the industrial capital of the world, and they wanted a piece of it.

The early summer day was already unbearably hot, and the air was thick with smoke when Thomas and Bob stepped off the train in Detroit at the downtown depot located at Third and Jefferson. A magnificent new depot was being constructed adjacent to the new tunnel. It would be called "Michigan Central Station" and could lay claim to being the tallest rail station in the world. Designed by the architects who created Grand Central Terminal in New York City, it was scheduled to open the next year.

The two men immediately noticed a gentleman holding a sign that read *CUNNINGHAM* standing at the back of the crowd that gathered waiting to greet disembarking passengers.

"I'm Mr. Cunningham," Thomas said as Bob and he made their way to the sign holder.

"Yessir. Welcome to Detroit. I'm Nathan, gentlemen. Please follow me."

Nathan led them to a waiting automobile and held open the back door. The auto was the largest, personal passenger vehicle Thomas and Bob had ever seen. It was a Winton Six Limousine. The driver and Nathan sat in a separate compartment from the passengers. The ride thrilled the two men, and they arrived wide-eyed at a mid-sized building in the heart of Detroit's financial district. The building was new and of a more modern design than that of its neighboring structures. It sported a large, brass revolving door entrance that was crowned by beautifully polished, brass letters that read:

TAFT REYNOLDS — ATTORNEYS AT LAW

As impressive as the building was on the outside, it was nothing compared to the opulence within. Carrara marble floors sparkled, mahogany paneled walls radiated warmth, and brass fixtures gleamed. The lobby had a thirty-foot high ceiling with tall, narrow windows along each side. At the end, opposite the revolving door, was a large desk with a sign that read "Reception." On the wall behind the desk was the law firm's insignia, "T R," recognized by everybody who was anybody. The entire building was designed for one purpose, and one purpose only—intimidation. T R was the biggest and best law firm in the country, and they wanted all who graced its interior to know it.

Thomas and Bob walked to the reception desk. "How may we help you today, gentlemen?" the receptionist inquired.

Bob cleared his throat. "We have a two o'clock appointment with Mr. Horvath," he said.

Upon hearing Mr. Horvath's name, the receptionist glanced to her left and snapped her fingers. A young woman dressed somewhat like a bellhop leapt to her side.

"Please show Messrs. Cunningham and Connors to Mr. Horvath's office. May I have a beverage brought to you gentlemen?"

"Thank you. Coffee sounds good to me," Bob answered.

"Yes, me, as well. Thank you."

The young bellhop led them to a spectacularly adorned elevator manned by an attendant.

"Mr. Horvath's office," she said as they entered the car.

The attendant nodded as he closed the elevator door and pushed the top button on the panel. The car rose quickly to the uppermost floor and slowed to a stop. The door opened to reveal a large reception room lined with tall, wooden doors. At the far end of the room was a desk flanked by sumptuous leather wing chairs. The elevator attendant motioned toward the desk, and the two men started walking toward it.

A professional looking, well dressed, middle-aged woman rose and greeted them. "Welcome to Mr. Horvath's office, gentlemen. Please have a seat. Mr. Horvath will be with you momentarily," she said.

Bob expected the perfunctory, *"I'm more important than you wait,"* and he was correct.

After about fifteen minutes, a buzzer rang on her desk. "Right this way, please."

She led them down the hallway to a pane of very tall, wide, solid mahogany doors. Opening the doors, she said, "Please go in; Mr. Horvath is expecting you."

Thomas and Bob walked into a large room obviously designed to mirror that of the ground floor lobby. The office was a tall-ceilinged rectangle of a room with long, narrow windows along each side. In the middle stood a massive mahogany table wide enough for two chairs at the ends and long enough for ten chairs on each side. At the end of the room was a mammoth matching desk facing four client chairs. Clearly, no expense was too great when it came to creating an atmosphere of superiority. The aim was to impress—and they did.

Sitting at one end of the huge conference table was a very distinguished, white-haired, older man. His face was deeply tanned and appropriately wrinkled with a big dimple in his chin. He had big, bushy eyebrows that sat perched above piercing blue eyes. "Please come in. Welcome. I'm Benjamin Horvath."

They walked toward the table and introduced themselves. Also seated on the far side next to the wizened lawyer were the two lead attorneys from the law firms who were suing Thomas. They'd had some heated exchanges with these two at depositions, so a simple *good afternoon* sufficed. They reminded Thomas of two Dobermann Pinschers told to sit and stay.

"Please, have a seat," Mr. Horvath said as a young lady dressed similarly to a waitress delivered their coffees. "That will be all," he said to her, dismissively. "I want to thank you for coming today. It is my hope that we can reach mutually advantageous solutions to what each of our clients need," he said looking at Bob.

Almost at that same moment, the intercom buzzed, and Horvath's secretary told him that Mr. Simmons had arrived. "Good," the attorney replied, "show him in, please." Mr. Horvath walked to his office door and opened it.

"Good to see you again, Hugh," said Horvath.

Simmons took the empty seat next to Horvath at the end of the table. "Hello, Ben. It looks like I'm a few minutes late," he said and reached out his hand to Bob and Thomas. "I'm Hugh Simmons, President of United Oil." He said the last part to no one in particular, yet expecting all to acknowledge his presence.

Simmons sat down and looked directly at Thomas. "The solution to everyone's problems is to agree to sell us the invention." His voice was persuasive, yet surprisingly gentle. It was immediately apparent why this man headed United Oil Company. Not only did Simmons command the room, it was clear *he* was the one to be impressed and intimidated by and that these fancy lawyers were merely his lap dogs.

Hugh Simmons then turned his stony gaze toward Bob. "You have done well advising your client to this point. Congratulations are in order; however, the time for fighting can be behind us now." He looked at the two lawyers sitting across from Thomas and Bob, both of whom were suing Thomas.

"You are both dismissed. Thank you for your service," said Simmons. The attorneys looked at each other, startled, and then looked at Mr. Horvath, who thanked them for their time and told them he'd be in touch, as he gestured toward the door.

This guy is good, Thomas thought as the two attorneys exited the room.

"Our information is that you now have a working prototype, and that you can demonstrate it harvests energy from permanent magnets. Congratulations," Simmons said derisively. "That is an amazing accomplishment. But due to the limited power of conventional permanent magnets, your device does not harvest *enough* energy to be of any use. Am I correct?"

Thomas was surprised and extremely intimidated that Simmons not only had that information, but that he appeared to be certain it was accurate.

"Don't be surprised," Simmons chuckled softly, looking into Thomas's eyes. At that moment, Thomas knew they were badly outmatched. "We know a great deal," Simmons said, looking down and folding his hands on the table, "more than you can possibly imagine.

"Your prototype has demonstrated problems that are beyond your abilities to correct, as impressive as they are. It's time to let the world's best take over. If this technology is what you think it is, it will take much more than your impressive talents to make it a reality. Please give us that chance." Simmons dramatically looked back into Thomas's eyes. That last part had sounded more like a command than a supplication.

Yet, Thomas wanted to believe every word. In a gut reaction, he said, "Thank you. That sounds great."

Bob put his hand on Thomas's arm. "Yes, it sounds good, so my client and I have much to discuss."

He then looked at Mr. Horvath. "Your letter stated that if Thomas is interested in selling, we should send you a proposed purchase agreement. No, *if* my client is willing to consider an offer, then you can draft it. I'll let you know if he's interested in entertaining *any* such offer later this week. Thank you for the coffee," Bob said. He stood and gestured to Thomas that it was time to leave. They exchanged parting pleasantries and left.

Simmons looked at Horvath. "So, this man Connors *does* has some savvy. My people tell me he has argued cases in the Michigan Supreme Court where he beat a large insurance company like it was an unruly army mule. Do *not* underestimate him! You negotiate with him, get the best deal you think you can get, and then contact me for approval. Get it done!" he shouted.

Out in the hallway, Thomas asked, "What just happened, Bob?"

Bob sensed Thomas's aggravation as they walked toward the elevators. He pushed the call button. "Once we found out all we needed to know, it was time to leave. That was one of the most powerful men in the entire world, and we currently have him where we want him.

"He made it clear he controls all the lawsuits against you and that they are willing to pay your price to control the invention. All that was left was for him to continue to take our measure, so it was time to go," said the lawyer. Plainly, Bob knew what he was doing, and Thomas smiled—comfortable in the knowledge that he had chosen the right person to help him.

Both men said little on the train ride back. They had a lot to think about and needed a more private setting to discuss matters. It was early summer, and nature had returned to life, replacing the colorless shades of winter gray with a profuse array of green. Almost as noticeable was the air. It was fresh and warm again. The stale, stinging air of winter was gone, and in its place was the sweet, oxygenated scent of flora in full blossom. It seemed to Thomas that *his* life was returning as well. Fixing his marriage and shedding the burden of the motor would be his own summer—a greening and renewal of all that was good.

They reached Bob's office in what seemed like a short amount of time. The attorney grabbed a pad and wrote some notes. After a few minutes, he looked toward Thomas. "Do you want to sell?"

Thomas had never been so unsure of himself. It was all he'd been thinking about since he'd said, "*Sounds great*" to Hugh Simmons. It seemed as if the entire world was waiting for his answer. If he sold the invention, the world would probably never hear of it again. However, continuing to try to do something that might be impossible, considering the consequences to his life, made it a lousy gamble. Most important of all, selling it to them would mean that the girls would be safe, and that was the clincher.

"I'll sell," he reluctantly mumbled. Thomas felt guilty and relieved at the same time.

"So, now we have to decide what you should ask for in return. In addition to settling the two lawsuits and dismissing the paternity action, you should be compensated for having to defend these frivolous actions and the grief they put you through. I'm thinking $100,000 just for that, together with documentation clearing title to the shop property. In return, you sign a release for all claims relating to those suits."

"But what about the written acknowledgment that it was all a lie, especially the paternity suit?"

"Well, that part may be a bit tricky for two reasons. First, unlike the two lawsuits, Simmons doesn't own the paternity plaintiff suing you; that is, United Oil owns the two plaintiffs' corporations who filed the real property and electromagnet suits, so he can make them settle *those* lawsuits. Unfortunately, they had to use a real person to allege the paternity complaint and controlling her may or may not be a problem for them. Second, such an admission, in writing, could end up in the wrong hands and be used to create a lot of damage to the lawyers, the company, and Simmons himself. Given these issues, I believe it is quite likely they will say it is a deal breaker. What do you want to do if that happens, Thomas?"

"Getting Joanna back is my priority here, and I believe having a written confession saying they fabricated the paternity suit should do it. If we can't get that, I'm not sure selling the motor makes sense. If I can't repair my life, I have nothing to lose."

"There may be another way. Our private eye is making some progress in unraveling that web of lies; he just needs more time. If he can prove it was all a farce, you won't need anything from United Oil. Besides, how much weight will Joanna give to such a writing when she knows it was part of the deal you cut with them? I think solid proof that it didn't happen will be much better than any letter."

"Thanks, Bob, you're right. Get the letter if you can, but we can still settle if they refuse. Regarding an amount, I'm thinking an even million sounds good. I want to hurt these scoundrels. And I think it makes sense to have an option to buy at least a half million in stock at today's rate. That way, if they do finish and produce the motor, myself or my heirs could still benefit from it by exercising the stock option. I'll leave it to you to negotiate over this; I just wanted you to have some parameters.

"Yet, getting the proof to convince Joanna is my top priority, so please do what you can to speed that along. Anything else, Bob?" But before Bob could answer, an intense Thomas leaned over the desk. "Do *you* think I'm selling out? Am I doing the right thing?"

"Candidly—no, no, and yes. I think we've covered the bases for now. No, you are not selling out, and yes, you are doing the right thing. The technology your invention has begun to discover has tremendous potential. I believe you have taken it as far as any one person can for now. It may be possible for you to make a more reliable switching mechanism, but creating a more powerful magnet is most unlikely. Why lose everything you have and hold dear over a mere possibility? In my opinion, you are absolutely doing the right thing," answered the attorney.

Bob was a fierce negotiator who took Horvath by surprise, despite Simmons's warning not to underestimate him. The first thing he did was obtain a sworn statement from Simmons's prior secretary outlining all that she had heard about plotting to force Thomas to sell. He then drafted a six-count complaint against United Oil that he sent to Horvath before filing it with the court.

As Bob anticipated, the first point of contention was the letter Thomas wanted that admitted the paternity allegations were a fake that they created to coerce a sale. Bob made it clear that any sale of the rights to the invention was contingent upon providing such a letter. In reply, Horvath threatened to take the deposition of Joanna.

Bob telephoned Horvath. "I got your response, and I'm calling to see if we're done trying to settle, because you should understand that any threats involving Thomas's wife ends the process. If he even knew you threatened it, he would never even consider a sale of his invention to your client." Bob surmised that Horvath was told to make the deal, so threatening to end negotiations should hit a nerve.

Horvath grew incensed at this small town lawyer with the temerity to return threats. "Do you understand the resources you are up against?" he yelled.

Bob hung up the phone while saying, "Bring it!"

Coincidentally, Simmons called Horvath just after the call from Bob. "How's it proceeding, Ben? It's been about six weeks since our meeting."

"Not good," Horvath said, and he explained that they had not even discussed any sale, because the letter regarding the paternity was a deal breaker.

Simmons started to see the end of their empire, stood up at his desk, and screamed into the phone, "Listen to me, you sonofabitch! You fuck this up, and I'll personally see to the end of your career. Is that clear enough?" With that, he slammed down the receiver.

The next few months seemed to grind by with no word from Bob. Still, an unusual peace enveloped Thomas—not working every spare moment on the motor, not constantly attending depositions or writing answers to endless questions from lawyers, not being haunted by the responsibility of having to save the world, and, most important, not worrying about Joanna's and the girls' safety—he hadn't felt this good in a long time, not since the last dream he'd had years ago on the night of the shop's fifth anniversary. Thomas thought, *Maybe this is the beginning of the end!*

The extra time gave him the opportunity to visit his beloved daughters more often and to occasionally speak with Joanna. With each visit, he could tell their relationship was getting better. Their love was too strong to simply be left behind, and the inevitability of this began to make itself known.

The following day, an exultant Bob showed up unannounced at the shop. "We got it, Thomas!" he cried.

"Got what?"

"Everything! *Everything!* Even a weak but written acknowledgment that the paternity suit now appears to have no basis in fact. Naturally, they will instruct her lawyer to dismiss the paternity suit and the other two lawyers to dismiss their lawsuits. They'll pay you $100,000 for the release of claims on the lawsuits and their related activities. They'll pay $1 million and a stock option to the corporation in exchange for the prototypes, all written material related to the invention, exclusive rights to the invention, and a nondisclosure confidentiality agreement from you, the company, and all its stockholders. This packet contains your copy of all the documents. Please read them over and meet me at nine o'clock in the morning at my office so we can go over them before they arrive at ten-thirty. We close then," said Bob.

"This is fast. What about the paternity investigation?"

"All I know is Matt is going to St. Louis to follow a lead. I expect to hear from him within the next couple weeks. I know he's going as fast as he can. I'm sorry, but it looks like they went to great lengths to set this one up, and it's going to take awhile to unravel. The people who put this together are the best, and they threw a ton of money at it. Unfortunately, it will take as long as it takes.

"Regarding tomorrow, bring all written materials regarding the invention with you, except for any letters from me. You'll have to review them with their engineer as well as demonstrate the prototype for them. After the closing, they'll go with you to your shop so you can show it to them, and they can take possession of it."

Hearing the words gave Thomas a sick feeling in his stomach. He thought, *If this is the right thing to do, why does it feel so wrong? I've never had this much doubt.*

He painted on a weak smile. "Alright, Bob, thanks, and great job."

"See you in the morning, Thomas." Bob headed back to his office to prepare for the closing.

Thomas arrived early the next morning, knowing Bob had already been there awhile. He knocked softly on the private entrance door, and Bob let him in. "I knew you'd be early, so let's get started." And with that, the two men reviewed all of the legal documents that were spread out on the gigantic conference table. Just then, Cynthia knocked on the door and said the parties had arrived. Bob told her to show them in.

Mr. Simmons entered first, followed by his lawyer, Mr. Horvath, and a third fellow who was obviously an engineer. Simmons walked directly to Thomas and offered his hand. "Congratulations. You're about to be a very wealthy man, indeed."

"Nice to see you again, sir." Thomas was nothing if not polite.

"Are we ready to begin, gentlemen?" Bob stated more than inquired.

"Certainly; however, it appears we have a slight change regarding the dismissal of the paternity suit," said Horvath.

Thomas went cold. "What change?" Bob and he asked at precisely the same time.

"We have to change the dismissal to a motion and order for withdrawal of counsel. It seems the plaintiff could not be persuaded to dismiss her lawsuit at this time, so her lawyer is withdrawing. It's the best we can do for now, but we will continue to do what we can to get it dismissed. Also, we'll cooperate with your private investigator. Finally, we have put as much as we can in the letter stating it now appears the paternity suit has no basis in fact and that the evidence available now clearly shows that her son is not your child. We hope this is acceptable, because there's nothing else we can do about it right now."

Thomas bit his tongue. He wanted to tell these people exactly what he thought of them. They created this Frankenstein of a story, and now they couldn't keep it under control. He wanted to say, "No!" He wanted to tell them to go to hell! He wanted to pound them into the floor. Thomas put the letter in his pocket, looked at Bob, and forced himself to agree. After that, all he could think of was finishing this. They signed the documents, he reviewed the written materials with only the engineer in the library, and then they drove to Thomas's shop.

Thomas wanted to make it absolutely clear to these weasels that no one, including his wife and his lawyer, knew anything about the design of the motor. Consequently, Bob did not accompany them to the shop where the prototype was hidden. Thomas had closed the shop and given his employees the day off so that no one would see the prototype. After the demonstration, they crated up the motor, and it was gone—just like that—a big segment of his life, gone in an instant.

Watching their vehicle pull away with the invention was painful.

Chapter 7

Deceived

Thomas was the country's newest millionaire, but all he could think about was taking the letter from United Oil Company stating that there was no basis for the paternity suit to Joanna. He hurried home wondering what her reaction would be. Thomas knocked on his front door, a necessary courtesy that always made him sad. Joanna opened the door.

"I know it's not one of my visiting times with the girls, but I came to see you. Please give me a little of your time."

Joanna smiled. "Of course. The girls are at my parents. I'm sorry, they aren't here, but that will make it easier for us to talk. Please come in, Thomas."

"I know how bad it looks, but you know I love you, and deep down inside, you must know I'd never, ever hurt you. You are and always *will be* my love and my life; I could never love someone else. The people who put these lies together are the best at what they do. While I could never get them to completely admit in writing what they did, I did get this letter from them as part of the settlement."

He handed the letter to Joanna as she wiped her tears with her apron. She read its contents.

"Thomas, I want to believe you, and while this helps, once again, it's not really proof of anything. I need more time."

"Of course. I don't mean to pressure you. I just want to get this behind us. I understand how you must feel. I wanted to kill that son-of-a-bitch this morning at the closing for what they have done to us.

"Someday soon, we will have proof that none of this ever happened, that this was just another avenue of attack they created to get me to sell. Well, it's sold; it's gone. So, her support from them has also ended. Without their cover, we will be able to find the truth. They all but admit that in this letter, because they couldn't get her to dismiss the paternity suit. They took her lawyer away, but she hired a new one, and they smell money. However, with the information they'll give our P.I., we'll get to the truth soon."

"I'm so glad that *thing* is gone," Joanna cried, defiantly. "It was nothing but trouble and was like a curse placed upon you. You changed, Thomas—constantly preoccupied and spending every spare moment and dime on that *thing*. I thought maybe we'd also changed, that you were gone so much because you found someone else. Now, I'm beginning to see that maybe my feelings are just another manifestation of the curse. I just hope it's gone for good."

She searched his face for a reaction.

"It is," Thomas assured her. "I've sold all the rights to it to them. It's gone. I'll be going now, but I'll be back as soon as I can with the proof you need," he concluded mournfully.

The next day, Bob contacted Thomas to stop by his office around one o'clock to sign the paperwork that finalized the transfer of the funds from the corporation to each of them. Thomas arrived promptly and was immediately taken into Bob's office.

"Hello," Thomas said.

Bob stood up and extended his hand, receiving a warm

hand shake. A bond often forms between a lawyer and client, not unlike that formed by soldiers during war. When people go through a lot together, and the struggle is intense at times, it forges a unique connection. Like war, when a lawsuit is over, everyone goes back to their lives and only occasionally have contact with their comrades in arms. So it can be with lawyers and their clients.

"Well, that's got most of it behind us. We still have to deal with the paternity action, though," said Bob. "She smells money, and I believe she thinks the lies are good enough to win the suit, or at least a very large settlement. I'm still waiting to hear if our P.I., Matt Springer, has received any information from United Oil's people, but he did report that he went to St. Louis and checked on her information about her prior employer. He said all he got was a bunch of vague answers and is convinced they were lying. I'm considering going there to take some depositions. It's one thing to lie to our private eye, but quite another to lie to me under oath."

Thomas was clearly disappointed, because he was hoping they were closer to getting the proof needed. "It will take as long as it takes, I guess." He was losing hope.

"Yes, but trust me when I say that it will be done as soon as possible. Moving on, here is your packet from yesterday's closing. It has all the documents, including the Option to Purchase Stock, which your heirs or you can exercise if and when you wish within the next twenty years. And, finally, the checks. Here is their check to you for $100,000 for the settlement of all claims relating to the two lawsuits. This is their check for $1 million to the corporation for the invention. I drafted the documents to disburse the money to the stockholders, you and me, in proportion to our stock ownership; being ninety percent by you and ten percent by me. As such, here is a check from the corporation to you for $900,000 and a check to me for $100,000. That's a total of $1 million in your hands. How does it feel?"

Thomas stood there with a blank look on his face. Bob thought of something that would cheer him up.

"By the way, I thought you should know about a house going up for sale by an estate I'm handling. It's a one-of-a-kind type of place up in the north end of the city built by a very well-heeled man for his mother about six years ago. She passed away, and the family is looking to sell it quickly. It's fully appointed with magnificent furnishings and ready to move in."

"Let's have a look. I'm really sick and tired of living in my shop, and I have nothing better to do for the first time in a long while."

Bob smiled sympathetically at Thomas. "Good, I'll get the keys. Cynthia, clear my afternoon. We're going up to look at the estate house."

On the ride up, Thomas spoke only about how much he missed being with his "girls" and how Joanna may be starting to see her way through the lies. Then, he noticed the terrain was more hilly.

"I didn't know these hills were up here."

Bob turned onto a street that seemed to appear out of a large hedge around a curve. "Oh, most don't," he said.

They were in a large, old woods that went on for a couple of miles to the north. The road wound through and around the hills so as to stay relatively level. It looked as though very few trees had been removed to make the road, with some being right next to the gravel edge. After a bit, the hills came to an end, and there it stood—the most beautiful house Thomas had ever seen.

By the time the men passed through the gates, Thomas knew he wanted it.

There could be nothing else like it anywhere in this part of the country, he thought.

A circle drive brought them to the sidewalk that serviced stairs to a porch that encompassed the front door. As they walked along the porch, the caretaker sauntered out to greet them.

"Good day, gentlemen. Have you come to look around, Mr. Connors?" the caretaker politely asked the attorney.

"Yes, yes, this is Mr. Cunningham, and he may be interested in purchasing this amazing house."

"That she is, that she is. Where would you like to start?"

The three men spent the next two hours going through every nook and cranny in the house, and it proved to be even more impressive inside than out. The house was designed and built by the best craftsmen in the country, and it showed.

On the way back to Bob's office, Thomas was unusually quiet. After a few miles of awkward silence, Bob finally asked, "Well, what did you think? I know it's a lot of house. They're asking $100,000 for it, but I know they have more than that into it."

"Make an offer of $90,000, plus $5,000 for the furnishings, on my behalf that expires in forty-eight hours. It's the perfect gift for my girls. They won't believe their eyes! It won't make up for all we've been through, but it will certainly help take their minds off it. While it's a bit of a hike from my shop,

I'm thinking of selling my business to my shop supervisor. He has the talent to make it, and I'd like to give him the chance."

They reached Bob's office. Thomas accompanied Bob into the office, so he could get his file and the checks. Bob told Thomas he'd contact him as soon as he had the owners' reply to his offer.

Thomas wondered on his way to the bank if he was being impetuous. He hadn't had the money in his hand for three hours, and he was already spending nearly ten percent of it! What good was the money other than to spend it in ways that improved life? Thomas knew he couldn't buy happiness, but he did believe money made life easier. He got to the bank just before closing and walked up to the receptionist's desk.

"Is Blaine here?"

The receptionist was annoyed due to the time, and curtly replied, "One moment, please, Mr. Cunningham."

Blaine followed her out of his office. The two men had been friends since prep school days.

"Hello, Thomas. Can someone else help you? I've got a meeting with the Board that I'm getting ready for tonight. I apologize."

"Maybe someone else *could* help," Thomas said with a broad smile as he handed Blaine the two checks.

"A million dollars! Are you serious? Hell, yes, maybe I *can* help. Please come on back." Blaine walked Thomas to his office and shut the door.

"Hmm, cashier's checks with one having United Oil Company as the payor. What'd you do? Strike oil?"

"I can't really say. I'm bound by a nondisclosure agreement. Can you help me with these?"

Blaine stared at the checks, wide-eyed, and responded, "Certainly. What did you want to do with them? You know, we couldn't possibly 'cash' them. I can deposit them and make funds immediately available up to a reasonable amount. Obviously, we don't keep that much cash here at this bank."

"My wife, Joanna, and I have a joint savings account here. Deposit the checks into that account, please. I'm considering a purchase of about $95,000 and may need that amount available in a day or two. My lawyer, Robert Connors, will let you know the specifics for payment. Now, I want to be absolutely clear about something. My wife can independently access this money without my involvement, correct?"

"Yessir, she's on the account and can withdraw any amount with only her signature. I will speak to the Board tonight about the interest rate we will pay on your account. Deposits like this are handled on an individual basis, and thank you so much for coming to *me* with it. This will certainly make to-night's meeting a great deal more fun!" Blaine blushed with a touch of lust, revealing his banker's love of money.

The next day came and went without any word from Bob. Thomas spent the day with the girls and hoped to hear that they'd accepted his offer, so he could tell Joanna about the house. It was hard not to, but he managed to make it. Joanna was clearly more warm toward him; however, it was equally clear that she was still torn about what to do. Thomas left that night feeling better and more hopeful.

When he returned to his shop, there was a message on his desk from Bob that read:

"They accepted your offer. Please be at my office tomor-row morning at 10 o'clock sharp."

Thomas arrived promptly, and the sale documents were already laid out on the conference table. Before he knew it, he was holding the keys to that magnificent home in his hand.

"You've made a really good deal," Bob told him. "Congratulations, *again*. It's been a good week for you. I'll be going to St. Louis on Monday and will be back Thursday or Friday, depending on how it goes. We should meet when I get back. I'll be in touch."

"Thank you, Bob." Thomas left the office in a hurry. He couldn't wait to tell Joanna about the house, and, optimistically, he hoped she would allow him to show it to her. He was so eager that he forgot to knock on the door of their house; instead, he just strode in.

"Joanna?" he shouted familiarly.

Joanna ran to the door. "What's wrong?"

At that moment, Thomas realized he'd just pushed his way in.

"Oh, I'm sorry; I'm so excited I forgot to knock! I bought us a house! Now, I know you're not ready for that yet, but you have to see it. Please, let me show it to you. It's probably best if the children don't see it until you're ready to move in, so there's no pressure related to getting it … . In fact, if you don't like it, I'll sell it … . I got a very good deal, so we could likely make a profit if we did … Joanna, what do you say? Will you come and see it with me?" Thomas practically begged her and was out of breath.

She feigned sternness. "You know you can't bribe me with a new house."

Oh, no! Thomas thought, but suddenly her faced softened, and she smiled.

"I know you do; I'm just pulling your leg. I'd love to see the house. I'll get someone to watch the girls."

Soon, they were on their way and spent a wonderful afternoon together, exploring one of the finest homes ever built in southern Michigan. It was truly a jewel set on an emerald mound that rose from the woods, and Thomas thought that Joanna made it shine. They were happy again, if only for the day.

When they got back home, Thomas helped Joanna from the car and walked her to the door. To his delighted surprise, she quickly kissed him on the cheek.

"Goodnight, and thank you for a wonderful day."

"You're so welcome. Good evening, my love."

Thomas bowed gallantly, like a swashbuckler, and backed away. Joanna giggled at this, turned, and went inside.

Thomas had decided he'd spent his last night at the shop and had packed his personal belongings to move into the new house. The sun set in an amazing persimmon-red glow that bathed the house and woods as Thomas arrived.

While it was certainly a large house, it could hardly be called a mansion. Indeed, it was quite small by upperclass standards. The classic Victorian structure had six bedrooms, including two master bedrooms, together with all of the customary rooms found in such houses. It was the quality, not the quantity, that made the difference in this home. The gentleman who built it could afford the best architects, engineers, carpenters, and tradesmen, and he brought them here from around the country to build this home. The result of their collective efforts was a masterpiece of design, function, and security. The more time Thomas spent there, the more certain he was that it was money well spent.

An entire week flew by before Thomas heard from Bob, and they met at the lawyer's office. Bob and Matt Springer were chatting as Thomas entered the conference room.

"So, how was St. Louis?" Thomas asked.

"Hello to you, too, Thomas. Great ribs and music! You remember Matt Springer, our private investigator, don't you? He has some interesting news. Go on, Matt."

"Yessir, I thought you'd be a bit surprised to learn that United Oil has a secret research project attempting to create a next-generation permanent magnet. Supposedly, it's been going on for quite awhile, and they are rumored to have made some significant progress. So, it would seem that the whole time they were telling you that a stronger magnet was either impossible or years away, they were, in fact, developing one."

"Those scoundrels deceived me. They knew the technology existed to make the motor work and covered it up," surmised Thomas. "I guess I shouldn't be surprised. The next question is, how can we find out what new technology they have?"

"I'll see what I can do. Industrial espionage isn't my specialty, but I know people we can hire. We should be able to find out something. These 'skunk works' types of projects have a very high level of security. It'd help if I had about three thousand in cash to spread around."

"That's not a problem. Bob will get you what you need — just get results. Speaking of that, what have your men got for me on the paternity suit?"

The private eye glanced at his file notes. "It appears to be a classic rebirth scenario where a person is given a completely new identity, like the government does for informants in high-stakes cases. Documents, ranging anywhere from birth certificates to diplomas, are forged, along with phoney personal histories, including family and employment. The key is figuring out who she *used* to be, then we can make it all fall apart. These people did a first-class job, but I'll find a flaw somewhere. I'm closing in on her. We did get a message that a Mr. Dawson wants to speak with me regarding United Oil. Hopefully, he'll tell me who she is, so we're getting closer. I'll let you know as soon as I know more."

"Thank you, Matt. Let me know when you want that cash," Bob said. "Right now, I need to talk with Thomas— alone." They shook hands, and the private investigator left the room. "And just what are you thinking of doing with any new magnet information?" Bob's tone made it clear to Thomas that he already knew the answer.

Thomas shouted, the veins in his neck were sticking out. He was visibly frustrated. "Those miscreants made a fool of me again! The uncertainty of creating a stronger magnet was one of the chief reasons I decided to sell it to them. Certainly, they knew that, and they actively concealed the fact that one may be just around the corner! That's why they paid so much; they wanted me to sell before information of new magnet technology leaked out. Can't we sue them for that, or *something?*"

"In theory, yes. You could sue to rescind the agreements based upon them concealing a material fact about the transaction. I say 'in theory' because such lawsuits are difficult to win, and I can't believe you're in a hurry to face their legal team and tactics again. Violating the confidentiality agreement or working on the invention yourself would violate the asset purchase agreement. It could cost you everything. I want all contact with Matt Springer on this to go directly and solely to me from now on to help keep it privileged and confidential. Any communications regarding the motor by you to anyone but me could prove to be disastrous."

Thomas nodded. "I understand. I do. Keep me informed. On a different topic, I have decided to sell my business to Joseph Thompson, my shop super. I'll send you the terms once we have them worked out. It won't be a cash sale; in fact, he won't be able to put much down. But I want to get out, and he deserves this opportunity. I think he'll do fine ... okay ... well ... thanks." It was obvious he had something else on his mind.

Thomas had several thoughts on the way back to the shop, *I can't let this happen! If I can get that information about the new magnet, I'm going to build the motor, and I don't care what they do to me. This time, I'll have all the money I need to get everything I need to finish it; once it's done and producing electricity for everyone to see, the public will never allow them to lock it up. The world needs it, and they will demand it once they know about it. But what will Joanna think about that thing being back in our lives?*

If Thomas got that magnet information, he'd have to work on a new prototype— somewhere secret, somewhere safe; he couldn't do it at the shop.

All the more reason to sell the shop to Joe; today is the day to tell him, he thought.

When Thomas arrived at the shop, he invited Joe into his tiny office and proposed an offer Joe simply could not refuse. Both men agreed upon the terms that Thomas sent to Bob with instructions to prepare the documents.

Another huge milestone in a month full of them, Thomas thought.

Soon, he'd be out of work for the first time since he was

fourteen. Now, he'd have the time to get the new house completely ready for the girls, including a playhouse, swing, and sandbox off the patio, and maybe even a dog.

Just when things were getting better with Joanna, the new attorney for the plaintiff in the paternity suit subpoenaed her to take her deposition. They knew that they could slam Thomas and turn up the heat in the hope of getting him to settle. As a party to the lawsuit, Thomas had the right to be present, but Bob was not thrilled about the idea of him being there.

"It will be nasty, distasteful even. They will make you mad and, probably, make her cry, or at least that's what they'll try to do. You have to stay calm and quiet. I'll explain to Joanna that you cannot come to her rescue at my insistence and that she has to be strong."

The deposition was brutal. It was the plaintiff's opportunity to tighten the screws on Thomas, and tighten them, they did. They paraded all of the false witness statements, birth certificate, affidavits, receipts, and miscellaneous lies in front of Joanna. The evidence seemed overwhelming, and at times, a tear would appear, but she remained tough and stoic. She denied knowing about the alleged events, but, of course, the plaintiff knew that already because none of it ever happened. The real purpose of this dog-and-pony show was to give Thomas a preview of coming attractions, to show him a small portion of what he could expect at the upcoming trial—all in an effort to get him to pay.

They wanted to settle for a $50,000 cash payment—$500 a month in child support and an acknowledgment of paternity. What they didn't realize was that Thomas would rather die than admit to a lie that would break Joanna's heart.

Chapter 8

Determination

Joanna was devastated by what she had seen at the deposition. Thomas saw that all of the ground he had made in the recent weeks was gone. Bob, his attorney, could sense Thomas's emotional decay and asked Joanna if he could speak privately with her. The plaintiff's attorneys were gone, and the stenographer finished packing up her shorthand machine. Thomas followed her out. Bob and Joanna were alone in the room.

"I would normally never interfere in a client's personal life, Joanna, but I've come to care a great deal for Thomas. What's happening between you two is killing him. He did not cheat on you, Joanna, and he certainly did not father a child with that woman."

Joanna was wide-eyed. "How could anyone manufacture all of that?"

Bob had a comforting demeanor and voice that calmed Joanna. "It's all a fake, and when we prove who she really is the whole thing will fall apart like a house of cards. Look, Joanna, the love you two share doesn't happen very often in life. Such a deep love is a joy to all because it's beautiful and rare and is living proof that two souls can mate—that we don't have to be alone—that there is hope. Evil people have interjected themselves into that beautiful union and, for their own purposes, are trying to destroy it. They will not prevail.

Please don't make up your mind until we have a chance to prove it's all a lie," he said.

She looked at him with a tear in her eye. "You *are* good. We're very lucky to have you helping Thomas. Thank you for your kind words, and please, please, do what you say you can do and get me the proof that this is all just a too-real nightmare," she said.

Then, Joanna gave Bob a warm but firm handshake and left the room.

Bob thought, *What a special woman. She's competent, confident, yet cordial and caring. I see why Thomas will never give up the love he has for her.*

On the way home, Thomas reached the only conclusion he could. They lied about the motor's potential, and they put in motion this paternity suit that ruined his marriage. He owed them nothing. Nothing! It was time to build a new prototype so it would be ready when the new magnetic technology became available.

I need a new shop, he thought.

Once at the new house, Thomas measured the garage and the yard behind it. *I need more room*, he thought. *If I add to the back of the garage, it would be less noticeable.*

He immediately drafted the plans and specifications to add a shop to the garage, and within a week, construction began. As soon as the cement, walls, and roof were complete, the machinery and materials, chiefly aluminum, arrived. Thomas commissioned a carpenter to do some work on the shop and to build a small box and a place to hide the box in the library.

It had been three weeks since the last meeting with the private investigator, but still Thomas had no word on the paternity investigation, and he was frustrated. Things had improved slightly with Joanna since her deposition, but to keep from getting depressed he kept himself busy with the garage addition and obtaining the materials and parts needed to make a new prototype. Thomas made a decision to have the permanent magnets and the electromagnets for this prototype made in Europe in the hope of avoiding detection and interference by United Oil. He hired a lawyer in Switzerland who had located a company capable of manufacturing the magnets to Thomas's specifications—a company who appeared to have no direct contacts with the oil industry.

Thomas finally heard from Bob that they would be meeting with the private investigator, Matt, on Friday at two o'clock. That was two days away—two days that passed agonizingly slow for Thomas. Finally, though, it was Friday afternoon. Thomas arrived early, which gave him a chance to tell Bob about his plan to build a new prototype, a topic he had avoided until now. Thomas's resolve to not tell Bob anything specific about the design of the motor was not violated by his decision to warn him of his intent to build a new prototype.

"This is totally my decision and has nothing to do with the corporation and you, Bob. I can't let them get away with keeping it from helping the planet. I can't let these ruthless villains rule the world with their energy monopoly. The stakes are too high to walk away. I couldn't live with myself! But I cannot put my daughters, Joanna, and you in danger!" Thomas cried.

The lawyer had a determined look. "I had a feeling it would end up this way. I'll dissolve the corporation we had and create a new one with you as the sole stockholder. When they sue, you can argue it is the corporation violating their proprietary rights to the motor and not you individually. It won't help much, but we should do what we can. Also, you should run all the expenses for the prototype through the new corporation. Parenthetically, I believe we will hear some news today about the new magnet technology.

"Cynthia, please send in Mr. Springer," Bob spoke into the intercom.

Matt Springer came in and sat down.

"I know you are most interested in the paternity investigation, so I'll start there," the sleuth began. "I still have not heard back from their Mr. Dawson, but I think we've found that flaw in their story that we've been looking for since St. Louis. The saga took us to Philadelphia and a possible witness who claims to know the plaintiff's true identity. She hired a lawyer who contacted me after she heard we were snooping around in Missouri. I meet with him on Monday, so I'll contact Bob right after that. I think we're getting very close." The P.I. had a look of satisfaction.

"Thank God," Thomas said and breathed a sigh of relief. "I can't tell you how good it is to hear that. Do what you have to do and get the proof we need to end this—now!"

"Yessir, we're doing all we can. It'll still take a little time to put it all together once we have her real name."

Bob looked at his calendar. "We have approximately sixty days before discovery ends and trial in three months. So, we must have what we need by then."

"I have a good feeling about this latest lead. Now, for the news on United Oil's magnet research. We got lucky." Matt Springer reached into his briefcase and produced a large file. "It seems they don't pay their researchers a great deal of money, so it didn't take much looking for us to find one in financial trouble. This is a copy of their research, including recent test results, which I have read through, and it appears to be quite complete. Essentially, they discovered that a rare-earth element combined with current magnet materials greatly enhances strength."

Matt handed the envelope to Thomas and said, "The element is neodymium, Nd, and it is element number sixty on the periodic table. It is an ore commonly found in monazite and lanthanite. The extraction process is far from perfect, but they're making progress, especially now that they have a use for it.

"They've found that creating an alloy of neodymium, iron, and boron increased magnetic power by well over ten times. They're trying to get purer neodymium to experiment with different combinations of these materials to make it several times stronger than that. This fellow told me that the lead scientist said one day a neodymium magnet the size of your fist will be strong enough to pick up and hold over a ton in the air for months, maybe even years."

"Oh, this is excellent news. Thank you. You did a marvelous job. Once I review this file, I may have some questions, so can you still get information from your contact?" asked Thomas.

"As long as the money holds out, and United Oil doesn't discover the leak. If that's all, I'll be leaving now and will be in touch as soon as I find out more about our possible witness. Gentlemen, good day."

Bob looked seriously at his client. "Now look, my friend, you start poking around asking about neodymium, and they'll be on you like a duck on a June bug," he warned Thomas. "These people will be extremely unhappy to learn that you are still a threat, and *they'll* stop at nothing to stop *you*. They're arrogant and sanctimonious enough to believe they're above the law. And they just *might* be right! They're capable of *anything*, so they cannot find out that you're working on the motor until it's ready to unveil to the public. It must be completed before they find out."

"Alright, Bob. Here's the name of the company in Switzerland that I hired with the expertise to build the new magnets. I'll go home and review this file now. If there's enough information, I want to wire them in the morning to see if they'd be capable and interested in making the neodymium magnet."

Bob glared at him. "Haven't you heard a word I've said? These people aren't stupid, Thomas, so we can assume they've been watching you ever since the day we closed on the deal. It's better if *I* arrange for the telegram. The telegram should only inquire as to their willingness to construct a magnet using a little-known element and nothing more specific. We'll take care of it. You must double your efforts at being careful not to do anything suspicious. Keeping your work secret is the only way to keep you, and us, safe. Are you absolutely sure you want to do this?"

Determination steeled Thomas. "Unequivocally, I've never felt selling it to them—knowing they'd keep it from the world—was the right thing to do. Guilt has a way of growing while it eats you up. I need to make this right, and they've given me everything I need to do it—the technology, the money, and an understanding of just how bad these people are. They must be stopped!

"Electromagnetic energy will one day replace fossil fuel energy. It'll provide the clean, abundant, and cheap energy we must have to power the future and preserve our planet. If they suppress this technology and continue their monopoly, their control over the world's only source of energy will give them power beyond measure. They will abuse the planet and the people on it.

"Unrestricted extraction and use of fossil fuels will pollute our air and water for at least the rest of this century. Evil is never satisfied, and they will not stop with the environment. Their control over our government, our economy—our very lives—will not be good. They must be stopped!" Thomas reiterated with a yell and pounded a fist on the desk as he stood. Bob was startled, because he had never seen Thomas this animated.

"Turning my back on this would be turning my back on all of humanity. Yes, I'm sure I want to do this, because I'm sure I *have* to do this. I don't like the fact that I'm breaking my word—even to them. My parents taught me that there's only one thing that can't be taken from you, and that's your integrity. I gave my word, and now I'm going to break it, and that goes against my grain—yet *another* thing I value that they've caused me to lose.

"Few people in history are given a chance to make life better for all. There should be a particularly nasty corner of hell waiting for anyone who walks away from a chance to do that. I have to try, and whatever happens to me is fair," Thomas concluded, patting the file. "I'll be in touch." And with that, he walked out the door.

In that moment, Robert Connors realized the depth of the man he had come to know so well.

Thomas got into his car and headed for home. It was near dinnertime, so he stopped at a diner Joanna and he had frequented before the children came along. Thomas sat in "their" booth, the one they had romantically shared back when life was simple. As he waited for his order, Thomas pondered how strange his life had become and how helpless he was to change that. Being in "their" restaurant depressed him, yet he felt oddly invigorated. Thomas ate quickly, so he could get home and review the United Oil file.

Once home, Thomas spread the file out on his work table. It contained very complete information about the new magnet technology that used neodymium and other commonly used elements. It showed test results from prototype magnets, together with proposals to create new prototypes with different compounds. Most important, it contained a description of the neodymium extraction process, together with proposals to improve it. Everything that any decent research facility needed to duplicate and enhance the technology was in his hands. He spent the remainder of the weekend working feverishly on the prototype.

Early Monday morning, Thomas headed to the hardware store for supplies and noticed that the same car had been behind him most of the way. It slowed and lingered when Thomas pulled into a parking spot near the store's door, and then it sped off.

Hmm, a bit obvious, Thomas thought. *Looks like Bob was right! They're watching me.*

After getting the needed supplies, Thomas paid the store clerk and drove home. This time, the same car followed him to his driveway—being very conspicuous and intimidating.

Hugh Simmons looked at Mr. Dawson in disbelief. "You're telling me it took him less than a month to break his word and start working on the motor again?"

"Well, not exactly," said Dawson. "He built a shop at his new home, which is not enough for our lawyers to go to court on, but it was enough for us to start looking into what he's doing with his time these days.

"Friday, after he left for his lawyer's, we picked the lock on his garage and got a look at his new shop. We found a lot of machines, but no motor. No sign of one. It was strange, because I was sure we would. There were some shavings, but no stock. We'll go back to see if anything has changed or if there's some other sign that work is taking place there."

Simmons took in all this information and said conspiratorially, "When you do, I want you to send a message. I want you to sabotage a few machines, nothing too destructive, so the police won't get involved. Short out some drive motors, stuff like that. Then, I want you to pay him a visit and make it clear how serious we are taking this, that we won't tolerate him breaking his word to us. Stick to him like glue. I want to know his every move, and keep me apprised. If he doesn't stop, I'm not sure a court order would help, and we may have to look to other alternatives. We simply cannot afford to have him breach our contract. Do you understand?"

"Absolutely, sir, you can count on us. If he's up to anything, we will find out and let you know immediately."

"See that you do, Mr. Dawson, see that you do. That will be all."

What no one else knew (except a well-paid carpenter, contractually bound to secrecy) was that Thomas had hired the contractor to not only make a box and a hiding place for the written materials about the motor, but he had also hired him to make a hiding place for the motor in the back of the shop. When the addition to the garage was complete, a false back wall was added with an immensely clever swiveling door disguised as shelving. A secret button unlocked the door to reveal a long, narrow, armor-plated assembly safe room big enough to contain the prototype and materials, yet small enough to go unnoticed.

After a few more days of work making parts, Thomas thought, *Just some finishing touches, and the prototype will be ready for the magnets.*

Bob called and said that the original order of magnets were built and that he hoped to get a response about whether the company was interested in making the new neodymium permanent magnet.

Several days passed, and Thomas completed the new prototype motor. Now, all he needed was the new magnets.

Three days later, a message arrived from Bob indicating that he needed to see Thomas at his office the next morning. It was the first time Thomas had left home since the last time he was at Bob's and, as expected, he was followed in a not-so-subtle way.

"Hello, Bob. What did Matt Springer find out?" Thomas blurted out, forgetting his manners. He was excited to learn what Bob had heard from the private investigator.

"He's got her. He's confident they've discovered her real identity. Now, they merely have to find people who know her and put her change of identity together. Proving her past will destroy her new identity, and then all of those lies will be obvious. It may take a few more weeks to find out who the real father of her child is. They'll create a final report with all of the evidence when they are done. Thomas, as soon as it arrives, I'll get it to you."

"I'm afraid it may be too late. It feels like Joanna believes them and doesn't love me any longer." Thomas could barely get those words out, and his eyes were filled with tears.

"Please, don't say that. Don't even *think* that. Joanna is confused, that's all, and soon we'll be able to reveal the truth to her. Don't ever give up on your love! I cannot believe that *she* has!" Bob cried.

"I hope you're right. Well, now, what about our friends in Europe?"

"More good news. All of the magnets arrived, and I'll have a courier pick them up and bring them to my office. Once here, I'll drive them up to your house.

"Regarding the neodymium magnet, the Swiss say they've heard that research aimed at improving the strength of magnets is happening and that they'd be very interested in starting such a project. I don't believe it would be wise to have any further unsecured contact with them. Perhaps we should have a courier take the file to *them,* or perhaps we should have Matt do it. If Simmons finds out you know about the new magnet technology, your life may be in danger."

Thomas was sullen. "Yes, I have to be sure Joanna knows nothing about this, and make that obvious to them. I want it to be perfectly clear that she is no threat to them. I have to stay away from her and the girls until this is over, which means I want it done yesterday. Contact Matt about him, or someone he trusts, getting the file to Europe as soon as possible. I can't thank you enough, Bob. And I mean that."

Both men stood and shook hands. "Thomas, be careful, my good man," Bob said earnestly. "Things are changing rapidly now. Watch your step. I'm also going to talk with Matt about a bodyguard for you. I'll be in touch."

The same car tailed Thomas home. It was a stark reminder of the forces at work against him. Thomas pulled his car into the garage and noticed that one of the machines was out of kilter. A quick inspection revealed that it and other machines had been tampered with to the point where they were inoperable. Someone had been in his shop while he had been at Bob's! The thought sent a shiver down Thomas's spine.

"They were in here," he said aloud as he shut the garage door.

Thomas hastily ran to the secret door and pushed a button in the back of the shelves that looked like just another knot in the wood. The wall pushed back, pivoted open, and revealed that the prototype was still safe and sound.

Good; I wonder what now? Thomas thought.

Shortly after dinner, Bob arrived with the magnets. Thomas had him drive his car into the garage so they could be unloaded without being seen—the new electromagnets and two conventional permanent magnets. Thomas was thrilled beyond belief. If felt like his birthday in more ways than one.

"I have to ask you to leave now, Bob, so that you don't see anything more about the motor."

Thomas immediately got to work and installed the new magnets in the waiting prototype, flipped the master switch, and ... *bam, bam, bam* ... it sprang to life!

He had made a few improvements over the prior prototype, but the mechanical switches still lasted for only about thirty seconds before they came apart. After about an hour, Thomas replaced five sets of switches, but was confident that it ran long enough to test. Now, all he needed was a set of neodymium magnets to install in the pistons in place of the conventional ones.

Late that night, he decided it was time to complete the written materials about the motor and put them in the hiding place in the library floor. Thomas meticulously copied all of the information that would be taken to the Swiss company and put that into the box along with all of his motor materials and the journal he had penned over the last few months. *Insurance,* he thought, *just in case they do get me. Maybe a descendant will find it.* He was closing the box in the floor when a sharp knock came at the front door.

Suddenly, Thomas realized how alone and unprepared he was. He thought, *But how could anyone know what he was doing?*

Now, he understood the value of the massive and solid front door with the small, elegant opening in the middle at about shoulder height. The previous owners knew security, and this door had been constructed to protect the matriarch of that family.

The little door mirrored the door into which it was set, and acted as a portal for small objects to pass, as well as to speak without opening the entire door. Thomas unlatched the little door, swung it back, and peered out. He saw two men in dapper suits, holding forth identification cards from United Oil.

"What do you want?" Thomas asked in a gruff, impatient voice.

"Just a few words, if we may, sir," one of the men answered. He wore a gray fedora and doffed it slightly. "May we please come in?"

Thomas saw a dried mustard stain on the man's necktie and decided that they were not so dapperly dressed after all. The food stain made him uncomfortable—Thomas was fastidious about personal appearance.

"No! Say what you came to say and be gone!" cried Thomas.

The man with the dirty tie was unfazed. "Mr. Hugh Simmons is concerned that you may have gone back on your word. He wants you to know that such behavior will not be tolerated." Boldly, the man then stuck his face in the little opening. "And you'd better not, if you know what's good for you. I've got a shotgun, a shovel, and an alibi," he said menacingly.

With that, Thomas slammed the little door in the man's face and stepped back. After a few moments, he opened it again to look out. The men had vanished.

Thomas thought, *Thank God! With all the things they've done to me, this is the first time they've threatened me face to face. This indicates a whole new level of attack.*

Later that week, Hugh Simmons put aside the balance sheet he had been perusing and summoned his henchman, Dawson, to his office. "What is your report?" he asked gruffly.

"Not good, sir. We've been watching shipments destined for this part of the state, and I received a call this morning that a shipment was delivered to the law office of Robert Connors from a Swiss magnet company. Worse, we were able to obtain a copy of a telegram to that company asking if they'd be willing to build a new-generation magnet."

"What? Are you sure? How could he possibly know about that? This changes everything. We *have* to stop him—now!"

Thomas awoke that morning feeling groggy after a difficult night's sleep. His worst nightmare had come true. United Oil's people might have him killed, and he needed to prepare. Thomas did two things that day: he bought two twelve-gauge shotguns and a very large life insurance policy naming Joanna as beneficiary. He took the guns home. Then, he delivered the policy to Bob's office for safekeeping. When he got to his attorney's office, Bob rushed out and said, "I've been trying to reach you. Come in, come in."

"Thomas, I learned this morning that Simmons knows you have their neodymium technology. Matt is sending over a bodyguard. He'll be here any minute. Matt has discovered that they're looking for an out-of-state hitman. He knows people with safe houses. And we both think you should go there now."

"No, I can't. I've just decided that I'm taking the file to Switzerland myself, Bob, and I have to go as soon as possible. I think I can speed the process along and bring the neodymium magnets back with me. When I get back, I can put them in and be ready to reveal the motor to the press in less than a week.

Once it's public, I'll be safe. While I'm gone, please keep an eye on Joanna and my girls for me, will you?"

"Of course, of course, I will," Bob assured him.

Cynthia's voice came over the intercom. "Mr. Springer and another gentleman are here to see you, sir." Bob pushed the button and told her to send them in.

"Good to see you again, Matt," said Thomas.

The private investigator acknowledged him. "Thank you, sir, and you, as well. Please allow me to introduce George Robinson. He owns a personal protection agency that provides security for many of the most powerful men on earth," Matt proudly explained. "I'm quite honored that Mr. Robinson himself has agreed to help you. You can't ask for anyone better."

Mr. Robinson was tall, and his broad-shouldered frame was clothed in a fine, woolen coat from a premier Italian design house.

To be wearing that, his company must be doing something right, Thomas thought. "Matt is too kind," admonished George. He shook Thomas's hand. "The honor is all mine, sir. You're very brave, and your effort is to be commended. We're happy to help keep you safe while you work on your invention. The tyranny that the *status quo* would bring cannot be condoned. A new energy source is United Oil's 'Achilles' Heel,' if you will, and the best chance we have at stopping them. I'll have our best men around you."

Thomas smiled and then laughed. "You'd better choose men that don't get seasick then, because I'm going to Europe to get the magnet I need to finish the prototype."

"Hmm, ocean crossings are difficult to secure," George said. "Are you sure you can't send someone in your place?"

"I'm positive," Thomas replied with a very determined look. "I leave as soon as passage can be booked."

"Again, sir, having very little time will hamper our ability to keep you safe, but we'll do our best. I have two men and a specially designed car outside waiting for you. One of the men will drive your car home. They're my best men. Please follow their advice," George directed.

"I will—so long as it doesn't interfere with my desire to get this done as soon as possible," Thomas replied curtly.

George said, "I'll book three tickets on the next available ship. Mr. Connors, I'll have the tickets delivered to your house this evening." He then looked confidently at Bob and Thomas. "Tell no one of the travel plans. After you've docked in Europe, Mr. Connors can notify anyone who needs to know that you've left. That includes your wife and the magnet company in Switzerland."

Thomas looked suspiciously at George and said, "You seem to know an awful lot."

"More than you need to know, Mr. Cunningham. That's my business. But we're looking forward to learning about your invention. Can you tell us more about it?"

Thomas avoided the inquiry and continued questioning George, his voice rife with fearful anticipation. "What about Joanna? Do you think she could be in danger?"

"Well, it appears quite obvious that your wife knows very little about the motor and *nothing* about the neodymium technology, so I doubt it. However, we'll keep your family safe. I have men watching over them as we speak. You have my word." At this, George proffered his hand, sensing how much Thomas was relying upon him for his family's protection. George's tone calmed Thomas.

"Thank you so much, Mr. Robinson. So, let's go meet my two new companions."

"We have an armor-plated car for you. Joe is the driver. Jim will drive your car home, and the two of them will go everywhere with you."

Bob turned to Thomas and said, "I'll drop the tickets off tomorrow morning at your house. Get everything you'll need for the trip on your way home."

"Come out and meet my men," George said to Bob with a chuckle. "I don't want them to shoot *you* when you show up at Thomas's house. Afterward, Bob, I want to speak with you."

As they approached the car, two men got out and walked toward them. "This is your driver, Joe, and our best body-guard, Jim," said Mr. Robinson. "That's not to say that Joe isn't also one of our best—it's just that he's also trained in protective driving. Both men will stay with you night and day until your project is done, and you're safe."

"It's a pleasure to meet you, Mr. Cunningham," said Jim as he vigorously shook Thomas's hand.

"Yes, it's an honor, sir," said Joe as he extended his hand in turn.

Both men appeared to be in their late twenties and in top physical condition. They were dressed in proper black suits, each with a holstered gun under their armpits that Thomas glimpsed when they shook hands.

Jim was tall, with a medium build and sharp facial features. His pointed nose and chin were separated by a bushy, black mustache that highlighted his set of large, white teeth. Those teeth gleamed when he smiled, and that made Thomas comfortable. Even more apparent was that Jim had an indescribable air of nobility—all three men did—as if they were infused with dignity and honor.

Joe was somewhat shorter in stature than Jim, but with a more husky build. His muscles tested the limits of his jacket seams whenever he moved. Joe was sandy-haired, with a neatly trimmed full beard and starling blue eyes that reminded Thomas, strangely, of an eagle's eyes. He could feel those eyes upon him now.

Thomas and George's men left. Bob and George went into Bob's office, and George shut the door behind them. "What I'm about to tell you few people have ever heard. Do you agree that my employment by Thomas renders what I say to you confidential and privileged under your attorney-client relationship with Thomas?" George asked him.

"Of course. What is it?"

"In addition to that, the information I'm about to reveal to you is confidential and you, right now, must take an oath to keep it so—under pain of death. What say you?"

"Yes, yes, I so *swear*," Bob answered, a bit annoyed. *As if I can't keep secrets ... in my line of work?* he thought.

"I'm part of a society secretly created by our Founding Fathers prior to the Revolutionary War," George described solemnly. "Our mission is to silently protect our democracy from all enemies, domestic and foreign.

"As you are now surmising, the personal protection agency is one of our many 'fronts,' if you will. Such businesses allow us to blend into society and, thereby, operate in secrecy. The personal protection business allows us to be close to powerful people without them knowing who we really are. Some we watch over—and some, we just *watch*.

"We interfere only when necessary to protect the foundations of our democracy and the government designed to foster it. Occasionally, power accumulates in the wrong places and poses a threat, requiring extraordinary actions to defeat it. Our members are placed in all segments of government, business, politics, education, and science all over the world.

"We've been watching Hugh Simmons and those scallywags who control him for some time now. Their energy monopoly has the potential for dominating the economy, which can then be used to undermine our democratic institutions. They've gotten too big to fight in the traditional ways.

"Thomas's invention will end their monopoly, and the threat they pose to all of us. I shudder to think what might happen if we can't stop them. This may be the greatest threat our country has ever faced.

"Most of us, including myself, are direct descendants of those who created what was then called, 'The Great Experiment.' We take an oath to reveal ourselves only if authorized. Given the magnitude of this quest, we've decided that we need someone on the inside—one of us. That someone is *you*, Robert Connors. We've investigated you from every possible angle, and we know you're a good man. Will you serve your country in this most unique way?"

"Well ... oh, my ... well," stammered Bob. George's request could not have surprised him more. Now, he knew why the man had asked for his secrecy oath. "You honor me with your invitation. Of course ... I will join." And with that, Bob graciously accepted.

"Excellent! Be at this address, in two night's time, at half-past seven—sharp. I'll meet you there," George instructed, handing him an engraved card with only an address printed on it.

The invitation that George offered, and that Bob accepted, was more rare than he could know. In over a hundred years, it had been given only three times. Membership in this group was inherited from those called the Founding Fathers and was not normally bestowed. It took the nomination by an executive officer and an affirmative vote by three-fourths of the membership to invite a nondescendant.

Bob was instructed that he could not share this knowledge with anyone else, including his wife, and not even Thomas—strict secrecy under pain of death. Period. No exceptions.

George said, "Once inducted, you'll be fully briefed. See you in two days."

On the way home, Thomas spoke to the driver, Joe. "You probably know I've been followed everywhere I go lately. I see the same car following my car behind us."

"Yessir. Keep watching back there."

Shortly thereafter, two cars raced up from behind in the other lane. One car pulled ahead of the car following Thomas's car, while the other pulled up just behind it. In unison, both cars pulled in—one in front and one behind the car. The front car applied its brakes, forcing the car in the middle to slow and pull off the road. Thomas did not see the car after that.

The next day, Bob Connors arrived with the tickets and announced they would have to leave within the hour to catch the train to the East coast. Bob shook Thomas's hand. Bob assured him he would watch over Joanna and the girls. From his briefcase, Bob produced a large envelope.

"I can't believe this came *now*. It's the proof that the

paternity case is a fake, Thomas. I'll use it to get the case dismissed before you get back!"

Thomas's face paled. "Take it to Joanna later *today*. I don't want you to be seen going directly from my house to her house, but I want her to see the proof right away. Tell her I love her more than life itself and that I'll be back when it's safe. Please don't tell her any more than you have to about what I'm doing. I want her to be safe. Thank you, my friend, and good-bye for now."

Later that day, Bob knocked on Joanna's door. Joanna opened it, saw Bob standing there, and knew something was wrong. "What is it?" she nervously asked the attorney.

"May I please come in and talk?" Bob asked her.

She watched him pat his briefcase, a gesture that indicated he had something to show her. Joanna prayed it was the paternity proof she had been waiting for and gladly welcomed Bob in.

"Where's Thomas?" Joanna asked, half expecting her husband to be one step behind Bob. But he was nowhere to be seen.

"Please, let me explain, Joanna. He's headed for Europe."

"What?" Joanna shrieked. "It's that motor again, isn't it! Not being around lately and then being distracted when he was—that was my first clue. I should've known! But why Europe?"

"I'm not sure," Bob lied unconvincingly. "More important, I've just received the report and evidence that the paternity suit is a complete lie!"

"Wh-what? What?"

Bob opened the entire file and showed Joanna how the

plaintiff was a lady of the evening who had a child at just the right time. She had been given a completely new identity and had fabricated *everything*. Thomas had never met her. When Bob finished regaling Joanna with the remaining details, she burst out crying, first softly—then with abandon. Suddenly, Joanna remembered that Thomas was leaving.

"I must see him," she snuffled loudly.

"I'm sorry. He's gone. He'll be back as soon as he can."

"No! If you meant what you said about our love, Bob, you have to help me get to him!"

"They left Detroit over two hours ago, Joanna. I'm sorry."

"Well, then, we'll drive there and catch the next train."

Bob had never seen such raw determination, and he knew right then and there that he was going to Boston.

"Mr. Simmons, it's Mr. Dawson for you," the intercom squealed.

Hugh Simmons picked up the telephone. "Yes, Dawson, what is it?"

"New information for you, sir, and it's not good. We just learned he's headed for Europe."

"Be here at one o'clock!" Simmons shouted into the mouthpiece.

Chapter 9

Disappearance

Thomas had packed the night before, so within an hour they were headed to Detroit to board the train for Boston. As part of his preparation to build the new prototype, Thomas reviewed all the materials retrieved from United Oil's neodymium magnet research. He then researched the elements they used to create the alloy that became the magnet and discovered that boron had only recently been produced in a form that was ninety-nine percent pure. Thomas obtained a sufficient quantity and had it securely hidden in his valise. Iron could be easily obtained in Europe, which left just neodymium.

Thomas's research revealed that neodymium —from the Greek *neos didymos*, meaning "new twin"—was discovered only twenty-eight years before, and isolating it into a pure form hadn't been accomplished to date. While neodymium was a relatively abundant element, it was found in extractable concentrations in only a few known places. He learned it was contained within lanthanite, which could be found in Pennsylvania. Subsequently, he made arrangements to have a sufficient quantity of the ore delivered to the new train station at Brockwayville, Pennsylvania.

Joe and Jim, the omnipresent bodyguards, were a tad out of sorts after hearing of this unexpected rendezvous—particularly with intelligence that they would likely be followed.

Picking up a container at the Brockwayville passenger depot would be impossible to conceal, and tracing the ore's origin would not be difficult. Once Dawson's men did that, there would no longer be any doubt about whether Dawson knew what Thomas was doing.

Dawson arrived at Hugh Simmons's spacious office headquarters exactly at one o'clock as directed.

"How did he get our research?" Simmons asked, brusquely. "He could only have obtained his knowledge of the alloy from us! We have a leak that must be plugged."

"He did, and we did! It has been eliminated. But the damage is done. It was a researcher, so we assume Mr. Cunningham knows everything *we* know, including the research on the process for extracting neodymium."

"That makes him too dangerous," Simmons snarled viciously, while sliding an envelope across the desk. "This is $15,000. And this conversation never happened. Cunningham must *not* reach his destination."

The oil giant's sources told him that Europe was on the brink of war. Traveling there was hazardous. The Europeans had increased military spending by fifty percent over the last five years. An arms race was on between Great Britain and Germany, and most of Europe was following suit. Espionage was everywhere, and disappearing foreign citizens was commonplace.

Simmons explained all of this to Dawson. "So, are we clear?" he asked him.

"Crystal, sir. When he leaves, we'll be following."

Simmons smiled, but his eyes remained hooded and cold. "Good. I don't want to see or hear from you or him again," he commanded. "Understood?"

The train steamed into the Brockwayville station on time. Thomas's trunks were loaded on the baggage car. Joe stayed with Thomas while Jim blended into the crowd milling on the walkway looking for anyone who might be following them.

"Say, Joe, that fellow in the brown suit appears to be following us," whispered Thomas.

"Yeah, I've been eyeing him since Detroit. Let's get back on the train. Jim will be along soon."

Meanwhile, Jim walked into the restroom and to the sink behind the door. He'd been watching the man in the brown suit following Thomas and Joe, as well as two other fellows on the train. One of them was now following him around the station. After observing that the man following Thomas and Joe met a fourth man, Jim entered the restroom to see if the man following him would tail him in. And he did.

"Looking for me?" Jim asked.

"No."

"Oh? You've been following us since we left Detroit, you and your two cronies there, and now you're following me. What do you want?"

"*You'll* see," the man snapped back. That was all Jim needed to confirm his suspicion.

"*You* won't!" Jim cried and broke the man's nose in the blink of an eye with a right jab . As the man fell back, Jim pushed his head into a concrete wall hard enough to knock him out cold, but not kill him. The "company" hired only the most well-trained people, and he was one of their best. Rather than kill the man, he gagged and tied him to a toilet. "That should hold you until we're gone." He patted the unconscious man's head.

Thomas and Joe saw Jim walking toward the train dusting off his jacket and straightening his tie. "Looks like Jim's been working," Joe smirked.

Thomas nervously laughed at this.

Jim sat down. "Well, one of those gentlemen won't be making the rest of the trip. Seems he can't get off the toilet!"

They all howled with laughter.

The train pulled away. After awhile, Jim looked at Thomas and said, "I know your invention might eliminate the use of fossil fuels for our energy needs, which is huge all by itself, but won't it also remove the need for all these power lines I see going up everywhere?" The question was very astute.

"Yes, but it's more than just elimination of the wires that are used to carry 'AC,' or alternating electric current. It'll mean the elimination of AC altogether, which is dangerous. AC starts fires and can kill, so replacing it with safer 'DC,' or direct electric current, will be a welcome change," explained Thomas.

"Wasn't that the debate between Tesla and/or Westinghouse and Edison?"

"Indeed, it was!" cried Thomas. "Tesla's AC current was cheaper to deliver to customers, so it won even though it's much more dangerous. The reason for this is that AC can travel down a wire for a very long distance without losing strength. This means that it can travel many miles from the power station to a customer.

"But, unfortunately, DC can't travel very far down a wire before it loses its strength. This means that the power station must be close to the customer, and this proved to be impractically and prohibitively expensive.

"Because my invention can produce DC power at any location, it no longer has to be delivered to a customer. A generator providing DC power will be located in each structure providing all of its power needs. This means that there'll be no need for wires or a power grid, as they now call it.

"More important, AC electricity will become a relic of the past, except for some possible industrial applications. DC will be used because it won't create fires or seriously injure someone if they accidentally came in contact with it. Clearly, a number of different companies will be hurt by this technology."

"It seems you might be the target of a number of people," Jim said forlornly.

The other two men following them kept their distance, and before long, they had arrived at South Station in Boston, Massachusetts—Beantown, The Olde Towne, The Hub, The Athens of America—the historical city had many nicknames. They got to the pier about four hours before departure, which gave them time to meet with two other employees of the company that employed Joe and Jim. They relayed that they'd been watching two of Dawson's associates and that those men had purchased passage on the ship.

"That makes four that will be joining us on a voyage across the ocean, and I assume more will be waiting for us in Cherbourg, France. Please inform Mr. Robinson of our situation and that I recommend additional men meet us in Liverpool to accompany us to Switzerland," said Joe.

Thomas did not like the feel of it all. He thought, *We can't hide on a boat, or a train, for that matter. Regardless, I have to try and get a call through to Bob to see how Joanna is and how she took the news. Damn, I wish I could call her myself.* But he knew that would likely put her in danger, and he could not risk that.

Being modern, the passenger station had a room with a couple of public telephones. Thomas eventually got through to Bob's office only to hear that Bob was unexpectedly away from his office for two days.

"I can't believe it," he said to Jim, who was seated a few feet away. "I've been waiting months for information that'll save my marriage, and it finally gets here while I'm away, and I can't speak to my wife!"

It's just like a curse, Thomas thought.

Bob and Joanna drove to Detroit and got on the next train headed east. "We're at least three and a half hours behind them, and by the time we get to the pier, it'll be close," she said to Bob, hoping for some encouragement.

"I know, but if you do catch him, he'll be very worried, cross even, that it may put you in danger. That's why he left without telling you. It was at the advice of very experienced bodyguards. Above all, Thomas wanted to keep you safe. It must be killing him to not be able to talk with you now that you know the paternity suit is all a lie.

"That's quite a man you've got there, you know. He loves you more than life itself, and yet he put his own desires aside to help his fellow man. I don't know if I could do that. I'm not sure if many *would*, but he has, and that must be recognized when you consider why he is doing this."

"Thank you, Bob. This is bigger than us, and I understand

that. But couldn't we have had just one night together before he had to leave? That's why it seems like a curse instead of a quest. I understand sacrifice, but does it have to be so harsh? That file couldn't get here one day sooner? It's so maddening!" she cried.

"No one can explain why things happen the way they happen. Good luck, bad luck, fate? Who knows? I don't know. Sometimes life's just hard for no particular reason at all. But feeling like a target doesn't help. Be optimistic. He'll be back before you know it, and, hopefully, you can say goodbye today."

"Oh, Bob, I was such a fool to ever doubt his love for me, and now I'm afraid I'll never see him again." Tears spilled down Joanna's cheeks.

"Please don't ever blame yourself for being ensnared by those evil bastards ... .I'm sorry ... evil men. They spent a lot of time and money to make that web of lies designed to fool a court of law. Your reaction to it was normal and measured, Joanna. You waited for proof that finally came. I know Thomas doesn't blame you, and you shouldn't either."

Their train reached Boston a little late. They took a streetcar to the pier, jumped off, and ran to the departure counter. Thomas's ship had left ten minutes before their arrival! Joanna, bitterly disappointed, collapsed onto a bench and wept uncontrollably.

Frantically gasping for air between sobs, she looked up at Bob and said, "I have a bad feeling about this ... I know I'll never see my Thomas again!" she cried hysterically.

Bob sat next to her and hugged her. Tears pooled in his eyes.

The crossing to Liverpool was uneventful. Three "company" men joined them there for the remainder of the trip to France and beyond. The ship was a sleek, luxury liner of recent vintage that had been refitted with more lifeboats in the wake of the *Titanic* disaster. Her decks were broad, her apartments opulent—every inch was palatial and well-appointed.

Nothing was seen of Dawson's henchmen on the last leg of the trip. Joe wondered if it was the calm before the storm and thought, *They should know by now that Thomas has the neodymium research, which makes him too dangerous. They will certainly attack before we leave the Continent.*

Winter was beginning to settle into Northern Europe. The countries were preparing for the possibility of war. And not just any war. This would be the biggest war the world had ever known—a world war. Preparations for such undertakings robbed resources that would otherwise be used to increase the quality of life in a country. It resulted in a Spartans existence laced with palpable dread. Europe was no stranger to war. They knew what was coming, and they knew what to dread, or so they thought.

As the ship approached the harbor in France, two pilot boats came out to escort it in.

"I miss my girls," Thomas said to Jim. "I wish they could see this."

"You have two daughters?"

"Yes. They're beautiful angels, and since only angels can beget angels, it all begins with their mother. Joanna is like no other person I've ever met—or ever will meet. She is love personified—my soul mate. One could not be any more lucky than that. I miss them terribly. It hurts."

"You are a lucky man, Thomas, and it's plain to see the magnitude of your sacrifice. Communicating with her between now and when you're done could put them in danger. We have men guarding them, but we don't want to do anything that could create any more incentive to go after them."

Another "company" man met them at the pier and made arrangements to rent the entire travel car next to the sleeping coach on the train. This gave them control over the section of the train they would be riding to Paris. Unfortunately, control did not mean exclusive possession. Security on a train was always a concern when, as here, passengers could walk through the secure sconce area to get to other parts of the train. But in Western Europe, rail travel was highly developed, and Thomas had never seen anything like it before.

The train, from back to front, was made up of a caboose, a baggage car, two sleeping coaches, four travel coaches, a restaurant coach, a public lounging coach or bar, and a coal car. The first-class accommodations in the last two travel coaches were luxurious beyond belief, boasting thick Persian rugs, Battenburg lace curtains, and brass handrails in the hallways. These hallways led to enclosed cabins that had sumptuous leather sofas, two facing each other with removable table trays between them for game and card playing, drinking, and *hors d'oeuvres*. The public lounging coach had dark, rich cherry wood paneling with library table lights for reading.

Ornately framed paintings by the likes of Jonas Lie and Henri Matisse adorned the coaches' walls. Extra attention was paid to these cars when they were built, and the exorbitant amount charged for their use was warranted. The lounging car had a large window and was constructed of state-of-the-art sound dampening and shock absorbing materials for a visually entertaining and comfortable ride.

Joe was not expecting any trouble on this leg of the journey, because it would take less than a day to get to Paris. He was much more concerned with what lay ahead. The stopover in Paris while they waited for their train to leave in the morning was when he feared an attack—if one were to come that soon.

Their train arrived at the *Gare du Nord* rail station in Paris just before sunset. The company rented three adjoining rooms in a hotel close to the depot. Joe and Jim stayed in the center room with Thomas. Two heavily armed men stayed in each of the adjoining rooms, all of which were connected by inner doors. No one left the rooms for any reason. Dinner was brought up from the hotel restaurant, and it was French cuisine at its finest. Thomas fell into a deep, food-induced sleep. It seemed like he'd just fallen sound asleep when Joe was shaking him awake because breakfast was on the way.

Suddenly, Thomas's door flew open as if it was off its hinges. Gunshots immediately rang out from the door and were instantly joined from the inner doors on either side of Thomas.

Joe was near the door when it was kicked open, and he threw himself in front of Thomas at the precise moment the shots were heard. Three bullets, not meant for him, riddled his body. Jim had just enough time; he grabbed Thomas by the arm and practically flipped him into the open door of an adjoining room. Bullets flew over Jim's head and struck the doorframe as he rolled into the room behind Thomas. And Joe, despite his wounds, returned fire as he fell. Having been caught in the crossfire, the assassins retreated in a hailstorm of ordnance. They'd lost what seemed like a platoon of men.

Predictably, the assassins attempted to kick in the door of the room to which Jim and Thomas had fled, but, luckily, it did not budge. That gave them just enough time to run to the far room before the door caved in and a barrage of bullets pelted the room that they had just barely escaped. As they ran through their room, Thomas saw his file on the desk and dove for it.

Can't leave without this, he thought as he scooped it up and pivoted to the door.

Jim yelled for Thomas to follow him and ran through the outer room and out the door into the hallway.

The contingent in the hallway was caught off guard, providing Jim the chance to shoot at least two or three of them and send the rest scurrying for cover. Jim's men followed and pushed Thomas into the hallway in Jim's direction, taking up position between them and the assassins to cover their escape.

Jim led Thomas down the hall to the first cross hallway and then down the stairwell. It sounded like a war back at the room. The unbelievable noise from a dozen guns being fired simultaneously echoed through the building like thunderbolts. Each adrenalin-spiked step took him further away, and then the noise stopped. That could mean only one thing. Jim's men bought a small amount of time for them and paid for it with their lives. Thomas followed Jim toward the street and out the hotel door.

A man in a truck parked out front shot a hail of bullets at them as soon as they emerged. One of the bullets split the door frame between them. Jim immediately sent two rounds at the man and killed him instantly. They took off running down the street.

As they turned the corner, Thomas couldn't see anyone behind them, only people running toward the hotel. It appeared they'd gotten lucky. Jim and he stopped running, and Thomas bent over while gulping in huge breaths of air.

Thomas gasped for air. "I - - don't - - see - - them," he said. His spastic breathing made it difficult to speak.

Suddenly, a shot rang out. and a bullet smashed into the brick wall behind them. Thomas felt the pieces of shattered brick hit the back of his hand.

"You keep running," said Jim. "There's a police station around the next block. I'm right behind you. I'll keep up!"

They ran like the devil himself was chasing them, but as they rounded the corner, a car door swung open and out jumped two determined-looking men with pistols blazing. Fortunately, they were not nearly as good with a gun as Jim was. He dropped the first guy and sent the other diving for cover.

This gave them time to make it across the street and into the back door of what appeared to be a brothel! Jim spoke enough French to calm Madame DuBois with a generous bribe, but they knew they could not stay.

Then, a lucky break happened. It seemed that this particular block of buildings had a long history of shady goings-on and, as such, came equipped with a secret tunnel connecting them. Madame DuBois quickly ushered them into the tunnel and shut the hidden door as two armed men kicked in the back door to her establishment.

"We know they came in here through this door," one man said, pointing his gun at the brothel keeper. "Where are they?"

"They went out the front door." The sound of multiple gun hammers being cocked echoed through the room. "That's right. You brought the *wrong* attitude to the *right* place! Those are four guns being aimed at your heads by my sons, and they're very good shots! If you want to live, you'll stick those guns up your asses and run out of here the same way you came in!" Madame DuBois smiled amiably. She was nothing, if not amenable. The two men promptly took her advice.

Thomas and Jim surfaced down the block in a tavern, of all places, that was not open yet. They looked out the back door and saw nothing.

"We have to hide out until help arrives," said Jim. "We can't go back to the depot. That's what they'd expect us to do. Let's stay put for awhile and look for a telephone." Unlike America, the telephone was not widely used in Europe. "Hmm, no telephone here. We have to make our way south toward the center of the city where we can find a place for reinforcements to meet up with us. Let's go! Stay low and right behind me, Thomas."

Slowly, they opened the back door and crept into a narrow alley. It was still early morning, and the shadows from the buildings were long. Jim and Thomas ran along the rear of the buildings, darting across streets as fast as they could. They were getting tired when they heard the screech of tires from a car with its brakes locked. Damn it! They were found!

Once again, they ran through the nearest back door and into whatever building it happened to be. This time, it was one of the many hotels in the area. They ran through the hotel's kitchen to a chorus of French profanity: *Connards! Merde! Chiant!*, accompanied by the chefs waving their arsenal of butcher, utility, and paring knives, into the hotel lobby, out the main door, and smack into a *gendarmerie* on routine foot police patrol.

Lady Luck smiled upon them again. Jim explained to the policeman, with great difficulty, that Thomas and he were being chased and needed to get to the nearest police headquarters to tell it all in detail. He knew they would be safe there until help arrived. The *gendarmerie* understood and agreed to take them to his precinct. They were saved! As he turned and gestured that Thomas and Jim should follow him, a car pulled up. Four men quickly leapt out with guns drawn and shoved Thomas, Jim, and the *gendarmerie* into the car.

None of them were *ever* seen again!

George Robinson called the executive meeting to order. As president of the Company, he personally assumed responsibility to run the operation helping Thomas. George was crestfallen. "This meeting of the executive committee of this Midwest Unit is hereby called to order. I have invited member Robert Connors to this meeting due to his connection to tonight's unfortunate, and probably the saddest, meeting we have ever held," he said.

"We have confirmation that Mr. Cunningham and all six of our men with him are dead." At this, Bob winced as if he'd been hit in the stomach. "We don't have specifics on Thomas and Jim, because they apparently made it out of the hotel. The other five of our men died there helping them escape.

"It was a battlefield in the hallway and the three rooms they occupied. According to our police contacts, they were attacked by at least twenty heavily armed men. Twelve were killed, and three were wounded. There were so many bullet holes that one of the walls collapsed!

"No one, except for Thomas and Jim, made it out of there. We know this because they were briefly assisted by a nearby Madame, and she'd said they were uninjured. She helped them get away, at least for awhile, through a secret tunnel connecting the entire block, and then they disappeared. What happened to them after that is unknown. Except, a contact of ours in the French spy division told us that their information is that they are dead along with one of the area's policemen. No other information was available.

"I thought it was my responsibility to tell Joanna. I'm sorry, Bob, but it was my duty. I told her you didn't know yet and that you would likely contact her once I told you. Because Thomas's body has not been found, I could only tell her of the circumstances of his disappearance and that we presume he was killed. She's a very strong woman and took the bad news bravely."

"That's because she knew it was going to happen," Bob replied sadly. "I don't know how, but she did."

George looked at Bob and said, "I told her that we will always be in her debt and will watch over her and all of Thomas's heirs until the evil that killed him is scoured from the face of the earth."

And so they did.

The world descended into darkness. The next twenty-five years saw two world wars, famine, disease, and millions of deaths. The need for oil to fight those wars gave the oil conglomerate dominance and unprecedented power. It controlled everything by the end of World War II, after which it became even more powerful.

Every industrialized nation had its assets obliterated in the war. Only America had its industries intact and at full strength. The war had ramped up production and facilities to levels never before seen, let alone contemplated. The world needed everything, and our corporations were poised to sell it to them. That took energy, and that required oil.

The evil that George Robinson feared came to complete fruition. United Oil Company's monopoly gave it free reign over the world, and every living thing suffered. Stopping them after the loss of Thomas's invention proved impossible.

Needless to say, Joanna never got over it. She raised Ethel and Dorothy in the house that Thomas bought for them and made their lives as normal and as happy as she could without their father. Joanna never remarried—she never even dated another man. Her heart was completely and utterly broken and could not be repaired. Joanna could never love again.

Bob Connors took over all of Joanna's legal affairs and stopped by the house often to visit the girls and her. Ethel and Dorothy called him "Uncle Bob." He had promised Thomas that he would look after them, and Uncle Bob did just that until the day he died at the ripe old age of ninety.

The money Thomas put in savings and the $1 million life insurance policy made Joanna and their daughters very wealthy women. Cunning use of the stock options added to their wealth. While the money made day-to-day life easier, Joanna hated the wealth because of what it represented. The only time she was happy was when she was giving the money away, and Joanna was known for her unselfish philanthropy over her lifetime.

Joanna had a deep disdain for all forms of prejudice and bigotry. She particularly hated the fact that women were not allowed to vote. She got involved early in the campus equal suffrage organization while in college. Joanna eventually became a delegate to several state and national suffrage organizations. She doggedly stayed in the fight until passage of the federal Constitutional amendment in 1920.

Known locally as a determined firebrand, Joanna and her friends always entered a big float in the annual downtown homecoming parade known as the "Lilly Float for Suffragists." The float was followed by dozens of local suffragettes in decorated cars. She was tireless in mailing out *VOTE FOR WOMEN* literature, flyers, and buttons.

An equal passion of Joanna's was fighting poverty and hunger. She was instrumental in creating shelters and kitchens in many parts of the city and even formed a number of private employment agencies that helped employers and employees find each other. You could say that Joanna knew about networking long before it became popular. During the terrible years of the Great Depression, she organized and funded soup kitchens and bread lines.

During Joanna's lifetime, she supported many charities, created charitable foundations, and established generous scholarship programs designed specifically for those unable to afford college tuition.

After Thomas's disappearance, United Oil's income went ballistic—exceeding all expectations. This sent the value of its stock into the stratosphere, and that meant that Joanna's stock options were worth millions. She shrewdly exercised the options over the next fifteen years, buying and selling stock at precisely the correct moments, right up until just before the stock market crash.

Her daughter Ethel's husband, while being a lousy spouse, was a very adroit stock broker who saw the crash coming. He convinced Joanna to sell all of her stock and buy gold, silver, jewels, and real estate. He also advised her to put a lot of cash in safety deposit boxes throughout the city—not in bank accounts. His advice saved her fortune, so she thought it fitting to give most of it away where needed.

In addition to her philanthropic pursuits, Joanna vigorously supported organizations, candidates, and politicians who were interested in furthering equal rights legislation and litigation. She lived through times of great social injustice and made a difference by helping change the many inequities that existed.

Despite Joanna's many activities, her greatest passion was raising her daughters, Ethel and Dorothy. The young girls often accompanied their mother on trips and became familiar with many East Coast and Midwestern cities. She kept them busy, because it was her way of helping her daughters not miss their father so much.

Toward that end, Joanna got a dog shortly after Thomas disappeared. Initially, the pet was for the girls, but it soon became obvious that Joanna had an affinity for this particular dog they had named "Misty." Misty was a spaniel and Labrador retriever mix puppy that Joanna found at the local animal shelter. They understood each other.

Misty never needed to be on a leash or tied up in the yard.

She stayed near Joanna unless told differently, because it was what they both wanted. A bond existed between them such that Misty always knew what Joanna wanted and was happy to comply. It was a gift that Joanna passed on to Dorothy, who also always had a spaniel-lab mix.

Dorothy possessed many of Joanna's traits but, physically, she got her body frame from Thomas's side of the family—most notably, her height and her flaming, red hair. Ethel looked like Joanna, but had Thomas's personality and inventiveness. Both daughters attended the best schools and knew "all the right people," yet they never let it go to their heads. They were always polite and humble and would have made their father very proud.

Dorothy married Henry Craft, an engineer she had met at a party. It was love at first sight, and this lasted for the rest of their lives together. He was a good husband and father who had many friends. They had a wonderful and blessed life and taught their sons, Dave and Tom, the meaning of true love.

Ethel fell in love with a man who had no idea what love was. For all intents and purposes, he appeared to be a "nice guy," but behind closed doors, it was a much different matter. He constantly hurt Ethel, because he was incapable of love and acting accordingly. She tried to make it work, but years of no progress eventually showed her it was over. She divorced and moved back home with Joanna, which was good for both of them.

Joanna filled her life with as much as she could to hold back the tears and the hurt. Her heart was broken by the loss of her soul mate, and such a wound could never heal. All she could do was try and make the girls' childhoods as normal as possible.

Strangely, they always felt that someone was watching over them.

Chapter 10

Change

Tom looked across the table where they were all seated and gently cradled Jane's hand.

"We won't know exactly what we are dealing with here until we get into the file, but we do know that Grandfather's invention involves energy and powerful people who will not be happy about our discovery. We have to discuss and decide, collectively, if this is really something we want to take on," he said.

Jane looked into Tom's startling blue eyes. "You know the answer."

She then turned her head to look at Dave across the table. "You both do. You know you have no choice, and neither do Sally and I. Your mother told me a great deal about this device. Granted, it was usually after a couple glasses of pinot grigio following dinner, but she said her dad's invention would have changed our world and that she believed he'd been killed to keep that from happening. That much you know."

Jane's eyes clouded. "She'd told me that her mother blamed the invention for destroying their business, their marriage, their very lives. She considered it to be a curse. The years after Thomas's disappearance made her extremely bitter, and she seldom talked about it. Your grandmother was always afraid someone in the family would take up his cause. One night, she sat Aunt Ethel and your mom down and told them about what she called the motor. Your mother, after at least one too many glasses of wine, told me a little bit about it, too."

Dave looked surprised. "Why haven't *we* heard about this? Grandma never spoke specifically about what the invention was, except to say that it had something to do with energy, that they were paid a great deal of money for it, and that she would give it all away if Grandpa had not disappeared. Mom didn't say much either, except that everything regarding the invention disappeared along with Grandpa."

"Why would *our* mom not tell *us* what she told *you*?" mused Tom.

Jane responded, "Like your grandmother, she feared you might end up doing exactly what you are about to do. Your grandmother implored her to not tell you anything about what the invention was and that everything about it went missing. She believed that if anyone in the family attempted to make this technology happen, it would result in more heartache and death.

"Dot was torn between that possibility and what the motor could do for the world. Grandma told her that if it works, the motor would use very little electricity to operate a very large electric generator. That means it could generate enough electricity to operate itself and other devices. It's literally a new energy source. This motor would be an energy source that is continuous, renewable, clean, and can be used anywhere to power anything. Such a device would mean the end of the most powerful corporation in the world, United Oil Company. Your mother was terrified of what might happen to you if you were to attempt to build this motor, but she was equally frightened of what will become of our world if you didn't.

"The unfettered production and use of oil and gas has devastated the planet and our atmosphere. This has to stop sooner or later when the oil runs out, but will that be too late? Let's not wait and see. The future of our issue and life on Earth depends upon finding an energy source like this device may turn out to be.

"In retrospect, I think that's why she told *me* about the invention and not either one of *you*. If it should resurface as your grandmother feared, someone had to know what was at stake. Or it may have been that bottle and a half of pinot grigio. Anywhooo, she thought telling it to you two may have started one or both of you looking for a way to pick up this quest to 'change the world'— especially you, Tom, with your engineering degree. She made me promise not to tell you unless and until you found out something about it."

Tom sat dumbfounded. He couldn't believe that Jane knew *the* family secret, or at least a large part of it, and that neither Dave nor he had ever heard it.

"So, what exactly is it?" Tom asked.

"All I know is that it's a motor that uses magnetic fields to operate instead of gasoline. She said no one ever knew if he finished it or if he'd disappeared when he was getting close. Grandfather either did it or was close to finishing it, and that's why he disappeared. I think it's likely that the file you have will tell us one way or the other, but he must have been working on a prototype that either worked or was close to working, or why else would he have been killed?"

Dave was pensive. "Something must have convinced those

who would be affected by this technology that their continued existence was in jeopardy, requiring the desperate act of doing the unthinkable to avoid worse, and I doubt anything has changed. This invention will be dangerous only as long as it's a secret. Even they won't be able to stop it once it is proven and in the public eye. The world won't stand for suppression of this technology once they know about it and can see it working."

"Proving it is the issue," added Tom. "I can't wait to dig into what that file contains, but the concept of putting 'x' amount of energy in one end and getting 'x plus 1' out the other end violates a number of indisputable laws of physics. It's a black box. However, the energy that obviously exists in the magnetic fields of a permanent magnet is equally indisputable. If Grandpa figured out a way to harvest that energy and apply it to a crankshaft, like a windmill does, then it wouldn't violate any laws of physics any more than a windmill does. It's interesting and completely confusing. I have to see that file!"

"Yes, you do," Jane replied, looking deeply into Tom's eyes. "*If* this thing works, it's the answer that the human race and the planet needs ... now! No one can turn their back on the task of bringing it to the world, of literally saving our civilization. There simply can be no debate. Your mother knew this, and your grandmother feared it."

Sally stayed out of the discussion as long as she could. Finally, she rose and said to the group, "I don't know why, but this task has fallen on us."

Turning pointedly toward Dave, Sally said, "Particularly, it's fallen on Tom and you. Maybe all the milestones in history occurred because someone made a decision to sacrifice what was necessary in order to do something that made a difference for all. We all know that nothing worthwhile comes easily, that there really is no such thing as a free lunch, that if you think you can't - you're right, yada-yada-yada. Here, we possibly have an opportunity to make a huge difference in the quality of human life, the repair of the environment, and quite probably the continuity of our civilization. This isn't just a better toaster we have here. This may be our ... *everyone's* ... salvation!

"I believe if the oil runs low before we have a viable alternative energy, the wars that will break out over what is left will end us all. Energy is required to sustain our economies, and we will, quite literally, kill to have it. I agree a way must exist, by design or providence, to solve our energy needs before this occurs, and this motor sounds very promising. It has to be pursued, and, collectively, our family now has the resources to possibly make it happen. Finally, we owe it to your grandparents.

"Tom's electrical engineering and education degrees clearly give him the credentials to understand and communicate the science behind the invention. Dave and I have the experience and contacts needed to bring the resources to bear to duplicate and modernize your grandfather's work. Our son, Mike, is a patent attorney for heaven's sake, so we'll have someone we can trust providing us with legal advice. Also, we have the money your grandfather made off Big Oil for this invention, so it seems fitting we use their money to help put an end to them. Jane and I can coordinate everyone's efforts and support you in every way that we can. So, do we do this?"

"Of course," Jane said.

"We have to," concurred Tom, but could not stop himself at that. He stood, arched his back, gazed past everyone as if he were addressing a large crowd, and doing his best, if not perfect, Mark Twain impersonation, said, "As my good friend, Samuel L. Clemens might have said,

> *'On the subject of Progress...*
> *Progress is Difficult...*
> *It is difficult because...*
> *not only is it hard to accomplish...*
> *by those who would better the human condition...*
> *It is easy to block...*
> *by those who profit from the status quo...*
> *yet progress must endure...*
> *we must soldier on.'*
> *"And endeavor to persevere."*

He then bowed, and in his best not-so-perfect Elvis impression, said, *"Thank you. Thank you very much."*

"Yikes. Sit the hell down, Fat Boy," chided Dave. "This is serious, but your point is well taken, if not that well made."

Sally leaned over and asked Dave, "What was that?"

"Oh, that's right. For a long time now, we've only seen my brother in settings where he's forced to restrain himself. Since we were kids—whenever he can—he loves to mimic Mark Twain. You know, sound profound, etc. Mom jokingly called it, *'A prodigious predilection to pontificate,'* otherwise known as a talent for talking out his ass. I doubt it's the last time you'll see such things."

"Anyway," Dave said, "we should not too easily decide

to leap into the unknown. We could get crushed like bugs if we're not very, very smart and lucky. I guess we do have a duty to try and better the human condition ... damn you, Tom. Alright, but you're not the only one who can wax poetic at times like these. As Alfred, Lord Tennyson said,

'We are not now that strength which in old days
Moved earth and heaven; that which we are, we are;
One equal temper of heroic hearts,
Made weak by time and fate, but strong in will,
to strive, to seek, to find, and not to yield.'"

Dave smiled and threw in the towel. "Well, it's not how I planned to spend my retirement—this is a big change for all of us—but you're right. We have to try and make this invention happen."

"So, that's it then. We do it," Sally said with satisfaction.

Sally had recently retired as CEO of a large technology company that brought cutting edge consumer products to market. She'd met Dave when she was Vice-President in charge of Financing. He'd been providing financial advice to one of her company's clients who'd invented a new antennae her company was helping to patent and license-out to manufacturers.

Sally and Dave fell in love over several coffee breaks and meetings, married, and had their only child, Mike, a chemical engineer and patent lawyer—blessed with near-genius left brain/right brain capabilities. Mike still worked at his mom's old company in their patent department in New York City. Sally was experienced at running a meeting, so she was the natural choice to now take the lead in organizing this endeavor.

"We should begin to identify, discuss, and delineate a series of steps we'll follow, as best we can, to get this done, beginning with Tom's review of the file. After that, if you feel it's worth pursuing, we need to decide a number of issues."

She rose and stared out the kitchen window at the gray haze that hung like a funereal pall. "I agree with Dave that our greatest period of danger is while the invention is still secret. Once it's out in the public, the need for it will outweigh and overcome anyone's efforts to stop us and suppress it. The environment has gotten so bad these days that any viable alternative to burning fossil fuels will be unstoppable."

The air outside was tinted grayish-brown, typical of an *Ev-Con 2* day. "*Ev-Con*," or Environmental Condition, was the scale used by the Environmental Protection Agency to describe the health effect of the air on a given day. *Ev-Con 5* meant that heavy metals permeated the air, posed a substantial health risk, and created very low visibility. Staying indoors was recommended. *Ev-Con 1* meant that the air did not pose a substantial threat.

The environment—soil, air, water—was heavily polluted from our dependency on carbon fuels for all of the planet's burgeoning energy needs. Large, oil-producing conglomerates created at the turn of the twentieth century had gotten so powerful over the past ten decades that they'd essentially taken over the world's economy and, thereby, all of the larger and most powerful governments. As such, these corporations controlled and prevented any meaningful regulations protecting the environment at the expense of business. This eventually resulted in the virtual destruction of the Great Lakes, the Gulf of Mexico, and numerous other sites along each coast from the extraction, transportation, and refining of oil and its byproducts with no environmental restrictions at all.

Controlling a large percentage of the capital of a country also allowed United Oil to control the country's scientific knowledge and endeavors. They prevented the legislatures from providing enough funding for research universities and, thereby, made their corporate grants to these institutions the only means of financing any research programs and projects. Obviously, this also gave the corporations direct control over curriculum and what research projects would take place at research universities and companies within their reach.

In addition to controlling the economy, government, education, and research, these corporations controlled the media, and they got very good at using the news to their advantage. They funded many studies and research projects at colleges of social science around the globe to develop and hone techniques of persuasion.

This knowledge was employed to convince most of the population that the pollution they were spewing out was a necessary consequence of our continued advancement and even our continued existence. It was, essentially, a restatement of the manifest destiny doctrine previously used for taking the land, except that in the twentieth century, it was used for taking the environment.

Additionally, everyone's jobs and their lives as they knew them, depended upon the continued success of the corporations. It was a beneficial symbiotic relationship. The corporations got what they needed and, in turn, provided everything the people needed. The environment was here for us to use and abuse as needed. Its degradation was simply unavoidable collateral damage.

"Nobody likes what's happened to our environment, and looking through this haze is a constant reminder that something has to change," Sally said dejectedly. "I believe we have to be able to demonstrate to the world, in an indisputable manner, that this technology *is* that change, that *this is* the technological advancement we need to stop and eventually reverse the damage that has been done. Now the question becomes: how would we do that?"

Tom answered quickly. "A prototype—a functioning motor that produces enough torque to run an electric generator large enough to then, in turn, run the motor, *and* another application such as a set of lights! It has to be an indisputable demonstration, as Sally said. We need to create a motor that is not hooked up to any outside power source providing electricity to a set of lights, endlessly.

"The scientific community will scoff at any claim that this can be done, so only an 'in your face' demonstration will suffice. It will look to them like we're proposing that our motor can *create* energy. And we know that can't be done. Instead, I believe Grandpa's invention harvests existing energy. And we know that's done all the time. I believe the only way to win this argument is to show it works with a functioning prototype."

"So," said Dave, "the sooner we can create this prototype, the sooner we'll be safe again. We're gonna need a factory, engineers, a design team, and materials for them to work with as soon as possible. A lot will depend on what's in Grandpa's file in terms of how complete any plans and specifications are and how close he actually was to building a functional prototype himself. Tom and I will take the file to my home office first thing Monday and start going through it."

"I brought a great salad. Who's hungry?" asked Sally.

Jane fondly hugged her sister-in-law. "I'll go fetch some fried chicken and lots of wine to go with that salad."

"That'a girl," said Dave. "How did you get so lucky, Fat Boy?"

Sunday morning progressed as usual, slow and easy. Each couple spent the day doing what they would normally do, but it really wasn't the same. Thoughts of the motor were always with them now. From this point forward, it would be their constant companion—always there, whether in conscious thought or in the background— but always there.

Few people are given the opportunity, as individuals, to change the world. History shows that many people often came together to create such a change, but seldom was a world-changing event the responsibility of just a few. The magnitude of such a task is difficult to overstate. The fate of mankind's future would be in the hands of a few reluctant but willing individuals. The weight of such a responsibility was always present, and their lives would never be the same. They knew this, and no one slept well on Sunday night.

"*Knock, knock,*" said Dave as he opened the door early on Monday morning. "You ready yet, Fat Boy?"

"Born that way, Jackass," Tom answered as he put down his coffee mug. "Let's go get it. I see you brought your briefcase."

Dave could not believe that Tom was ready to go, because he was always late.

He looked curiously at Jane, who just shrugged her

shoulders and said, "Sally and I will see you guys at your house."

On the way to the bank, both men were looking in every vehicle near them. The bank had the normal Monday morning business crowd getting ready for the work week. Tom grabbed Dave's briefcase and retrieved the file without anyone seeming to notice. The trip to Dave's was equally uneventful. It was an *Ev-Con 3* day, so the added smog seemed to give them cover.

As soon as they got to Dave's house, they hurried downstairs to his office to open the file. There it was! It was like looking at the Dead Sea Scrolls, or perhaps even the Holy Grail or the Shroud of Turin. The future of everything seemed to hang in the balance. Tom pulled back the leather folder's flap to reveal about three to four inches of papers, some in their own folders. The smell of old paper filled the air. The last one to touch these documents was their grandfather, who hid them, knowing it was his final, desperate attempt to save the world.

Dave and Tom emerged from the basement about four hours later feeling both amazed and bewildered. Tom looked at Jane and Sally. "It's all there—everything we need to build it," he said.

"If we build it, they will come!" cried Dave.

A silence fell upon all of them. Eventually, Sally smirked at Dave and asked Tom, "How complete is the file? Are there plans with specifications?"

"Yes," said Tom. "Specs and drawings for the motor and each of its parts. It also has Grandpa's notes, a sort of journal he kept ... to the end. Obviously, there is nothing in the file that says what happened to him, but the last journal entry says they threatened his life unless he stopped working on the motor."

"Who threatened his life?" Jane asked.

"Thugs sent by the oil company that bought the invention from Grandpa," answered Dave.

"He wrote that he could no longer continue his work here because the danger to Joanna and the girls, Dorothy and Ethel, was too great. Also, he couldn't build the magnets he needed here, so his only option was to go to Europe and, hopefully, find help that he could trust. He said they were following his every move, so getting there without being noticed was unlikely. Grandpa left for France with two bodyguards and, as a precaution, he hid his complete file here and took out a million dollar life insurance policy for Joanna," Tom told them.

"The journal said he planned to go to Switzerland where he would be able to find help creating a more powerful permanent magnet. Amazingly, Grandpa then described a more powerful magnet made with the element neodymium that he was trying to have made. The oil company was making sure he didn't get any help with that here. He said they controlled and, thereby, prevented all research in the United States on using neodymium to make a much stronger magnet.

"They knew that a stronger magnet was required to make the prototype effective, so they did everything they could to suppress technology in this area. Grandpa discovered that the strongest magnets made at the time were not powerful enough to have any significant energy to harvest. It was like having a windmill without enough wind to make it work. Just like lack of enough wind made a windmill appear to not work, lack of a strong magnetic field from the permanent magnet made the magnetic motor appear to not work. As long as he had only weak magnets to work with, critics could point to its lack of power and say it was useless."

Tom paraphrased Grandpa's journal words. "He wrote that he later realized the oil company recognized the neodymium potential early on and actively suppressed any effort to employ, or even look for, a stronger magnet. They told him his invention wasn't important, because their testing showed the motor would never produce enough torque or power to do anything useful, let alone replace the internal combustion engine. The file has the copies of their studies and research showing the motor does harvest a little energy from the permanent magnet, but concluded it would always be too little to do any useful work.

"The file also contains a legal folder with the contracts and letters from his lawyer regarding the sale of the invention to United Oil Company." They all looked at one another. "That's right, *the* United Oil Company—the one that now owns everything. That's who we're up against. Grandpa wrote that while they showed him the motor had some potential, it was really just a toy that could never replace existing motors. After the sale, Grandpa discovered *that* was a lie when he somehow got their neodymium research file. Shortly after that, he started working on it again."

Sally looked at Dave. "United Oil Company. Really? Are you kidding? Well, that explains a lot. Who else could make people and research disappear without a trace? No wonder the women in your family were scared that the motor could resurface. Fighting *that* corporation will be like fighting the devil himself," she said in desperation.

Dave handed Jane and Sally the note that had fallen from the file when Tom first opened it. The women finished reading it, and Tom said, "I think he always believed the motor would work, so he never completely believed their lies. They wore him down and then offered him a lot of money to sell them the rights to it. He sold out. Deep down he knew it and felt guilty. Then, he got proof of their lies and treachery. I think that's why he wrote the P.S. on his note."

"According to his journal," said Dave, "when he discovered they were sitting on the magnet technology the motor needed, Grandpa decided to rebuild the prototype and attempt to find someone, somewhere to build a neodymium magnet to operate it. He added a machine shop to the garage at the house and built a *new* motor with some improvements over the original design. The results were promising, but the best permanent magnet he could find was still lacking.

"United Oil found out about Grandpa's rekindled efforts and sent some ruffians to threaten him. Shortly after that, someone broke into the machine shop and damaged some machines, but didn't find the prototype. At about that same time, he apparently got a tip from a friend at Michigan State University that a lab in Zurich might be working on a compound using neodymium. It looks like he decided quickly to go there, creating this file to hide in the library as insurance and hoping an heir might one day find it if he didn't return."

Sally looked at Tom. "Obviously, Dave read the journal and other folders while you reviewed the specs and drawings for the motor. Do you think it will work, Tom?" she asked.

"I must admit I was skeptical, thinking it was just another attempt to create the mythical perpetual motor. Energy cannot be created, so no device will allow you to end up with more energy than you started with. It's simply not possible. Then, I read Grandpa's paper entitled, *The Evolution of the Reciprocating Piston Motor*. Let me read it to you." Tom reached for the yellowed paper and read aloud to them.

'*Movement is the force from which we derive all work. If something is moving, it has energy which can be utilized resulting in the production of work.*

The Ancients observed that nature created movement, and if that "natural movement" could be captured and harnessed, it could be used to produce work. Windmills capture and harness the movement of air, and paddle wheels do the same with moving water. This is "natural energy." These devices produce work, and the movement that they capture is provided by nature, which is, therefore, free; however, it is not available everywhere and at any time. Additionally, the amount of power that such devices can produce is limited to the amount of force behind the natural movement being captured. As such, natural movement and the free energy that could be produced from it was simply too limited.

Lack of portability, consistency, and power brought about the need for a device that could produce the same rotary movement as a windmill or paddle wheel, but could do it anywhere, at any time, and with much greater power or torque. Such a device shifted attention away from natural movement to "created movement." That is movement created with "applied energy" rather than by capturing natural movement. Created movement made such a device possible by using fuel, which is portable, consistent, and powerful; however, the design for the device to effectively harness this movement was illusive until the invention of the reciprocating piston motor.

It was known long ago that steam could provide very forceful created movement, but it took over two thousand years to invent the piston design that harnessed that movement. Instead of using natural movement resulting from natural energy, the piston steam engine produced work using created movement resulting from applied energy supplied by a fuel. For the first time in history, it turned fuel into significant motion and made the Industrial Revolution possible. The next step in the reciprocating piston motor's evolution was the creation of the internal combustion engine, which is even more portable and powerful.

This advancement in the reciprocating piston design allowed work to be done anywhere and with great power. We owe much of what we have created to the reciprocating piston motor, and the time has come for the next step in its evolution -- the use of natural movement instead of created movement for its operation. Natural movement that exists abundantly and with great power is the only answer. The natural movement of wind and water have been captured and harnessed to the limits of our technology and are simply not enough. There is, however, another type of natural movement that is available anywhere, anytime, and with great power, but its capture and harnessing are not as obvious as they are for wind and water. This other type of natural movement is from magnetic fields.

Presently, we use only the effect a magnetic field has upon an electron to create movement, which is an electric motor. The natural movement that a magnetic field creates upon another magnetic field or objects such as steel is irrelevant to this process. In an electric motor, electricity is causing the magnetic fields (and the magnet generating it) to move. Without electricity (i.e., applied energy), there is no created movement. By contrast, in a magnetic motor, natural movement is caused by the interaction of the magnetic fields with other fields and/or objects (i.e., natural energy) and not by electricity. This distinction is all-important, because only the latter can capture natural movement where the former has none. As such, an electric motor can never produce more energy than it uses, while a magnetic motor can do so by capturing and using natural movement to create work just as is done by a windmill or paddlewheel.

The purpose of the above discussion was solely to point out that it matters where the movement being harnessed originates. Is it natural movement already in existence, or is it created movement resulting from applied energy? If the most efficient electric motor in the world were coupled with the most effective electric generator in the world, that generator could never produce enough electricity to operate the electric motor on which it runs. This would be the mythical "perpetual" motor and would violate accepted laws of physics. As the electric motor uses only applied energy, some of this energy is converted or lost in the process of producing work; therefore, it cannot sustain itself. The magnetic motor can sustain itself without violating any laws of physics, because it captures and harvests natural movement.

By example, a hydroelectric generator operated by a river/ reservoir is not considered a "perpetual" motor, because it captures and harvests natural movement resulting in the free production of work or natural energy from the moving water. The source of free energy it is capturing and using to do this is obvious. A magnetic motor is no different in that it also captures natural movement resulting from natural energy, but because its source of energy is not so obvious one forgets it is, in fact, capturing free energy. Additional confusion comes from the fact that a magnetic motor uses a small amount of electricity to actuate the magnetic fields that manipulate the natural movement being captured. This use of magnets and electricity often results in the assumption that a magnetic motor is just another electric motor bound by the same laws of physics. But, it is not.

The reciprocating piston design is the best way to harness movement, and attempting to operate it with natural movement is not a new idea. However, a design operated by the natural movement created by permanent magnets has eluded inventors for decades. Prior magnetic motor designs are unable to manipulate the fields to create appropriate reciprocating piston movement, and previous patents reveal painfully complex and inefficient designs that produced very little work. This design uses the reciprocating piston to capture and harness energy existing in magnetic fields. It is, in essence, a windmill in a box.

T.C. 1913

Tom finished reading their grandfather's paper. It was like a voice from the past, as if Thomas was reaching through the years to explain his scientific theory about how the motor can be a new energy source. "In looking at the design, I do believe it is possible that the motor may actually work, especially with the technology available today.

"I looked up neodymium online and found very little information. The research in Grandpa's file on neodymium magnets simply doesn't exist anywhere else. It shows that such a magnet can be made that is capable of lifting over a ton of weight. That is a lot of energy, and if it can be harvested efficiently and applied to turning a crankshaft, it may be possible to operate a generator capable of producing more electricity than is needed to operate the motor. This is the concept of exceeding unity, and that has never been done. It would be such a game changer."

"Wait, wait, wait ... you used the *internet* to search for neodymium?" cried Sally. "That could lead them directly to us!"

"Oh, shit! It never occurred to me, but I suppose it's possible."

"*Too* possible," Dave said. "Grandpa's journal mentioned how effective the security department at United Oil Company was, and I assume they have only gotten better."

"We need to start watching our backs," said Sally. "One brief online search of an element by some science teacher may go unnoticed, but we have to assume it didn't, and we have to assume we will be watched."

"Okay, now I'm scared," bemoaned Jane. "These people will stop at nothing, and that makes me scared. No, wait a minute—that makes me *mad*. If they think they can threaten my family without risk, they have another thing coming!"

"We need to plan our strategy for this war, and the first tactic is misdirection," said Sally. "We must appear as if nothing has happened and that our lives have nothing to do with the motor. For now, let's make three copies of the file on Dave's copier and return the original to the safety deposit box. Remember, we must look as if everything is normal."

"Oh, one other thing I forgot to mention," Dave said. "The file contains a description of a secret room in the garage where Grandpa Thomas kept the prototype—*the* prototype! We have to go check it out!"

Chapter 11

Concealed

"Do you really think the prototype is still there?" Jane asked Dave, with a hint of excitement in her voice. She loved an adventure, even while admonishing others to keep both their feet firmly planted.

"We're talking nearly one hundred years ago. It's hard to say. I've spent a lot of time in that garage, and I didn't see anything that made me suspicious. Given the history of the house, I always thought we might find some hidden passageways and even a secret room, but we never did ... . You know, the kinds of things you think of when you're a kid. Learning that one exists is no surprise to me! If these builders wanted it not to be found, it won't be, and it's that simple. These guys were craftsmen of the highest order, and that's apparent throughout the house."

"I have one more question that has been bothering me since I first heard about your grandfather's invention. Why hasn't someone else thought of it by now?" asked Jane.

"Well, I have some thoughts on that," said Tom. "It's been concealed. A number of factors had to come into play to stop others from discovering, and then creating, this technology. Most of these factors have been created by United Oil in the hope they would delay its discovery, and they were incredibly successful. Most significant among these was their exclusive knowledge—early on, according to Grandpa's file—of neodymium's magnetic properties."

Tom went on to explain that they then used their influence on the scientific community, fertilized with massive grants and scholarships, to discourage any magnetic research using neodymium. That discouragement kept neodymium, one of many elements not fully understood, on the sidelines. It was mainly used to color glass then later used in laser technology. But using it to create extremely powerful magnets has been successfully suppressed.

"In addition, the mechanism to harvest the energy in a permanent magnet—the motor—quite simply has not been thought of by anyone else yet—at least not by anyone we know. Maybe others met a fate similar to Grandpa's. It took over two thousand years before someone thought of using a reciprocating piston to capture the movement made by steam. Taking a few hundred years to think of a design to capture the movement created by magnets doesn't seem out of line to me. It's been said, 'The obvious is only obvious once it is obvious.' And it is no surprise that, once again, a reciprocating piston design is the mechanism used to capture this energy."

Tom suddenly looked annoyed. "But possibly most important is that any incentive to experiment with this technology is stymied by what I call scientific arrogance. Once they are convinced that a scientific principle prevents a certain result, it is virtually impossible to show them that such a result can still be achieved. One is literally considered a heretic for proposing such a thing, let alone thinking it. It's a career stopper."

Realizing that he may have gotten a tad too serious, and in an effort to lighten the mood, Tom reached his hand partially into his shirt, *a la* Napoleon, assumed his Mark Twain pose, and pontificated,

Regarding scientific endeavors;
Science is a fickle mistress,
Revealing her secrets only when and where
she sees fit; and never to those
who do not beg the chase.
As such, if we decide we know
all there is to know about something,
we will be right!
Convincing the scientific community
that they are mistaken,
is like swimming
Against the Current,
It can be done, but only by the
best, strongest and luckiest,
most will drown.
Sir Isaac Newton was a Science God
To appear to violate his principles
is heresy, period.

Tom finished with his Elvis voice, "Thank you, thank you very much!" and sat down.

Sally seemed both amused and confused. "But what principle says it cannot work, and why is it wrong, Tom?"

"Let me explain. In essence, the principle holds that energy cannot be *created*. It's not that it's wrong, it's that it simply doesn't apply … . Wait, let me start at the beginning. Movement is the source of all of our energy."

Tom told them how electricity was the collective movement of electrons across a conductive material. "In order for it to occur, some process was employed to cause the electrons within the conductive material to move. Further, the conductive material, that is, a copper wire, must form a loop so that the electrons keep moving endlessly in a circle, that is, a circuit.

"The process used to cause electrons to move employs the magnetic fields produced by simple magnets. Basically, electrons cannot exist in the same space as a magnetic field. If a magnetic field, or the magnet producing it, is moved toward an electron, it'll cause that electron to move—just like a tennis racket hitting a tennis ball.

"The simplest form of this process was to move a conductive material next to, or within the magnetic field of, a permanent magnet. This movement caused the electrons to move in the direction that the magnetic field moved and, thereby, produced electricity.

"As such, movement must be created to generate electricity, just like any other form of work. How we create that movement is what pollutes the environment and expends tremendous amounts of resources. Heat is used to create movement for the simple reason that it causes gases to expand. An expanding gas causes whatever is in its way to move. Producing heat is done in a variety of forms and ranges from burning wood to igniting explosive mixtures—all of which result in the movement required to generate electricity. It was what Grandpa Thomas called *created movement.*

"By contrast, Grandfather used the term *natural movement* to describe movement that came from nature, such as the wind or water flowing downhill. These types of movement are free, do not pollute, and are also used to generate electricity. We use windmills to capture, harness, and convert the wind's natural movement into mechanical energy in the form of a rotating shaft, which is then used to operate an electric generator. The same process is used by a paddle wheel in a river.

"A windmill and a paddle wheel are mechanisms created to harvest natural movement by turning it into something useful—mechanical energy. These mechanisms harvest only natural movement, and before now, no such mechanism existed that uses both natural movement and created movement together. Apparently, this bifurcation of types of movement resulted in the scientific assumption that such a mechanism combining both doesn't exist. It appears that they've not considered the possibility that a small amount of created movement could be used to release a large amount of natural movement. This is exactly what a magnetic motor does, and it is why they don't see it. And United Oil has done everything possible to keep it that way."

Tom's eyes grew even bigger as he explained further. "Engineers and physics students are taught that producing created movement expends more energy than the energy resulting from that movement, including electricity from a generator, and that, therefore, the desired result of positive production or gain of energy from such a device is impossible, pointing to the law of physics that says we cannot create energy. But this law does not apply because of the addition of natural movement to aide in the process of the operation of such a device.

"An engineer who hears of a claim that a device can result in the generation of more electricity than it uses immediately dismisses the possibility as a violation of accepted and indisputable laws of physics. Such a device would even exceed the mythical perpetual motor, which would only produce enough energy to operate itself. Perpetual motors can't exist, although often attempted. Every attempt has failed, and the U.S. Patent Office maintains a collection of perpetual motion gimmicks. If that's impossible, a device that operates itself and has energy or electricity generation left over is crazy and reveals the ignorance of the claimant. Such a prejudice prevents consideration that there may be a way *around* those laws.

"Again, that's what a magnetic motor does. By harvesting natural movement within magnetic fields, a device like a magnetic motor coupled to a generator can be made that can result in the generation of free electricity, just like a windmill. The obvious difference from a windmill is that such a device can be portable and used anytime, anywhere, because the energy it harvests is contained within itself—in the magnets."

Tom told them that Grandpa Thomas created a type of magnetic motor that used a reciprocating piston. "It harvested the natural movement of magnets that in turn caused the piston to move instead of using heat or explosive gasses to make it move. This was revolutionary! If enough energy could be harvested to be useful, it'd be nothing less than a new energy source!"

Sally was mesmerized by Tom's explanation. "Wow. Wow. I can see why your students loved you so much. That was *wonderful*. I wish I'd had a physics teacher that could make such complex scientific information so understandable—almost sexy—yikes, I guess I have my own problems," she said.

Dave smirked. "Yeah, he's a wonder alright. We often wonder about him. I thought he'd *never* shut up. Let's go look in that garage!"

Sally and Jane ran to the windows. Jane looked back at Tom.

"There's a dark-colored van with tinted windows parked across the street! I've never seen a car parked there before. I don't like the look of it!" cried Jane.

Suddenly, the van pulled away and drove down the street. "Whew, that was weird," said Sally.

The group waited about fifteen minutes, watching the street. Nothing seemed unusual. Finally, Tom and Dave could wait no longer. They had to go and see what was in that garage. Grandpa had conveniently included a drawing with the description of the secret entry door in the back wall of the shop he'd added to the garage.

About halfway to the house, and right before the S curve, Tom noticed the dark-colored van with tinted windows trailing behind them. Dave was at the wheel of his new Corvette C5-R and in no mood to be threatened or followed to where they were going, so he nailed the seven liter, handmade, monstrous Detroit power plant that faithfully roared to life with a prolonged twin squawk from the rear tires. In an instant, they were pinned to the back of their seats while the roar of the engine increased in intensity with each passing second and each passing car. They blew easily through the S curves as the 'Vette jumped to over one hundred twenty before Dave backed off a bit while he traversed through expressway traffic. The dark van behind them disappeared into a thick curtain of smog.

Once the two were far enough ahead, Dave hit the brakes, downshifted, tweaked the emergency brake, popped the clutch, and entered an exit ramp in a power slide or drift.

Tom thought, *The boy can drive!*

What Tom did *not* know was that Dave attended every corporate seminar and/or perk that taught advanced driving skills. Kidnapping of corporate executives as hostages was becoming more commonplace, so much so that many were offering various types of *How to Avoid Trouble* seminars, such as a weekend of training with the Michigan State Police driving instructors. Dave loved driving and attended many such training sessions where he acquired very impressive vehicular skills.

A love of driving fast manifested itself in the cars he owned. Dave had to have the latest and greatest, which he then sold, often at a profit, to acquire the next latest and greatest. This 'Vette was the culmination of a lifetime of owning cutting edge vehicles. It was built and made street legal by Pratt & Miller, who built the car for General Motors Racing. It took connections and lots of cash to own one of these.

And worth every penny, Tom thought as they carved the exit ramp.

Instantly, they were off the ramp, under the bridge overpass, and in the parking lot of a gas station convenience store. Once the brothers were convinced they'd lost the van, they took the back roads to the house.

Tom peeled himself from the back of his seat. "It occurs to me that those guys were not trying very hard to hide themselves. It was like they *wanted* us to know they were tailing us. It also seems likely that they'd know the location of the house, so I think we should get there as quickly as we can, bro—I mean, Jackass" he said.

"So be it, Captain—I mean, Fat Boy. Aye, aye. It's my

pleasure. Let's see what this baby can do through those curves!"

And with that, the 'Vette leapt forward and undulated gracefully over the curved, well-maintained roads leading to the house's neighborhood. In one fell swoop, the sports car sprang up the driveway and into the garage, closing the door behind it. Both men quickly exited and carefully looked out the garage windows. Nothing—no cars—no movement of any kind.

Eventually, they went down and closed the gates. Dave was morose. "This is the first time we've had to use these. It's like now *we're* walking in our grandfather's footsteps," he said. And what he didn't say aloud was, *Hopefully, not our grandfather's deathly path.*

The gates' locks had ceased to function long ago, so only a center latch held the two tall, wrought-iron skeletons closed. Tom shrugged. "Better than nothing, I guess. Let's go see what we can find." Just then Tom stopped, tapped Dave on the arm, and said with a smile, "Remember the dogs? I almost looked for them. Ours and Grandma's always came with us to lock the gates at night and then outrace us to the porch. God, I miss having a dog."

The two turned and ran up the driveway, sort of like the way they used to when they were kids visiting Grandma and Aunt Toot, except they were way slower and hobbled now. To a kid, the best part of that mausoleum of a house was the *outside.* The grounds were spectacular! But age made the run up the drive turn into more of a labored trot for the brothers. Still, youthful memories flooded over both of them as each felt the excitement of exploration upon entering the garage.

They went in, locked the door behind them, made their way through the garage to the shop located at the rear, and headed to the back wall.

It was an unremarkable wall save for a tool bench running along its left half and big, floor-to-ceiling wooden shelving beginning at the end of the bench and continuing to the wall that was next to the house. It all looked extremely solid and unmovable. Dave pushed at various points along the wall, but nothing gave.

Tom took out the diagram and walked over to the center of the shelves. He craned his neck into a shelf at about chest height, reached in, and *clunk*—the middle section of shelving swivelled open. A slight push with his finger kept the massive piece of wall moving back, which revealed a cool, dark room with an ancient, musty odor. The air was stale with a sterile quality about it. This was to be expected for a room that had been unoccupied for nearly a century.

He could barely make out the shop's back wall, which was about fifteen feet away. Drawings and diagrams were hanging on the walls. Tom spotted a light switch to the left and flipped it. An impressive array of lights came on, and there *it* was. In the middle of the room, on a stand made of angle iron topped with thick aluminum, sat the prototype.

"To think it was last touched by our grandfather, who we never got a chance to meet, but owe so much. Picking up where he left off and seeing his work in front of us makes me proud and honored. This task is now ours," said Tom.

Together, the brothers explored the room that looked more like a museum display due to all of the antique machinery. Because the electromagnets used DC (direct current) electricity, a rudimentary electric motor operated an even cruder electric generator that provided the needed DC electricity for the prototype. It was a two cylinder motor made of aluminum with one cylinder placed horizontally on each side of a crankshaft. At each end of a cylinder was an electromagnet with a piston in the center, supported by four rods, one dissecting each corner of a square piston housing that contained a permanent magnet protruding from each side toward the electromagnets.

The DC generator was connected to two big batteries that in turn were connected to four on-off power switches. All of these were connected to a bar so that they could move in unison. Wires from these switches led to four three-way switches—each connected to the body of the motor at the center of each cylinder. From these switches, two wires connected to each electromagnet. These switches were located so that a trip bar connected to the piston housing would flip the switch back and forth as the piston went back and forth. This caused the electromagnets to reverse polarity, resulting in the piston continually moving back and forth, or reciprocating.

Dave looked questioningly at Tom. "You don't suppose it could still work, do you?" he asked.

"No, I don't think so. The batteries surely have had it, but with new ones, it might ... ."Tom flipped up the bar operating the power switches. *Just making sure*, he thought. *You never know.* To his surprise, the pistons moved about half an inch. "Shit, that's a really good sign!" he cried.

Dave walked toward the wall nearest the house. "What the hell is this? It looks like a door handle or something," he said.

He turned the handle, and the door swung in. It was a secret entrance to the house! *Clang!!!!!!* They heard a noise from the direction of the front gates. The brothers ran into the garage, and peering out the garage windows, they saw that the gate stood open.

"Oh, my, God! They're here. They've found us," Dave whispered.

Suddenly, they saw two men walking down the porch stairs toward the garage. One held a pistol in each hand, while the other shouldered a twelve-gauge shotgun.

"Hide in the room!" both brothers whispered at the same time as they ran toward the room. They reached it and tried to swivel the door shut, but it would not budge. It was stuck open. Tom saw the two men walking past the big garage doors toward the side entry door. Soon, he heard the door handle rattle and the lock being tested.

"Here it is!" whispered Dave. With no time to spare, he pushed a lever that allowed the door to swivel shut.

Tom thought he heard the garage door open just before the *clunk* of the secret door slamming shut.

The brothers leaned tight against the door. "Do you think they saw the door close?" Dave asked. Suddenly, they were startled by a knock on the shelving.

Chapter 12

Curious

"They must have seen the door swivel shut," whispered Dave. "I'll call 9-1-1."

"No! Wait a second," Tom said. He put an ear to the door. When he felt cold steel against his cheek, he realized the door and walls were paneled in steel plates. "This is a safe room! Let's see what they're doing before you call the police."

Tom looked around on the wall and spotted what appeared to be a hand-sized piece of steel made to swivel up to reveal whatever was behind it. He unlatched a steel hook holding it shut and swivelled it up out of the way. Behind it was a pencil-shaped slit about eight inches long and approximately half an inch tall.

Looking through it, Tom saw that it was hidden by a ventilation grate on the wall over the tool bench. It provided a view of the entire shop and the two guys who were looking over the place where the door was concealed in the shelving.

Unexpectedly, one of the men made an announcement to the shelves. "We are glad to see that you're safe. My name is Alex, and this is Steve. We're not here to harm you; we are here to help you. I'll leave our business card on this work bench. Call us," he said. The fellow then turned and walked directly to where Tom was watching from behind the hidden peephole and placed the card on the bench. The men tucked away their guns and left the garage, locking the door behind them. Eventually, Tom and Dave heard the gates slam.

"That was freaky. So, who do you think those guys were?" Tom asked as he looked out the peephole again just to be sure they were gone.

"I don't know, but Grandpa Thomas built one helluva room here," Dave said. He looked around and patted the steel wall.

The wall was double-lined with steel plates that rose to about waist level and provided a bulletproof zone to that height. The single steel plate from that point to the ceiling would stop a round from most guns, he thought. Dave looked at the second door that led into the house and pulled it open. Like the door leading to the garage, it was double-lined in steel and swivelled on massive steel hinges so perfectly balanced that the impervious doors operated with the slightest push of a finger. They were secured shut with large sliding bolts that could never be moved from the outside.

Dave went through the concealed house door and found himself in the back of the kitchen pantry. This door utilized shelving to conceal its location—much like the one that led to the garage. He walked through the kitchen, down the hallway to the back door, and looked out its peephole.

"Nobody around," he whispered. Again, the door was constructed to allow a good view while preventing any intrusion.

Dave thought, *This place is built like a fortress; they didn't miss a trick.* He surveyed the driveway a bit and noticed the gates were closed and latched.

Meanwhile, Tom retrieved the card the two men had left behind and handed it to Dave. The card was blank save for a local phone number engraved on it.

Dave said sarcastically, "How clandestine of them. What should we do, Fat Boy?"

"I don't know, Jackass," Tom pointed to the card in Dave's hand, "but I'm sure not ready to give *those* two guys a call. I checked that outside door in the garage, and it was not damaged. That means they picked the lock *and* opened that door about as fast as I could with a key. These guys, whoever they are, are pros. Anyway, it looks like they're gone, so let's check out Grandpa's prototype."

Dave thought about their wives. "I'll call Jane and Sally and tell them what happened. They're probably starting to worry about us. After all, we really don't know to what lengths these people are willing to go to stop us. Hopefully, the dudes here today aren't the bad guys, but who else could they be?" he asked without expecting or needing an answer.

Tom and Dave spent the next few hours looking over the motor and the drawings displayed on the wall. Tom made a list of everything he needed. The list was not too extensive. Mainly, he needed electronics.

"It's so cool to see early 20th century technology in a pristine and unaltered condition," said Tom. "Even the two permanent magnets still have an amazing amount of strength left in them. I can tell from a few wear marks and a wastebasket full of busted switches that Grandpa had this motor running, and running fast! Grandpa described in his journal that he had trouble keeping the mechanical switches from busting apart from the quick and constant switching the motor required of them."

The switches looked like they could take that punishment for only a minute or so before they came apart. That meant it would run long enough to test, but not long enough to effectively demonstrate its potential. Using modern technology, Tom could fix this issue using a position transducer—a computer and solid-state relays to switch the polarity of the electromagnets without moving parts. This would also allow him to control the motor's rpm and timing. Modern electromagnets could create and collapse the magnetic fields much faster while using less electricity than these relics. Add a new DC generator and two new twelve-volt batteries, and it would be ready to run!

"I know a magnet manufacturer up by Petoskey that might not be on their radar, not yet, anyway," said Tom. "An old classmate of mine works there. He can be trusted. Ohhhh, darrrrn, you know what that means, don't you, Jackass? I mean, Old Man? A road trip up north! I'll call my friend later today and set up a visit for this weekend."

Dave smiled broadly. "Mmm, I love that neck of the woods! I have connections at a beautiful, old hotel on Little Traverse Bay; maybe we can stay there. We need to get back to our wives, Fat Boy. I don't like leaving them alone anymore," he said.

"Regarding security, I think we should finish up the few remaining renovations we'll need to make for all of us to live in this house. I didn't really notice before, but this place was built with security as a top priority. That must be a major reason why Grandpa bought it. We'd stand a better chance of keeping everybody safe here, Tom."

"Agreed."

Together, they walked back through the kitchen, the pantry, and into the safe room. Dave locked the door handle and slid the upper and lower steel bars of the pantry door into place. This was the same design that was on every exterior door in the house. They exited through the garage's shelf door, and it closed behind them with a resounding thud as the push-button locking mechanism engaged.

The trip back to Tom's passed in silence, except for the throaty sound of the 'Vette's engine. Doing *anything* was anticlimactic after what they had been through. There was so much to tell their wives and a lot to do if they were going to get the prototype working again. When they pulled into Tom's driveway, they noticed the same van that they had dusted on the freeway parked across and down the street a few doors.

"Don't like the looks of that," Dave said ominously as they got out of the car and glared at the van. The vehicle's windows were too dark, and they couldn't tell if anyone was inside.

They walked into his house where their wives were apprehensively waiting. Tom grabbed two Cokes, handed one to Dave, leaned on the kitchen counter, and said to Sally and Jane, "There was a time today when I thought you two were about to become widows."

Sally was beyond anxious. "What are you talking about?" she cried.

Dave explained what had transpired, about being followed, the two men with guns and the card, the safe room, the prototype, and what they needed to get for it. The two women stared at each other and then at their husbands.

"Jesus H. Christ!" wailed Jane. "What if they come here? This is getting serious. I'm scared. What should we do? What about the kids? Will *they* be targets?"

Dave tried to calm Jane. "That may one day be a concern,

but for now, I think we're alright," he said. He was trying to convince himself as well as Jane.

"I agree," said Sally. "They couldn't possibly know what we have just learned ourselves. The faster we move, the more we can accomplish before they get wind of what we're doing. We have a window early on, maybe a couple of days, before they would know enough to where our safety may become a concern. We must try and cover our every move, beginning with getting the new electromagnets. You mentioned a place up north to do that? Really? That seems like an unlikely place to find a state-of-the-art magnet company."

Tom reassured them. "Yes, I know it seems an unlikely place, but that's what makes it good. I've known Ed since Caltech, and I know we can trust him. Besides, we won't tell him what we're doing. I'll just tell him we can't—for his own good. Most importantly, he is really, really excellent at this stuff. If anyone can make what we need, he can." Tom was confident about that.

Sally took it all in. "You have to go see him and explain what you need. Phones and the internet cannot be trusted with this information. Dave and I can get us reservations at an adorable hotel on Little Traverse Bay. No one said we can't enjoy some of this; besides, it'll make great cover for your meeting with him. You're simply meeting an old friend for dinner while in the neighborhood. Nothing inherently suspicious about that," she said.

Tom's mind was racing a mile a minute. "I should be able to get a propane-powered DC generator in Detroit. We can drive there tomorrow," he said, glancing at Dave. "Look, girls, Dave and I think we should make Grandma's house livable for all of us and get moved in right away. It's the safest place to be."

"Well, that sounds like my territory," Jane said. "Sally and I will go to the house tomorrow and check out what has to be done first. I'm thinking a good cleaning and new appliances to begin with. We can get that done quickly. I'll contact a cleaning company today; Tom will call Ed to see if his wife, Candace, and he can meet us for dinner this Saturday night at the hotel. Dave, please make our reservations for Saturday night in Petoskey. Road trip!"

"Sounds like a plan," conceded Sally. "Dave and I will head home for the evening and meet you back here around ten in the morning if that's alright with you guys?"

"It's all good," Jane said.

"I'll be ready when you get here," replied Tom.

"*That* would be a first, Fat Boy," Dave's voice trailed off. "In the meantime, find out where we need to go to get you that generator. Goodnight, all, see you around ten."

Tom followed them to the door. "G'night, you two. Drive carefully and watch for a tail," he warned them. "I see that van is still parked there. I'll watch to see if it moves when you leave. Don't forget to call us when you get home," he said.

"Will do, Bro."

The van did not move and showed no signs of life when Sally and Dave pulled out of the driveway. They didn't notice anyone following them on the drive home. Once parted, all four of them set about their appointed duties in preparation for the next day.

In the morning, Dave and Sally arrived at his brother's house promptly at ten o'clock. As expected, Tom wasn't ready.

"My truck is gassed up and ready to go," Tom said as he finally entered the kitchen and kissed Jane good-bye. "Seems like I'm always waiting for you, Dave. Let's go, Jackass!"

Dave eyed his brother and disgustedly shook his head. He got up from the kitchen table, grabbed his coffee cup, kissed Sally, and pursued Tom out the door.

The parked van they'd seen before was nowhere in sight, so they felt a little better about leaving their wives alone again. "It took me awhile to find a DC generator," Tom told Dave, "I was beginning to think I wouldn't when I came across a generator used for cell phone towers. It's on the south side at a factory distributor."

Reginald Forsythe pushed the intercom button on his telephone and said, "Please send in Mr. Johnson."

"Yessir," replied Ms. Flanigan, the secretary.

Mr. Forsythe finished reading the dossier marked, *Top Secret*, that Hugh Simmons had put together over eighty-five years ago about the motor. As president of United Oil Company, Forsythe was aware of the "project," but up until now, had thought it was merely a policy directive to actively discourage research in the area of magnetism and electromagnetic energy, in general. However, Mike Johnson was head of security and was entrusted with monitoring the heirs of Thomas Cunningham—and the scientific community, *in toto*—for any signs of new research.

"Hello, Mr. Forsythe," Johnson said as he entered the office. "I have some curious news. It seems the grandsons of Thomas Cunningham may be poking their noses around their grandfather's bane. We've been watching them closer since they started remodeling their grandfather's old house on a hunch they might find something. It seems they found something, alright, because on Monday, one of them did some online research regarding neodymium."

"*Curious* news? I'd call it a lot more than that ... we have to know exactly what they're up to, AND NOW!" shouted Forsythe. "Make this your first priority. I don't want one of them to even breathe without us hearing and smelling it. You got me?"

"Yessir. We already have surveillance on them, but I'll step it up to a full court press. We'll be watching and listening to everything they do and say from now on."

What Forsythe did not know was that Johnson had a *Top Secret* portfolio of his own from Hugh Simmons. It was handed down to each head of security since Simmons retired. The file contained clear orders that its contents were to be revealed to *no one* and that the existence of the file was known only to the head of security and the chairman of the Board of Directors. Any violation of this directive would result in immediate dismissal, together with every punitive measure that United Oil was capable of inflicting, regardless of cost and effort.

Hugh Simmons had known many, many decades ago that the survival of the megagiant depended upon the suppression of electromagnetic technology. This meant efforts to prevent and surveil any research in the area had to continue in perpetuity. To insure this happened, Simmons created a secret wing of the security department, unknown to all but the head of security and the chairman of the board. Quite simply, it was charged with the task of doing whatever was necessary to suppress and prevent the technology.

As this mission often involved illegal activities, the secret, separate wing was created to protect the oil company—a shadow agency that specialized in espionage, misinformation, bribery, extortion, arson, physical persuasion, even murder—codename: Watchdog!

The secret file revealed the concept of the motor and the neodymium research. It detailed all known information about the Cunningham family. It contained any research institutions known to have considered or to have begun any research involving either the mechanism or the element. The file also held information about what was done to stop any such research, including what happened to Thomas Cunningham. Finally, it was continually updated by each successive head of security The import of the file was clear to Johnson and all his predecessors: Do not let this technology happen, no matter what it takes.

Johnson could not tell Mr. Forsythe any of this for his own good, but he'd gotten his marching orders eons ago from a long-dead president of the company. If these guys were working on their grandfather's invention, they had to be stopped!

Dave and Tom got on the expressway and headed for Detroit. They didn't detect anyone tailing them, which they thought was odd, given how much had happened.

"Maybe they know the motor can't work, that the technology is unusable or, worse, worthless. Maybe that's why they're no longer following us," Tom hypothesized.

BARRY COLE

"I think I know the answer to that one," Dave replied, intently looking out the passenger side mirror and seeing the van behind them. The tiny writing on the bottom of the mirror made him laugh: OBJECTS IN MIRROR ARE CLOSER THAN THEY APPEAR. *No shit*, he thought.

Tom was in the left lane coming up on slower traffic when the van came quickly up alongside them in the right lane next to Dave's window. It was clear they wanted to make their presence known. Aggressively, they veered behind Tom's truck and tailgated them down the freeway.

"What do we do now?" Tom asked in an angry, yet determined, voice that Dave had rarely heard his brother use.

"Just keep driving. Screw them, whoever they are. What can they possibly do to us out in public in broad daylight?"

"If they follow us to the generator distributor, they'll know that we're working on Grandpa's motor. The visit from that gun-toting pair yesterday made it crystal clear *someone* knows we are and that they're taking us seriously. I can't figure out who those guys were, but I don't think they're the same people following us now. They could have followed us when we left the house yesterday, but I don't think they did. So, why harass us now?"

"I think you're right. Those guys behind us are clearly communicating a threat—that they're watching—so we'd better back off, or else. I'm guessing the company they work for *owns* this world, and they won't loosen their grip. We're nothing but a couple of ants to be crushed, and they don't care if they do it in public! Right now, they've got nothing solid to go on, but after our visit to Detroit, that will change."

The brothers grimly drove on to the Motor City distributor

with the van in tow. Once arriving, they immediately backed the truck into a loading bay and were greeted by employees taking a cigarette break, while the van parked across the street. As quickly as was possible, they got the new generator securely loaded in Tom's truck and headed back home. This time, Dave drove.

"So far, so good," Dave said and breathed a sigh of relief. "I see our friends in the van are still with us. I may not be able to lose them in this truck, but I can sure have some fun with 'em."

He suddenly swerved across two lanes of traffic and took a right.

"The van stayed behind us, but left some pretty agitated drivers back at that intersection," Tom laughed. "Here it comes!"

The van pulled in behind them, not keeping the distance between them that it had kept since getting to the city. Dave signaled a right turn and waited in the right lane at the stop-light for just the right moment. Swiftly, he turned left across all four lanes and slid between two cars that had the green light. The van was forced to either wait until another such break occurred or until the light changed.

"*That* will really piss those guys off," chuckled Dave. "They'll catch back up to us if we get on the expressway now, so let's get some lunch. I'm starving. How 'bout you, Fat Boy?"

"I could eat, Jackass," Tom countered.

Dave quickly took another left, drove through a strip mall, and found a tiny diner at the far end.

"I don't think they'll see the truck here," Dave said as he

tucked the pickup between two parked semis. "Ah, yes, always eat where the truckers eat. That's my motto."

After their delicious lunch of mile-high BLT sandwiches made with thick slices of homemade bread and a ridiculous amount of bacon, they belched satisfactorily, got on the freeway, and headed west. Tom's head was on a swivel looking for the van.

Dave looked at him and cried, "It's amazing how that glob of mayonnaise can stay on your chin even with your head moving like that!"

"Thanks, Jackass! You know they didn't give up, right?" Tom asked his brother as he wiped his chin.

"Yeah, and sadly, they know where we're going. So, somewhere between here and the house, they'll probably show up. They've got what they needed and what we were hoping to avoid giving them this soon—the proof that we're working on the motor. There aren't many uses for a DC generator these days. Everything runs on AC. I think they've already reported our purchase to those in charge. Things may get a little dicey from here on out."

As if on cue, the van roared up behind them just after they'd passed a rest area. Here they were, out in farm country, between cities, and feeling way too alone. The van pulled up alongside and stayed there, like it was waiting. Dave alternately sped up and slowed to keep them from being window to window as much as he could.

The van slowed and veered to the right, hit the left rear end of the truck in a pit maneuver, and caused it to slide. Dave masterfully gained control and straightened out the vehicle while the van pulled in behind.

Tom's cell rang. He looked at the phone's screen and recognized the number; it was the same number from the business card left on the tool bench yesterday.

"It's them," he said, "the guys at the house yesterday."

Tom answered his cell, "Hello?"

The voice at the other end spoke in a clear and commanding tone. "That van is going to force you into an accident, unless you do exactly what I tell you to do. Understand?"

"Yes." Tom's teeth were clenched. He put the cell on speaker.

"There are two cars coming up behind you. One will stay behind the van, and the other will pull up next to you. As soon as it does, hit your brakes for two seconds, then floor it. This will make enough room for our car to get between the van and you. When that happens, just keep the pedal to the metal until they're out of sight. Got it?"

"Ten-four," answered Dave. He thought of the movie, *Smoky and the Bandit*.

"Ten-four? Seriously? Jackass!"

"It seemed appropriate." Dave was grinning.

Two dark sedans with tinted windows appeared in the rear view mirror. They'd seen one of the vehicles before—it was the car that had followed them to their grandmother's house. Just as the voice had said, one car pulled in behind the van and one pulled up next to Dave's window. Dave braked, then hit the gas, and the sedan next to him darted in behind them. They watched as the car behind them slowed; the one behind the van rear-ended it, causing it to careen off the pavement and flip over in an ostentatious cloud of dust. Soon, both cars were flanking the truck, and the brothers felt safe for the first time in days.

Jane and Sally had spent the day preparing the house. They had new appliances installed and hired a cleaning company to get at every nook and cranny. The final trip to the mall had been for linens and towels.

"Sally, I'm starved," stated Jane. "It's not the best time to get groceries, but the pantry needs restocking. Let's see how much we can gather in one trip."

Sally did not respond at first. She kept staring into her rear view mirror.

"We're being followed, Jane. It's a van like the one parked near home!"

Jane's stomach growled. "Fine, then they can follow us to a restaurant. I have to eat something. I'm weak and very cranky."

Sally pulled into an old café that had been in business for over a century.

"This is one of Tom's favorite eateries," Jane said fondly. "I'm not sure why ... the food is alright, but nothing to write home about. He said it makes him feel good. Comforted. I don't think the place has changed since it opened."

The owner greeted them and told them to sit anywhere.

The women chose a booth. Little did they know they were sitting at Thomas and Joanna's favorite table in their favorite eatery. They finished their lunch and strolled out to the car. As they approached, the van that Sally thought had been following them earlier pulled into the handicapped spot by the front door. Sally and Jane took off running for their car.

The van began to back up and looked as if it was going to chase the women. Suddenly, out of nowhere, a dark sedan with tinted windows pulled behind the van and boxed it in.

Jane and Sally got to their car and drove away as fast as they could, not daring to look back.

"Let's get home fast," Jane cried. "I hope the boys are back in town by now."

On their way home, Sally and Jane saw that a car similar to the one that had just helped out in the restaurant parking lot was behind them. The offending van was nowhere to be seen.

Chapter 13

Challenges

D ave drove into Tom's driveway, and the two dark sedans parked on the street on either side of the drive. The brothers looked at each other after Dave pulled the truck into the garage, neither saying anything, but both wondering if they should greet the occupants of the cars who had just saved their bacon on the highway or run inside and lock the doors.

Finally, Dave said, "I've gotta find out what the story is with these guys. Let's go see what they want."

Both jumped out of the truck and cautiously walked toward the two men exiting one of the vehicles.

One of the men met them, held his arms out in a placating gesture, and said. "Please, don't be alarmed. As you can see, we are here to help you. My name is Alex Weston, and this is my associate, Steve Robinson. Those two guys in that other car are Ron and Terry. You can meet them later."

"Okay ...," Dave said cautiously.

"Two more of our associates will be arriving shortly, because they're escorting your wives here," Alex continued.

And with that, Alex Weston extended his hand. "Glad to meet you, Dave and Tom," he said as Steve and he heartily shook each brother's hand.

"Do you mind if we come in to talk?" Steve asked. "We have a lot to tell you."

At that moment, Jane and Sally arrived. And as Alex had

said, a third dark sedan had followed the girls home, but kept going down the street after Sally parked the car. Dave introduced their wives to Alex and Steve, and the group headed inside the house to talk.

"I'll put on some coffee," Jane said lightly.

"Please, don't go to any trouble," Steve said.

Alex chuckled and said, "Speak for yourself. It's been a long day already, and I could use a little caffeine. Besides, we have a lot to tell them and probably a lot of questions to answer as best we can."

"No problem. Now, just who the hell are you guys, anyway?" Jane said sharply, but with a gentle smile.

"Good first question," remarked an amused Alex.

"Jane, dear, these are the guys that were at the house on Monday," said Tom. To Alex and Steve he said, "I saw you in the garage when you left your card."

Alex offered an explanation to Tom. "Yes, that was us. I apologize for startling you, but we were concerned that the bad guys may have gotten to the garage before us. Cool hidden room, by the way; never tell anyone anything about it. It's your best insurance."

"Back to Jane's question," said Tom. "Who are you guys, why are you here, and what do you know?"

"This is going to sound a little odd, but maybe not after the couple of days you've just had. We are part of a group that dates back to before the American Revolution. The information I'm about to reveal to you is confidential and all of you, right now, must take an oath to keep it so, under pain of death. What say you?"

Sally looked at the other three. "Our lives apparently are

already in danger, and these guys want to help. Seems somewhat odd, but I say, why not?" She looked at Alex, raised her right hand in pledge fashion, and vowed, "I so swear."

Immediately, Jane, Dave, and Tom, virtually in unison, raised their right hands and pledged, "I do, too."

"Close enough," said Alex gravely. "Only the highest level of our group can authorize divulgence of any information regarding the group and its activities. I have been authorized to tell you only on a need-to-know basis about who we are, our pursuits, and our history. In well over two hundred years, no one outside of our group—except for a few heads of state—has been told what I am about to tell you.

"Our group is a secret society whose name is known only to its members. You can refer to it as the Company. Our founders are some of the same founders of our country that signed the Declaration of Independence and later penned the U.S. Constitution. Our members are either direct descendants of these founders or those nominated for admittance by such people.

"Our mission is, quite simply, to covertly preserve and defend our democracy and our government as created and envisioned by our Founding Fathers. We have the resources to secretly intervene when and where it is deemed necessary to protect 'The Great Experiment' as it was known back in their day. Historically, we had done reasonably well ... until one catastrophic failure that has led to our country being controlled by an oligarchy.

"United Oil and a handful of other corporations control our economy, pollute our environment as they see fit, and predestine our elections to manipulate, coerce, and pervert our government. Energy consumption is what has allowed them to accomplish a coup d'état that extends past our government and into our daily lives. Energy is what runs the Industrial Revolution. They exploited their monopoly over oil and used it as a springboard to world domination.

"We saw what they were up to early on and did all we could to stop them. But as long as oil was used to run the world, their control of it made them unstoppable.

"Then, along came your grandfather, Thomas Cunningham, and his invention. Our scientists were searching for an alternative energy source when we were made aware of an inventor who claimed to use the power of magnets to energize a motor instead of fossil fuels.

"We investigated your grandfather and discovered that because of his invention, United Oil was doing their level best to ruin his life—in nearly every way possible. Big Oil's big efforts to stop him convinced us that your grandfather's invention was a threat to them and, therefore, valuable to the country. We intervened, but it was a case of 'too little, too late,' I'm afraid.

"Your grandfather and several of our key men were killed in Paris before we got any substantive information about the invention. Its design eludes us to this day.

"We do know that it used electromagnets, together with permanent magnets, because we were aware of Thomas's efforts to obtain them. And we know he wanted to have a permanent magnet made with an element called neodymium. That's why he went to Europe in the first place."

Dave was astonished and said, "That's the first time we've heard anything about what *actually* happened to Grandpa Thomas!"

"He and our men with him were outnumbered in a shoot-out

at a Parisian hotel and were never seen or heard from again. Your grandfather's body was never found. The same was true for all information about the invention. United Oil literally buried every bit of knowledge on the invention and has prevented any research in the area ever since.

"That moment in history, the death of your grandfather, likely changed our world in a very bad way for nearly a century. His loss was our crowning failure, because the suppression of his invention has unleashed worldwide suffering. Had this new energy source happened back then, things would be very different now—how much, we do not know. Some have said that the Earth would be a paradise by now.

"We have striven to right that wrong! We have watched over your family ever since. We have also scrutinized your activities since you began remodeling the house on the hunch that you might find something. And we were concerned they may have had the same hunch, and it now appears we were correct. They started tailing you right after you researched neodymium online. That's what tipped us off. I assume they saw that, as well.

"Anyway, I have to ask. Did you find some of your grandfather's research?"

"You know we must have, but I appreciate your tactfulness," said Dave. "We're going to need help, especially now that United Oil knows we're gathering parts and that a third party may now be involved. Thanks again for your help today."

"What help today?" Sally asked Dave.

"I'll tell you later."

Jane broke the ensuing awkward silence. "Please thank your associates for helping us today."

"What help today?" asked Tom, repeating Sally's question.

"I'll tell you later," Jane answered sarcastically.

Sally smirked at Tom and said, "We have to have help, so we have to trust someone. They have trusted us, and these folks are our only offer. What choice do we have? I say we take a chance, go out on a limb, and trust them back. If they aren't here to help, we're screwed either way."

"Thank you, Sally, I think," said Steve. "I know this has all happened quickly, which requires making rapid decisions. And that's always unsettling, but you *can* trust us. That will become clear with time. I can't wait another minute." He glanced at Alex, then at Tom. "I have to know. Was the prototype in the secret room, Tom?"

"Yes."

"Drawings? Specs? Notes? Written materials?" Alex asked all at once.

Tom wore a huge grin. "Yes, yes, yes, and yes! We found a file with everything in it!" he cried.

"Do you know what this means?" Alex asked, rhetorically. "If we can make it work, we can lift the evil that lays like a blanket of soot on the whole planet. We can undo all the environmental harm and return our government to the people. We can restore the promise that was once 'The Great Experiment.' We now have that chance! Our forefathers demand that we take it!" he cried. "As Thomas Paine said, 'We have the power to begin the world over again.'

"As I see it, our role in this is twofold: Protect you folks and help you build that thing. First, do you have any thoughts on how we can do these things?"

"We move into Grandfather's house, and you guys guard it," Dave said, simply enough.

Tom went next. "Help me get a neodymium magnet."

Sally said, "We feel that the sooner we can complete a working prototype, the sooner we can feel safe. United Oil is far more powerful now than when they killed your grandfather and stopped this technology. We have to be smarter, faster, and stronger this time around. And I'm working on a plan. We will have many challenges to overcome."

Mike Johnson answered the summons to go to Mr. Forsythe's office in the stately United Oil headquarters—an impressive, but decidedly understated, lair for the fellow who could arguably be called the most powerful man on the planet.

"What do you have to report?" Forsythe asked him.

"The brothers are definitely working on it, sir. We just can't be sure of their progress at this point in time, but that really doesn't matter. We know they're working on it, and we know what we must do. Toward that end, there was an incident earlier today."

"Oh? An incident?" Mr. Forsythe asked this in a tone and with a look that clearly showed he had instantly surmised this was not going to be good news. The people who owned the most powerful corporation on Earth chose this man to run their business. He was the latest in a line of extraordinary men handpicked to continue the dynasty. Very little got past Reginald Forsythe.

"Yes. Our men have been tailing the brothers and their wives in a way that, shall we say, was intended to send a message. The women were working on the grandfather's house this morning while their husbands drove to Detroit. We followed the guys to a generator company where they bought a DC generator!"

"That means they must have already built a prototype or found one."

"Uh-huh, I agree. It was thought that if an accident were to happen on their way back home, the generator would likely be destroyed—and maybe the brothers dissuaded—permanently. As this was being carried out, two vehicles interceded, and our men were dispatched. Someone with expertise and resources appears to be guarding and/or helping them."

Forsythe said, in a low, ominous tone, "Not what I wanted to hear. Nope. Not at all! This invention is a terminal cancer that has been in remission for nigh on a century. It'll be the end of everything if we do not stop them. Not on *my* watch!" His voice kept rising. "Do it!" he cried.

"We have the best people money can buy. It will be done," Johnson said as he left the office.

Tom looked at Alex and said, "We're making plans to drive up north to see about having electromagnets made. I'll get you the name of the hotel in Petoskey where we plan to be staying Saturday night."

"Why up north?"

"I know the perfect engineer to build what we need. And, obviously, few would expect us to go up there for cutting-edge *anything*, let alone magnet technology. We also thought we'd make it look like an innocent weekend visit to a place worthy of the journey. Now that the jig is up, so to speak, I'm not sure how that affects our plans?"

"You need the magnets. Getting them made in the usual places would be easily detected, so I like the idea," said Steve. "We can provide adequate security to make it happen. I'll start right away. We'll arrange for your reservations. What time on Saturday did you want to leave?"

Sally mentally ticked off the miles and calculated, "It's about a three-hour cruise, as it were. We should leave around noon. That'll get us there near check-in time."

"Good," said Alex. "Next order of business—when can you move into that lovely, old house?"

"Today. We'll fake what we don't have," said Jane.

"Fantastic! We have your backs ... and that means a few changes to what you're accustomed to. Number one is that we will always drive you wherever you want or need to go in one of our vehicles."

"What?" Dave interjected. "Wait just a minute ... ."

"Look, I know you're one helluva vehicular dynamo, Dave," Alex conceded. "And that 'Vette of yours has to be one of the fastest cars ever put on the road. But we have professional drivers specifically trained to operate our security equipped vehicles. We provide security for heads of state, and your required level of security is no less than theirs. That means we handle all transportation and will provide a ring of protection around you, twenty-four seven. Your lives have changed, and you no longer have the option, or the luxury frankly, to go back to the way things were.

"Make no mistake about it, this is a war for the future— a quiet, private war—but war, nonetheless. And the stakes couldn't be higher. If that thing *is* a new energy source, we cannot be defeated again. The world cannot take another century like the last one."

"Well put," Sally said. "Welcome aboard, Alex and Steve!" She stood and enthusiastically shook each of their hands. Tom and Dave followed suit. The handshaking seemed to signify the agreement or pact they had made.

Jane gave them each a big hug. "You're both heaven-sent. Thank God! We totally underestimated the danger we're in. And I want to thank you from the bottom of my heart for helping us—for keeping our family safe," she said with a tear in her eye. "Please tell us what you need, and I'll make damn sure they do it."

Her face suddenly hardened from her usual soft, loving look. Her eyes blazed; her chin protruded. With her teeth somewhat bared, she said, "Those bastards have to come through me to hurt them!" Jane was in full-blown, mother-protecting-her-cubs mode.

"Yes, ma'am!" they both cried. Alex and Steve were the best the military could create—special forces—and with further private training, their skills were off the charts. Alex spent eight years in the Secret Service on the presidential detail. They knew *attitude* when they saw it, and with Jane, they knew they were looking straight at it.

"And finally," said Alex, "we have new cell phones for each of you." He put his hands in both of his suit coat pockets and gave one to each of the brothers and their wives. "Here you go. These are secure lines with a panic button. Push the red button three times, and we'll be there. Our names and phone numbers are loaded into the *Contacts* along with standard emergency contacts.

"Keep in mind that the phone you are calling must also be a secured phone for the call to be completely safe. And your phone numbers will not appear on caller ID. All calls to your current cell phones and land-lines will be rerouted to your new phones. Any questions?"

"What about our children? Are they safe?" asked Jane.

"We have people watching them, and we'll bring them in at the first sign of any trouble. At this point, they have no apparent involvement in any of this, so let's keep it that way for their own safety. Any time you want them fully protected, you should have them move into the big house. Speaking of which, let's get you moved into what will be your new digs for the foreseeable future."

"Sally and I have been packing, so it won't take long to get the rest together. But we'll need to get foodstuffs yet."

"Make a list of everything, and I mean everything, you want, and I'll see that it's delivered to the house," assured Alex. "A security vehicle is in the driveway ready to take Sally and Dave home to gather their belongings and take them to the big house. Another vehicle will take us when Jane and Tom are ready. Just leave your suitcases by the door, and they'll be loaded into the escort vehicles."

Within a few hours, the four were at the big house and ready to settle in. One of the house's unique features was that the upper floor was basically divided into two master bedrooms. The house had been built with two purposes in mind: first, to provide a secure home for the family matriarch and second, to provide a secure place for her son when he was in the area for business.

The big house faced south, and both third-floor bedrooms

were oriented in the same north-south fashion. They shared a large deck that hung high above the main entrance. The four, second-floor bedrooms were oriented in an east-west fashion, each with its own balcony on the east and west sides of the home.

The staircase that serviced the two floors was nothing less than a bona fide work of art. It was uniquely hand-carved from two humongous, white oak trees and had taken craftsmen nearly a year to complete. Its first step up from the floor was wider than the others and rounded. This bullnose step, as it was called, gave the balusters or stair sticks a strong base with which to support the elegant, curled gooseneck banisters with intricately carved, mammoth end posts where the curls terminated. The flight of stairs rose gracefully from the end of the grand entrance foyer to a landing that joined three other sets of stairs—two short flights of stairs that led to the left and right accessed the second floor bedrooms on either side of the house and then a grand continuation of the staircase from the back of the landing led to the third floor.

The stairs ended at the third floor with a huge, north-looking window directly facing the stairwell. On either side were big, bird's-eye maple doors for the two bedrooms.

The interior woodwork of the house was the best available from 19th century Michigan lumber camps. Red and white oak, ash, beech, walnut, and birdseye maple were utilized to give each room of the big house its own distinct ambiance. Perhaps the most intriguing wood used was the birdseye maple. Its grain pattern resulted from wood fibers growing in different directions that distorted the sugar maple's growth rings. It was relatively rare, and that made the wood valuable and its look prized.

Doors that divided the rooms were made of wood on each side to match the rooms they faced. Rooms on the first floor were divided by eight-foot tall pocket doors capable of disappearing into the twelve-foot high walls topped with wide, hand carved wooden crown moldings. All of the wood trim and fixtures in the house were made with the same care and attention as fine furniture.

"The bedrooms on the top floor are the same. Which one would you guys like?" Jane asked.

"If it's alright, I'd like to have Grandma Joanna's room on the west side. I have a lot of great memories of her in this house," Dave reminisced.

"It's settled, then. Tom and I will have the east bedroom."

"Now that we have the hard work done, I say it's time for a drinkipoo," drawled Dave. "I assume you ladies put stocking the bar high on your list?"

"You bet we did," replied Sally. "And the bar is open. What's your poison, gentlemen?" She stepped behind the beautiful oaken bar tucked into the corner of the library.

"Scotch, and lots of it," yelled Dave.

"CC and wa-wa for me," Tom ordered sheepishly. "And Jane, my dear, what sounds good to you this afternoon?"

"Vodka tonic, please," she purred.

They sat at the bar and discussed the remarkable house.

"Tom and I spent a lot of time in this magnificent place as kids," reminisced Dave. "Mom and Dad would drop us off almost every Friday evening so that Grandma could babysit us while they went out on their date night.

"Remember the summer we built the tree house in the side woods? We wanted something to do while waiting to be picked up Saturday afternoons, so Grandma Joanna bought us what we needed to build a tree house that we'd designed for a big maple tree. It's still there."

The couples relaxed and imbibed, regaled by competing stories from Tom and Dave about the tree house.

"Tom got the bright idea that we needed a rope swing to get down from the tree house instead of using the crude ladder we'd made. He spotted the perfect branch in a tree next to the one we built the house in, got a rope, and climbed to the branch. He tied a good knot and left plenty of slack.

"He climbed down that tree, grabbed the rope, and climbed up to the tree house. Then, he stepped out on a limb, gave his best Tarzan yell, and jumped—clutching the rope. Unfortunately, the rope was a little too long, and so was Tom's position on it. He did a face plant under that tree that still makes me laugh to this day," Dave said with a chuckle.

Storytelling, and listening to endless stories, can be thirsty work. The four ended up getting a bit wasted, so they decided to order—what else?—pizza!

"We'll have to say something to someone if any pizza is going to find its way through all that security. Oh, hey, yeah, order two extra ones to share with our new friends," insisted Dave.

A knock came from the back door that led to the driveway. Jane looked out its portal and saw Alex and Steve standing there. "Please come in. I hope you brought food!" she said.

"The groceries should be here any minute," said Alex. "I wanted to brief you on our security measures here at the big house. To begin with, a state of the art security system is being installed tomorrow. All cameras will be monitored from a small command center in the safe room. A security vehicle will be in the garage to take you where you want to go. One of our cars with two agents will always be parked right outside the gates. A driver bodyguard will be posted in the garage at all times. On top of that, an agent will constantly man the command center.

"That makes five agents always on site. We operate in three, eight-hour shifts per day, which means we have a total of fifteen agents, plus Steve and myself, of course, available at all times. We got lucky and were able to rent a house suitable for all of our agents just down the street from here. All in all, I'm very happy with your security here. This house was built like a fortress. It's perfect!"

"Yup. And what's more perfect is we have pizza for everyone on the way! Could you have someone take this cash to the gate? It should be here any minute," Jane slurred.

After dinner and a short nap, Tom took off for the safe room and immediately began removing the antiquated generator. Out of the blue, he felt a *deja vu*: he swore he'd done this before, but of course, he hadn't. Instead of feeling creepy, the *deja vu* comforted him.

"Hey, how's it going, Fat Boy?" asked Dave, poking his head through the pantry doorway.

"Good. Good. Thought I'd hook up the new generator to see if the motor might turn a few rpm. You know, for old times' sake. After that, I thought I'd remove one of the electromagnets and take it up north with us. Having it there in person, so to speak, may help in designing the new ones."

The brothers worked well into the night connecting the new generator and the batteries.

"There. That should do it," said Tom. "The propane motor on the generator is way too noisy to fire up tonight. Time to hit the hay."

Chapter 14

Continuation

The next morning, everyone gathered for coffee while Jane cooked breakfast. Tom and Dave filled the ladies in on the progress they had made with the motor the previous evening and the plan to fire up the new generator to see if the prototype still worked.

"Hey, Tom, after all these years, do you think the permanent magnets in the pistons have much strength left?" asked Sally.

"I can tell they still have some power by the way they attract my screwdriver. They never had much strength even when new, but I *am* surprised how little they appear to have lost after all these years. Grandpa wrote that perhaps being constantly bathed in the magnetic fields from the electromagnets replenishes the permanent magnets, so they may *never* lose strength. As the amount of energy being harvested from the permanent magnet is directly related to its strength, this part of the theory is huge." His stomach growled. "Anyway, we plan to see what happens after breakfast."

"Attracts your screwdriver? Please, dude, not in the presence of womenfolk. What the hell?" teased Dave. The cell phone he'd been given suddenly rang, and they all jumped. "Hello?" he said.

"Good morning, Dave. This is Steve."

"Hey, good morning, Steve. How we doin' today?"

"Great. The reservations in Petoskey are all set. We leave Saturday at high noon. Do you know if Tom contacted his engineer friend up there yet?"

Dave looked pensively at Tom and asked, "Did you get ahold of Ed yet?" He handed the phone to Tom and mouthed that Steve wanted to know.

"Hey, Steve," said Tom. "Yes, I called him last night and simply invited them to meet us for cocktails and dinner. I told him to contact me when they get to the hotel. I didn't say anything about *anything*."

"Excellent! Everything is a go, then. I'll see you Saturday morning, unless you need me before then."

"Thanks, Steve. See you then," Tom said as he flipped the phone closed, ending the call.

Jane sat a plate of scrambled eggs made with crumbled bacon and freshly grated cheddar cheese with a side of hash browns in front of each brother. The breakfast smelled yummy.

"Thank you so much. With your passion for cooking, Jane, I think you missed your calling" said Dave with a mouthful. "Yikes! I'm surprised Tom doesn't weigh 500 pounds by now, Fat Boy!"

"Aww, you are very welcome, *Dave*," she said pointedly and glared at Tom. Jane sat plates down for Sally and herself.

"Oh, I'm sorry, Sweetheart," Tom said sheepishly. "It's just that I'm absorbed in the computer programming I'll need to write to operate the motor. Breakfast is fantastic, as always. Thank you!"

Jane was familiar with Tom's absorptions. It wasn't the first time she'd witnessed her husband's obsessions, but this was downright extreme. It strangely seemed as if he was not just *continuing* his grandfather's work, but that he was *becoming* his grandfather. "You're welcome. I understand. You know I do, love."

The brothers inhaled their breakfasts like two kids anxious to get back outside and play. "Let's go fire that bad boy up," Tom tried to say to Dave, inhaling the last bite of potatoes.

"Right behind you, Fat Boy!"

"Eat my dust, Jackass!"

They went to the safe room and were surprised to see a guy watching three banks of television monitors. "Good morning. You must be Dave and Tom. I'm Jerry. Please ignore that I'm even here."

"Wow," said Dave, "when Alex said the system would be installed tomorrow, I assumed he meant during the day. You must've done it while we were sleeping. Do you guys moonlight as Santa's elves?"

Jerry grinned broadly and said, "Not anymore, but we're pretty fast at set up. From here I can monitor every entry point to the house and the grounds. A squirrel couldn't enter the property without me knowing about it. And this is the coolest room I've ever seen to have a command center. It's a steel fortress that even a cell phone signal can't penetrate. We drilled a small hole to run cable and found that the bottom layer is hardened steel. It took two carbon steel drills to get through it! No bullet could possibly come through that part of the wall. Very cool!"

"Yeah," said Tom, "Grandpa was big on security. I hope us lighting up this generator won't disturb you, but this is where we planned to work on the motor."

"*No hay ningun problemo.* I expected that," Jerry said, putting on a pair of earphones.

Tom looked at Dave quizzically. "What'd he say?"

"Duhhh. He said, 'No problem.' Jeez-o-Pete, Tom."

Tom looked over the connections, and after satisfying himself that everything was in order, he walked over to the generator and pushed the starter button. It roared to life and settled into a rhythm. He then checked various contact points with an electrical tester. "Looks like we're all hooked up. Here, put these on," he said, handing Dave a pair of safety goggles. "Stand back a bit ... I don't know what this puppy is going to do, but I think it's going to do it with gusto. Watch your back over there, Jerry!"

Tom flipped the bar controlling the four electromagnets and *bam ... bam ... bam ... bam ... bang!* The two pistons slammed back and forth, abruptly changed direction at the end of their stroke. They did this four times before the mechanical switches that controlled the electromagnets blew apart. "It works!!!!" cried Tom. "It actually works!" he yelled again while dancing a little jig.

Dave looked at his brother with a puzzled smile. He'd never seen Tom do that before.

"Nice work, Tom!" Dave yelled excitedly. "Did you see that crankshaft turning? Just by watching it, I could tell it had a lot of torque. What happened?"

"The mechanical switches can't take that much abuse for very long. I have an electronic solution that didn't exist back in Grandpa's day. I just wanted to see if the motor might still work. Now, I want to go get what we need to solve Grandpa's switching problems."

"What do we need?"

"A position transducer, computer, and solid-state relays

should do it. Essentially, the position transducer will be hooked up to one end of the crankshaft to tell the computer the position of the rotating shaft. The computer will use that information to tell it when to signal the relays to change the magnetic field of each electromagnet from attract to off to repel so as to cause the pistons to reciprocate."

Dave said, "I think I've got it, Fat Boy. You're saying the piston's permanent magnet is attracted to an electromagnet that is switched to attract while simultaneously being repelled by the other electromagnet that is switched to repel. As the piston approaches the attracting electromagnet, *that* electromagnet is switched to off and then to repel to send the piston back the other way. At the same time, the repelling electromagnet is switched to attract to pull the piston toward it."

"Yes, you've got it, Jackass!" cried Tom. "All that switching is done in microseconds once the motor's rpm get higher. And these mechanical switches can't handle that speed. They simply weren't built for that. Modern technology allows me to use what is basically electronic switching that will also allow me to control the motor's speed. I know just the industrial electrical supplier where I can get everything we need. Let's go!"

Dave and Tom went out into the garage and toward the man ensconced at the front window. "Hello. My name is Frank. What can I do for you?" he asked them.

"We need to get to an electronic supply dealer on the south end of town," Tom answered.

"No sweat." Frank spoke into his sleeve, "Get ready to roll." He turned to the brothers. "Right this way, gentlemen," he said, opening the back door of the black Suburban for the brothers.

"I feel like royalty," said Tom.

"Quite," Dave said. "You can be my court jester."

"Yeah, right."

They pulled out of the garage and drove down to the gate. One of the two men stationed at the gates opened the brand new lock; the other got in the vehicle's passenger side. That was when Dave spotted the shotgun attached under his side of the dashboard and said, "Adds a new meaning to the phrase, 'I've got shotgun,' hey, Fat Boy?"

"Hi, guys," the new addition said, turning back toward Tom and Dave. "My name is Ron. Where're we going?"

"To the industrial park south of the mall," said Tom. Ron repeated that into his sleeve as they drove through the gates. As soon as they cleared the driveway, one of the dark-windowed sedans pulled in front while another pulled in behind.

The brothers purchased the equipment they needed without incident and with no apparent tail.

"Do you see anyone following us?" Dave asked the driver.

"We've not detected any surveillance, but it's there—somewhere," the driver said sullenly. "They've stepped up their game a bit. I just received a report that two of them went into the supply store you just visited. I assume they were curious as to what you purchased. A Benjamin or two would likely get the clerk talking. They won't show themselves to us again unless they ... ."

"That's enough," said Ron, the other Company man. He turned to the brothers. "I hope you've got everything you need. If possible, we can get what you want for you so that you won't have to leave the compound any more than necessary. It's always a security concern when you're out in public."

"Alright," said Tom. "It's a bit of an adjustment. It's hard to believe these henchmen would make a move out in the open."

Ron's face went cold, and he said, "Remember what happened to the Kennedys? You can't get any more out in the open than during a public appearance. It's actually a preferred venue for assassinations because there are crowds to blend into and create chaos after the event."

"Hadn't thought of that," said Dave as they drove through the gates of the house.

Tom unloaded the new equipment and immediately got to work. He went into full obsession mode—working well into the night, removing the mechanical switches and all electrical connections. He also removed the electromagnets, packaging one for the trip north.

Over the next two days, Tom connected the transducer, rewired the motor, finished programming, and connected the computer. He was ready for the new electromagnets and could not wait to see his old friend tomorrow evening.

Bright and early on Saturday morning, they all got ready for the trip north. Tom, as always, got up after Jane, walked into the kitchen, and announced, "Road trip!"

"Road trip!" was the instant reply from the already-assembled group.

Tom said wistfully, "I always wanted to move there after we retired. Still mean to," he added with determination.

An all too familiar knock came at the back door. "Come on in, Alex," said Jane. Steve and he appeared in the hallway.

"Good morning. It's a beautiful day for a ride. Are we too late for breakfast?" Alex asked Jane.

"Not if you like Eggs Benedict. Or Eggs Robert if you prefer. Have a seat."

"Eggs *whoever* are fine with me!"

Alex reverently carried an enormous apple pie into the kitchen that screamed an odiferous invitation to partake in a moment of bliss. Mouths watered, and pulses quickened. Everyone had all other thought immediately evicted from their heads.

"Plates!" cried Tom.

"On it!" Jane shouted. "Hand me that bad boy. Who wants whipped cream?"

"My, oh my ... pie," Tom began. "Pastry's ultimate and divine culmination. Clearly, pie is a gift from God. Anyone who makes and gives such a thing is a minister of the soul. I love food, and my favorite food is pie."

After breakfast Steve and Alex asked Tom to give them a brief review of the prototype and materials. "We don't want to make the same mistake again," said Alex. He took out a small camera to videotape the presentation. "This time the knowledge of the technology will not be lost."

"Sure," said Tom, "but first, Jane and I need to finish packing. Dave can show you the file we found and the prototype for you to videotape until I get back. Come on, Jane, let's go finish."

Jane looked puzzled, but played along anyway. "Sure, Honey," she said.

Dave led Steve and Alex to the library where the file contents were displayed on the huge ornate desk. Alex videotaped the drawings, the specifications, and the journal.

Meanwhile, upstairs, Tom said excitedly, "Jane, I wanted to tell you, but didn't want anyone else to hear. I had another one of those dreams last night! Grandpa was standing over the library desk. It was so real! I can still see the sunlight filtering through the big front window and shining on the side of the desk. Its mahogany finish glowed—spectacular! There was Grandpa, smoking a pipe, looking over the research file from United Oil's neodymium project. The aroma of the pipe tobacco was delightful. All of a sudden, he looked straight at me and said, 'The compound is the key.' I woke up saying that—'*The compound is the key*'—as if it was being drilled into my head. I have to make one of those neodymium magnets ... actually, two of them." Tom smiled. It was *deja vu* all over again.

They finished loading into two vehicles for the trip north—Jane and Tom in one along with Alex and Frank, and Dave and Sally in the other along with Steve and Ron. Each auto had a two-car escort, each with four men. It was a regular convoy! The two groups left about fifteen minutes apart. The Company was outgunned years ago in Paris, and they were not going to let that happen again. They reserved the two best suites and the adjacent rooms at the hotel in Petoskey. That meant paying for substitute rooms, meals, and other gratuities for those who had already reserved rooms. Money was no object at this juncture.

The Company was founded by several of the wealthiest colonial families who wanted to break with the crown. They put large tracts of land around many East coast cities into trust after the Revolutionary War. The subsequent sale of these lands created vast amounts of money that the company used for national emergencies.

"I've never been to this part of the state before," said Steve. "I'm a California boy transplanted to Chicago, so I'm looking forward to seeing what it's like around there. I've heard it's nice, but I hail from the land of nice. When we think of Michigan, we think of Detroit. Southern Michigan, away from the cities, the factories, and power plants is pretty, but nothing special in terms of scenery. It seems like the Ev-Con is always pretty high."

Sally looked at Steve with a big smile and exclaimed, "Well, you're in for quite a treat!"

The groups passed through the farm fields of central Lower Michigan, and Steve looked out the window as if to make the point that so far, he was not impressed with the scenery. This pissed off Sally, so she decided it was time to enlighten this young "foreigner."

"Summer glows nowhere like it does in Michigan," she began. "The girdles of freshwater lakes that surround its two peninsulas protect and nurture the land and its people. Nowhere in Michigan does it glow the way it does in the northwest Lower Peninsula—northern Lake Michigan's sunset coast. The dune-swept shore of its southern reaches slowly merge into shores of broken limestone that surround the Tip o' the Mitt, where the Mighty Mac *bridges* the two peninsulas—a passage used by man since long before any history was noted here." Sally continued her Chamber of Commerce-like campaign, but paused to sigh comfortably.

"It's hard to pick the most amazing example of beauty. Is it the view of the Manitou Islands from the lofty peak of a sand dune that cascades hundreds of feet directly down to the ribbons of varying shades of blue that is Lake Michigan's shoreline? Is it the turquoise waters of its large, near-coast inland lakes, the crown jewel of which is, in my humble opinion, the world-renowned Torch Lake, where the rainbow stores its colors? Or perhaps it's the cherry trees blossoming on the hills surrounding Grand Traverse Bay and its two peninsulas—their white petals set against the deep blue of the lake and sky in the background? Some say it's the sunset viewed from the cupola atop the Grand Hotel on Mackinac Island. The list could go on and on … Native Americans, early settlers, its current residents, and frequent visitors know of its magic. I am very proud of this—our—land."

The group listened intently to Sally's dreamscape description. "Little Traverse Bay may be able to lay claim to being the most unique in this very distinctive area. It's a good-sized bay oriented in an east-west direction and, thus, perpendicular to the western coast of Lake Michigan. Its northwestern shore contains a natural harbor that provides unparalled protection from the fury that Lake Michigan can unleash when weather conditions make her angry.

"This natural port, eventually called Harbor Springs, was arguably the capital of the local indigenous peoples—the Ottawa, also known as the Odawa tribes—for hundreds of years. Settlers began homesteading land and the wealthy from Chicago discovered its rejuvenating air and water. Soon, the harbor was bustling with Great Lakes schooners that whisked passengers out of the putrid, stale, sticky, city air to paradise.

"A camp built by the Methodists, called Bay Colony, sprang up across the bay just outside the growing city of Petoskey, named after a prestigious Odawa chief. Families, like the Hemingways, built cottages on Walloon Lake and

Lake Charlevoix—the area is said to have inspired the famed author's fictional alter ego, Nick Adams.

"It may be the world's best kept secret. And nestled on the east side of Petoskey, surrounded by Bay Colony, is an old hotel built to accommodate the wealthy visiting or looking to buy a little slice of heaven. It has always been well maintained and staying there is an experience. You'll love it!" she cried.

Steve was convinced by Sally's words and said, "I know I will! I understand a passion for the land, and I can see that you clearly have that. Who knows? Maybe I'll become the area's newest fan."

The remainder of the trip went by quickly as the scenery progressively changed and the air began to clear. Just south of Petoskey, hills appeared and the highway started to roll up and down. Suddenly, at the crest of a hill appeared Little Traverse Bay and Lake Michigan. The vista was jaw dropping! The topography sloped down to the water where the city nestled on the shore.

Upon arriving at the hotel, Steve hopped out to look at the breathtaking beauty before him. The sun was high in the sky, and it made the tops of the small waves undulating in the bay sparkle as if covered by diamonds. Between the waves was a deep blue that appeared to turn white as it rode up onto the shore. The sound of screaming seagulls and the smell of water in the air made him homesick.

"I'm so glad to see there are still places in our world like this!" Steve cried. "I could *sooooo* live here." He turned to Sally who had joined him. "I'm sorry for being a bit snarky when you were talking about this place ... I had no idea. I should have known better. I've been all over this globe, most of what *was ... is* no longer. Pollution and greed have devastated every place I've been, especially in this country. I never expected to see a place like this, here, in my lifetime. How is this possible?" he asked her.

Jane overheard Steve as she walked up to them. "Luck," she answered, "pure, beautiful luck. The factories that've desecrated Lake Michigan are far enough south to have had less of an effect here because much of it is drawn out through the Chicago River and ends up in the muddy Mississippi. Any pollution put in the water to the north or in Lake Huron flows out through the St. Lawrence Seaway into the Atlantic. While the water is fairly clean, it is really not potable, and eating many of its fish isn't advisable, but it still *looks* good. So, while some toxins are still present, water clarity is good in this unique quadrant of the Lower Peninsula.

"In fact, the air is so clean here they don't even bother with Ev-Con ratings! The prevailing wind is from the west-northwest, which takes any windblown pollutants across the filtering effect of a very wide route of water to reach here. The eastern shore of Wisconsin at that point upwind has relatively few sources of pollution, and the same is true to the northwest all the way through Canada—forming a corridor of unspoiled air that flows through this land.

"The luck of location has resulted in an island of virtual immunity from the poisons we emit every day," Jane said, "but that's only half of it. The jaw dropping beauty of this area is the luckiest part. Together, it is a sight to behold, even for a world traveler like yourself, Steve."

"No doubt, no doubt," concurred Steve. "Thank you!"

They all walked in through the main entrance to the

hotel, which was guarded on either side by tall, white fluted columns that supported a roof for arriving guests to avoid the rain. Thick, red carpet greeted guests at the entry and ran directly to a reception desk carved out of a single, virgin white pine. All who entered the hotel for the first time automatically stopped to look at this incredible creation.

The carvings etched into the wood facing the room were ornate beyond description. In the center was a view of the bay from the same vantage point they'd just enjoyed outside. To the left of this was a Lake Michigan sunset delicately carved and painted. At the right end was a woodland scene—masterfully detailed right down to the veins on the leaves.

Alex came back from the desk with two keys. He kept one and handed the other to Jane. They were good-sized, brass keys with a "1" and a "2" affixed, respectively.

"Please follow me," the bellhop said to the entourage as he walked them to the elevator. They emerged on the top floor of the grand old building in the middle of the hallway. "Suites one and two are this way," he said, sweeping his hand to the left.

The hallway was lined with photographs of the area from long ago. At the end of the hall toward the water was a big wooden door that said, "Private" in gold script. The bellhop unlocked it and pointed out that their room keys would also unlock it. On the other side of the door was another hallway, and at the end of it was a picture window nearly as big as the wall into which it was set. It looked out on the patio below, followed by the grounds, the beach, the bay, and the lake. It was like a giant postcard. The doors to the rooms were in the walls on either side of the massive window.

These were the presidential suites—the best that the best had to offer. The rooms were mirror images of each other, both designed to equally embrace, inspire, and delight those fortunate enough to stay there. Each presidential suite had a large, private deck showcased by front windows that looked out on "God's Splendor" from a spacious living area.

"Okay, so you're in one, and we'll be across the hall in two," instructed Alex. "The rest of us will be in the rooms across from the stairwell and elevator. When your friends arrive, call me, and we'll send someone down to bring them to your room." Alex was very direct about this next part, "Please do not leave your rooms without calling me first. I'm sorry for this inconvenience, but it's for your safety."

"Not a problem," offered Jane. "Right, guys?"

"Right," they said in unison.

Jane smiled.

Their luggage was brought up to the rooms, and they decided to relax before dinner. "Unless I miss my guess," Dave said idiomatically, "this room probably has a well-stocked bar." He headed for it. "Yup, it's five o'clock somewhere! Who's ready for a drinkipoo?"

After each mixed their *own* cocktails—being familiar with Dave's lack of palatable cocktail preparation skills—they repaired to the deck with drinks in hand to fully contemplate the view. It was the first relaxing moment they'd had together in what seemed like four score and seven years ago. They let the moment linger for a few hours. Left unsaid was the common thought that it might be their last chance to relax and savor the present for a very long time.

The room phone rang, and Tom dashed in to answer it.

"Hello. Glad you two could make it," he brightly said into the receiver. "Please grab seats, and a dude will be there shortly to bring you up to our room. Hmm? I know. I know, I'll explain when you get here. See you in a few, okay?" Tom hung up and used his cell phone to contact Alex.

In less than five minutes, they heard the suite's door knocker. Tom opened the door, and there stood his old friends, Candace and Ed—not that they were old, necessarily. He marshaled them into the room.

"What the *goddamned* hell?" asked Ed as his head did an owl-like perusal of the gorgeous presidential suite.

"I *know*—quite the place, indeed!" replied Tom in his best, but still not good, British accent. "Like it?"

"Jolly good. Jolly fucking good," laughed Ed. The group was completely unfazed by his f-bomb. They were used to his potty mouth. He looked at Jane, who hugged him fondly. "What's the occasion?" asked Ed.

Jane deferred to Tom.

"Well, let me make you guys a drink, and I'll tell you what I can," divulged Tom. "You remember my brother Dave and his better half, Sally, don't you, Candace and Ed?

"Yes, yes, of course," they said. "It's been a long time— Chels's graduation from Michigan State, wasn't it? I remember because it was also Mother's Day that year."

"That's right," chirped Tom. "I'll wager that curiosity is biting you two pretty good by now and, boy, do we have a job for you, Ed. Do you feel like helping to save the world?" he said to the new arrivals.

At this, Ed looked at Tom and thought, *Hell, yes, who wouldn't want to have a shot at playing Superman?*

Tom returned his gaze and said, "Do you remember, way back when we were at Cal Tech, I told you that my grandfather had an energy-related invention that disappeared?"

"Kinda ... you said it must have had something to it because it made him an awful lot of cabbage before he also disappeared. It's not something you hear every day so, yeah, yeah, I remember. Why?"

"That's right! Well, we found it!" Tom cried. "I'm rebuilding the prototype as we speak, and I need your help."

"Me? Tom, how could I possibly help?"

"Well, it uses *electromagnets*."

"What? Seriously? Really—how?"

"For your safety, I can't tell you that, but what I *can* tell you is that I need you to build four of them, twenty amps each, that can reverse polarity as fast as possible. Here's one built around nineteen thirteen, a museum piece, but it shows the physical size we need and how they designed it."

Tom's friend surveyed the old electromagnet and said, "Reverse polarity magnets are nothing new. But I've never heard of a high speed design," he mused as he rotated the object Thomas had built. "However, some ideas do spring to mind. I suppose you need them, like, yesterday?"

"You got it. Here's a $20,000 advance that I hope will convince your company of the urgency. Also, here's another $3,000 in cash for you. Call it a bonus. We need your best work as fast as you can do it. I'm after expertise and results. Cost is not an issue."

"My boss will like the sound of that!"

Tom's face clouded. "The question becomes, can we

trust the people you work with to keep this quiet?" he asked seriously.

"Yes, I believe so. I won't tell them anything, except the design goal to make it fast. That should satisfy their initial curiosity. Why can't you tell me more, Tom? Maybe I could help you. You know you can tell me anything. We go back a long way."

"I know, I know ... I can't even tell you that, except to say the less you know and say about anything, the safer both you and we will be." Tom handed a cell phone to him. "Here's a phone you can use to contact me that can't be intercepted," he said. "We'll send some folks to pick up the electromagnets when they're ready. How long do you think it will take?" Tom was obviously in a hurry.

"I'll crack the whip on Monday and stay in touch, but I'm thinking I may have something worth testing by the end of the week."

"You're the man!" cried Tom. "In an effort to keep our little meeting a secret, we'll have dinner sent up. I'll get the wait staff."

The group enjoyed a private and delicious dinner of planked whitefish surrounded by a piping of duchess potatoes; a vegetable side medley of fresh asparagus, zucchini, and carrots; and crema catalana for dessert. Then, Tom and Ed spent hours discussing the design of the electromagnets and the solid state relays to operate them. After they finished, Tom called Alex to let him know that Candace and Ed were ready to leave. Seemingly within seconds, a GQ-type young man appeared and announced that he'd escort them to the lobby and bring their car around.

After his friends left, Tom knocked on suite two to talk with Alex. "I'm concerned about their safety, Alex," he said in an ominous tone.

"Of course, you are. I didn't want you to tell them, but we'll be watching over Ed until the magnets are built and we're confident he's not of interest to the bad guys. It's better that he not know we're around. Remember, we've been doing that with *your* family for nearly a century," Alex reassured him.

Chapter 15

Convalescence

Tom awoke and noticed, as usual, that Jane had already risen and was gone. He threw on jeans and a sweatshirt and stumbled out into the living area. It appeared that everyone was gathered out on the deck enjoying the summer morning—convalescing. He spotted the coffee pot on the counter and was pouring himself a steaming mug when there was a soft knock on the door. Tom unlocked and opened it, and to his extreme delight, a hotel employee came in pushing a serving cart.

The entourage had heard that the hotel employed its very own *patissier*, or pastry chef, directly from Belgium. As such, there were *patisserie* of every mouth-watering description; brioche *au chocolat*, orange sugar Danishes, iced Nun's puffs, blueberry strudels, croissants, crescent-shaped rugelach, bear claws, red tart cherry pinwheels, beignets, cinnamon twists, blackberry jam straws, raspberry pastry braids, vanilla cream Long Johns, brioche raisin snails—yes, it's a pastry! and rose rolls.

Tom had never seen breakfast treats like these before. Despite swimming in swirling, strudeled sweetness, his singular thought was, *Where are the glazed doughnuts? That's what I really want—a simple glazed doughnut.*

"Good morning, sir. I'm here to take your breakfast orders," said the nattily dressed server as she pushed the oversized, delectable display to the center of the room. She read his mind and pointed to a rose roll. "You look like a glazed doughnut-type of man, but I'm sure one of these will make a more than acceptable replacement."

Tom's attention immediately shifted from the pastries to the woman tending the cart. She looked at him with eyes that innocently stared directly into his soul.

Tom winced uncomfortably, but could feel her warmth and presence. Obviously, she was Native American—her round, full, unblemished face beamed with wisdom and innate goodness and with a youthful healthiness that belied her maturity. He felt that she must be descended from the leaders of her people.

"Pardon my boldness, ma'am, but may I ask you ... are you Anishnabe?" asked Tom.

This caught the server off guard, because that was a term not used by many outside the tribes.

"Why, yes, I am *Anishnabe Odawa.*"

Tom went on to tell her that his love of the area caused him to read whatever he could get his hands on about its history—especially its earliest inhabitants—and how he'd particularly enjoyed Andrew Blackbird's book, *History of the Ottawa and Chippewa Indians of Michigan.*

The server looked startled and said proudly, "Thank you, sir. Blackbird, *Mack-E-Te-Be-Nessy,* or Black Hawk in our language, was my great-great-grandfather on my father's side."

"Oh, my," said Tom with the utmost humility, "it's an honor to meet you, ma'am. Out on the deck, Jane, seeing the cart practically groaning with its load of perfect pastries, came into the room and immediately sensed how her husband was reacting to the beautiful, older woman who stood theatrically erect. "Jane!" Tom shouted a bit too loud. "It is my great pleasure to introduce you to a direct descendant of Blackbird."

"Oh, my God," Jane gasped, "it is indeed a privilege to meet you. The history of your ancestors is as fascinating as it is tragic, and he was one of the few who documented and preserved it. It is truly an honor to meet you."

Sally and Dave joined them and also expressed their respect and admiration.

After taking their breakfast orders, the stately woman thanked them and then looked directly at Tom and said, "Do not stray from the path you have been put upon." She then turned abruptly and left the room.

"That was a bit odd," said Jane.

"Yeah. I don't know why or how, but I know she was talking about the motor!

"I remember reading about one of their teachings that was passed on from generation to generation regarding something called the Medicine Wheel. In addition to depicting the four sacred directions, the wheel also refers to the four races of men—red, yellow, black, and white.

"This particular story from the wheel tells that many thousands of years ago all of mankind lived together until the Great Spirit sent them out in the four directions, each with instructions and guardianship over one of the four basic elements.

"To the East, he sent the red man with guardianship of the earth and minerals. To the South, he sent the yellow man with guardianship over the air. The black man he sent to the West with guardianship over the water. The white man was sent North with guardianship over fire.

"All four races kept their teachings and guardianships by developing and preserving the functionality of the elements in their charge. Regarding the white man, some regard fire to include electricity and the many inventions using the power of fire.

"Essentially, this teaching holds that the Great Spirit originally ordained and tasked the white race to develop the energy mankind will need. This is what they believe, so there is history and tradition at work here.

"It is also said that some among them continue the spirituality of their ancestors and possess knowledge and abilities we are not privy to and do not understand. That amazing woman is a direct descendent of a chieftain, and her abilities—her gifts—should not be discounted."

"Yes," said Jane. "She certainly had an aura around her. When she said, 'Do not stray from the path you have been put upon,' her bearing was regal, and the look on her face was as though she knew you from the past. Really strange. It sent a chill down my spine!"

After breakfast they set their suitcases in the hallway and enjoyed a little more time on the deck. Soon, Jane and Tom decided to take a brief walk around the hotel and its grounds. Alex arranged for an escort. Tom experienced *deja-vu* that he could not explain around every corner. Dave and Sally had stayed here before, but their descriptions of the beautiful hotel could not explain Tom's feelings.

Then, there it was, hanging on the wall near the front desk in a birdseye maple frame. The original hotel registration book was open to page one, and right in the middle, they saw written, "Mr. & Mrs. Thomas Cunningham, August 16, 1901 - Room 1." The boys' grandparents had stayed at this hotel when it was new and had stayed in the very same room! Tom and Jane looked at each other in amazed disbelief.

"That's more than a little freaky," said Tom.

"Ya think?" asked Jane.

Before long, and before they wanted, they were headed south to home. Tom was consumed by his next phase—finishing the electronic switching to replace his grandfather's mechanical switches. He started sketching schematics of a solid-state relay that could operate at high speed. By the time they got home, he had a rough draft of what might work.

Part of the other evening's brainstorming session with Ed had been about the switches, because they would be operating the new electromagnets. He'd given Tom the name of an engineer he could trust to build it who lived in Chicago.

The suburban pulled into the driveway of the grand old home, and the guards opened the gates. One escort car followed them up to the garage while the other parked in its usual position on the street. The car entered the garage as the door was opened by the posted agent.

"Welcome back," he said with a smile. The vehicle's occupants knew they were safe.

Alex rolled down his window and said, "I'll see you tomorrow. Have a nice evening. We're all good here."

"Thanks, Alex, you too."

The suburban backed out, headed down the driveway, and out the gate just before the other suburban with Sally and Dave inside pulled in. The timing was perfect.

"Watching these guys choreograph everything we do is a sight to behold, isn't it?" said Tom as he took Jane's hand and squeezed it in his.

"I hope they're as good as they appear to be," she murmured.

Tom spent the rest of his day finishing what he could on the design of the solid-state relays, as well as going over all of the other moving parts on the prototype. Before long, he discovered a small flaw in their grandfather's prototype regarding the use of materials near the piston. The support rods upon which the piston rode to move back and forth were made of steel, as were the ball bearings on which the piston housing rode. The *gauss* meter indicated a significant amount of magnetization of these parts had occurred.

Not as much of a problem for Grandpa, thought Tom, *but a new piston magnet a thousand times stronger is a whole different ball game.*

It would magnetize those parts to an even greater extent, which would then act like a brake on the piston. They had to be changed to authentic stainless steel. By the time he disassembled the motor enough to remove the rods and bearings, it was time for bed.

Tom spent the next day looking for manufacturers for the parts he needed. Ed's friend in Chicago seemed to thoroughly understand the design for the solid-state relays. He'd also agreed to build them right away—estimating seven to ten days for delivery. The ball bearings were a different kettle of fish. They had to be the exact same size used in the motor to avoid more extensive reconstruction. Unfortunately, they were an unusual size, and that made them difficult to find.

After an exhaustive search and hours of phone calls, Tom found a place in Muskegon that could manufacture the bearings he needed, but not for at least sixty days.

"That's totally unacceptable," Dave said in exasperation when he learned of this setback.

"We have to come up with another option even if it takes a sack full of dead presidents—whatever it takes to get what we need now. We have to think of something."

"Will do ... Jackass."

"What's your report?" Forsythe bellowed at Johnson.

"Good news and bad news, I'm afraid, sir," said Johnson. "The good news is we can see no indication that they're getting the magnets they'd need to build a motor. The bad news is they have apparently hired a top drawer security company. These people are very good at what they do and, therefore, very expensive. I don't see how they could afford their services indefinitely."

Forsythe stiffened. "They know that if they can complete and make public a working prototype proving itself to be a new energy source, killing them at that point will do us no good. *We'll* be dead. They can certainly afford security for as long as it takes to complete it. Don't be fooled," he said, wagging his finger, "they're working on it alright, and they need to be stopped! Putting our legal team on them will just attract suspicion toward us when they have an 'accident.' We are depending on *you* to solve this! Dismissed."

Johnson left and immediately called a meeting of his own. This group held its meetings off company grounds in the conference room of a local law firm to ensure confidentiality and privacy. The secret wing of the security department had Johnson at its helm; four "lieutenants," each with five men to command; and a four-person electronic surveillance department. The wing's code name was "Watchdog," but they referred to themselves as "dawgs."

"The problem is getting acute," Johnson said to his assembled lieutenants. "We have to eliminate this threat, and we have a short time to do it in. Strategic use of overwhelming force will likely be our only option. If they leave that compound," he said ominously, "we need to be ready to strike at a moment's notice. They will need parts to build a prototype, and sooner or later, they have to come out of there."

Sally was sitting alone in the library staring off into the distance. Dave came in, sauntered over to her, and began massaging her neck. He cooed softly by her ear and asked, "What you thinking about, Sweetheart? You look miles away."

"These people are ruthless and, hopefully, that'll make them careless. It may also make them predictable, and we can use that to our advantage. I know they're planning something. Maybe we should help them along," she mused in a barely audible voice. "Oh, love, that feels *so* good. You can stop in an hour or so."

Tom programmed the computer so it would be ready when the parts arrived. His phone rang. It was Ed. "Hey, hey, Tom, old man. I think you'll like what I've made here. It's the fucking best I can come up with, so I'm making four of these bad boys for you. They'll be ready to pick up by the end of business on Tuesday."

"Nice job, man. I knew I could count on you, my friend.

Someday, I look forward to showing you what I'll be doing with your handiwork."

"Thank you. I'm looking forward to that day, too. Be well and keep your ass safe, *mi amigo*."

"We shall, and I will be in touch. You can depend on it. G'bye." Tom ended the call.

"Who was that, Tom?" asked Jane. She had entered the safe room through the open door into the garage.

"That was Ed. The magnets can be here next Tuesday night! I've got a lot to do before then." He glanced toward the workbench that was covered with parts. "I have to get the parts I need to replace now, so that I can put the motor back together over the weekend. A company in Muskegon could produce the parts, but it would take weeks—even months— to make what I need. However, I did find a local distributor who deals in a lot of stainless steel. I have to go *there* and see what they have and what I can make work." Tom called Alex to see how soon they could leave.

Tom and Jane walked into the library where Dave and Sally were talking. "I just heard from Ed, and I'll have the electromagnets next week," Tom informed Dave. "That means we can't wait to have any of the stainless steel parts made. I'm headed over to a local distributor now to see what I can come up with from their stock. Alex should be here any minute. If I wait until Monday, I'll never have it ready to install the electromagnets when they get here." Tom's sense of urgency made the others nervous. "I'll need up to two days to install the solid-state relays that I've heard will be arriving on Monday morning. It's all coming together now!" he said like a kid anticipating Christmas.

The front doorbell rang. It was Alex with the suburban parked next to the sidewalk off the front porch.

He gets here in a New York minute, and that's a good thing, thought Jane.

Tom left without saying good-bye.

"I've never seen Tom like this," she said to her in-laws with a concerned look on her face.

"I know it," said Sally. "He's starting to really freak me out a little."

"I see it, too. He's completely and utterly obsessed," agreed Dave. "It's not normal."

Tom trotted down the porch stairs and into the waiting open door held by the driver. He sat in a rear seat. Steve was in the other rear seat, and Alex took up shotgun. They took off, but Tom noticed only one escort vehicle behind them instead of the normal front and back. "Did you guys lay some people off?" he asked.

Steve smiled and told him they'd damaged the other car this morning and its replacement would catch up to them soon. He was a bit concerned, because it was coming from Detroit, and Fridays were always crazy-busy on the highways. Additionally, the distributor they were headed to was about ten miles south of the city and located on a county road. Steve did not like having only one escort car on a road with unlimited access. He was relieved when they arrived at their destination.

Tom met with the owner's son, who was in charge in his father's absence. Tom explained what he needed and that he'd have to take whatever was available that day. "It's a good thing you came in today while the old man is gone," said the son.

"We keep a bone yard of our mistakes that my father doesn't know about, and we don't want him to. Just one less thing for him to yell at us about. Let's go see what we can find."

Tom was feeling lucky, and that feeling was well founded. Out in the bone yard, they discovered some long, discarded stainless steel rods that could be quickly cut to size to replace all of the piston support rods. He thought that part would be easy. While those were being cut to size, both men scrounged around to locate the hard-to-find ball bearings of the correct size. At the bottom of the pile, they found what they were looking for sealed within a part that had never been claimed by its owner. They took the part into the machine shop where the bearings were extricated.

"Perfect," exclaimed Tom as he handed the young man his credit card and examined the shiny stainless steel orbs in the box.

The stainless steel rods were boxed and loaded into the back of the suburban. They headed back to the house.

About a mile down the road, Tom noticed that the driver sat up and focused on his rear view mirror with a tense expression. Alex and Steve spoke into their sleeves, and the driver floored the suburban—it was stupendously fast. The vehicle leapt forward and approached a car going the speed limit. As the driver moved left to pass the car, a second vehicle in front of the one they were going to pass moved over into the left lane—both cars completely blocked the road ahead. A man in the back seat of each car leaned out the window and began shooting at them!

Bullets ricocheted off the suburban's bulletproof windshield and grill. Steve threw Tom to the floor and laid on top of him. Their driver stomped the brakes, and the escort car roared past, all the while returning fire.

Suddenly, one of the blocking cars locked its brakes, and it and the escort car collided. Both were sent careening off the road. Alex retrieved the shotgun from underneath the dash—a military-issued automatic twelve-gauge with a twenty-round mag—and unloaded the beast on the remaining vehicle. It swerved in an attempt to avoid being hit. Alex was able to shoot one of the rear tires at precisely the right time, sending the vehicle into a spin.

At that same moment, the suburban approached a dirt road intersection where a cloud of dust betrayed a car hurtling straight at them—too late to avoid. They all crouched down anticipating the impact when, *kaboom*, they heard a huge crash. But they felt no impact!

The driver yelled, "Alright, Ron!"

Tom looked up and saw that the second escort car had caught up to them and steered directly into the oncoming vehicle's path, t-boned it, and sent both cars flipping off the road.

Suddenly, there was dead silence. "We're clear," Steve shouted, and the driver punched it again. Almost immediately, they were back on the expressway, headed north.

"Holy shit, Steve!" cried Tom. "I hope your guys are alright!"

"It didn't look too bad, and, besides, Alex called for ambulances ... that's all we can do for now. Those escort cars have much of the same reinforcement as their stock car counterparts."

Tom trembled like a leaf in the wind. He wasn't sure if he

was scared or angry—or both. "Nice job, guys, thank you."

The two off-duty escort cars joined them for the rest of the trip home.

The clang of those gates closing behind us has never sounded so good, Tom thought.

One escort car followed them up to the garage while the other parked sideways across the driveway down by the gates, blocking the driveway. It reminded Tom of a scene out of *The Godfather Part II*.

Jane noticed the commotion and ran to the garage to greet the suburban. "What happened *here*, Tom?" she demanded after seeing the bullet-damaged front end.

"I've just heard all of our men will be fine. The bad guys that survived are under lock and key, for now."

"What the hell happened?"

Tom hugged her close. "We had a close encounter. Alex and his guys were *phenomenal!* There's no other word for it! All is well."

"All is well? All is well? Are you kidding me? Guns, shooting ... nothing is well. Those sons-of-bitches tried to kill you! What the hell is next, Tom?"

Sally heard them. "What's going on, Jane?"

"Those assholes tried to kill Tom! Look at the front of the truck!"

"That's it!" growled Sally. "It's time. Let's talk in the library!" She organized a meeting between the two couples and Alex and Steve.

Sally, as CEO of a growing global company in a very competitive market, was an effective leader and a formidable war chief in such times. The big difference was that her corporate battles never involved physical violence. *Although, there had been the occasional cafeteria food fight*, she thought with a smile.

"Tom will be completing the prototype next week," she told those assembled. "Then, we'll know if it really works and whether or not it's worth pursuing neodymium magnets. As Alex probably knows, I've been in contact with some old acquaintances in the Netherlands who can help us with that.

"United Oil knows we need those magnets to make it work. They also know they've closed off every domestic site to obtain them. This forces us to go overseas where they hope to bury you guys and the motor again—just like they did with your grandfather. Knowing what they'll be planning gives us the advantage we need to end these bastards."

Everyone gathered looked at Sally with wide eyes—they'd never heard her swear before.

Tom spoke first. "I just survived a shootout that would've shaken up Doc Holliday. I want to know how the police are going to react to what they find on that road!" he said in a somewhat accusatory tone directed at Steve and Alex. "I assume we won't be seeing anything about that little incident on the evening news?"

"No. We won't," responded Alex.

Steve and he looked pointedly at one another. As an aside to Steve, Alex said, "I don't care. These people are risking their lives for the 'cause, and they deserve to know a little more."

"Alright. It's your call," said Steve.

"The Company is very old and very entrenched. After all, we brought you this country you love. Did you think we'd just go away? Our country has always been under our protection.

We have many members deep within every corner of it. We operate with the same immunity as the CIA, except that very few know we exist. We were created to do that which known governmental agencies could never do without investigation and probably prosecution."

Alex continued the history lesson. "Our system of government is based upon the concept of freedom—more precisely—the preservation of freedom. Up until the United States, no form of government existed to do this one thing—to ensure the endurance of freedom. And not just for the few, but for everyone. Sure, racial, gender, and other forms of equality issues hadn't been figured out yet, but they understood that the richest few could not be trusted with the control and operation of society. Greed would always corrupt—will always corrupt—and will always happen. Democracy, with control wielded by the average citizen, was the only way to remove this inevitability. Unfortunately, in their day, the average citizen meant all landowning white men. But the vision and ideal of power vested in the many, rather than the few, was born. It set the stage for further enlightenment.

"Creating a system of government immune from this corruption was their immediate goal, and it required something different than had ever been done before. It required an innovative approach never seen before, a system that prevented the usurpation of power by the most powerful. We all know absolute power corrupts absolutely, and such power will always seek absolute control. It has never been stopped before. This new approach was aptly called *The Great Experiment*. Never before had control been vested in the heretofore controlled."

The couples sat transfixed. They'd never imagined a body-guard could be so eloquent.

Alex continued, "Experiment? I should say so. Monarchies, oligarchies, and tyrannies are all the world had ever really known before that tiny little moment in history. This group of individuals had an opportunity, albeit blood-bought, to change life on this planet. And they had one fleeting shot that they staked everything on—their ingenuity. If they failed, it meant certain death at the hands of the old guard—with a hardy, 'I told you so'. If they succeeded, it meant nothing less than the beginning of the eventual enlightened evolution and salvation of mankind.

"Please understand that this is our mission and has been our sole reason to exist—to keep this dream alive in the face of relentless evil that only seeks to undue this glimmer of hope. We are everywhere. We'll never stop and will always endeavor to preserve this experiment. The evil's latest incarnation is in the form of faceless gangs of cretins called corporations. These entities allow those who would rule us to remain anonymous, blameless, and completely without accountability. The people who control these entities are ghosts who pass unnoticed through our society in every possible way.

"This is not our first battle with corporate power. In fact, corporate abuse sanctioned by governmental authority was one of the reasons behind the Boston Tea Party. In addition to taxation without representation, you could say that fighting usurpation of power by a company helped bring about the Revolutionary War.

"The East India Trading Company was British-chartered and controlled the trade of most goods in the American colonies, including cotton, silk, salt, and tea. It was *their* tea that was dumped in Boston Harbor by the Sons of Liberty— the company was hated by the merchants and consumers for their monopoly and the abuses they callously inflicted on the colonists.

"The spirit of distrust of companies is older than our government and is ingrained in our organization. United Oil is merely the latest incarnation of the East India Trading Company. We have fought their kind before and will probably do it again in the future."

In conclusion, Alex said, "Their power cannot be directly defeated, because it is based in the existence we have created. Technology means a good life, and its lifeblood is energy. As long as they own the access to energy, they will own the world and destroy freedom. Evil can only beget evil, and so shall it be unless we constantly fight against it.

"An alternative energy source is their Achilles Heel. It would bring them down and restore order to this troubled planet. You have many, many people behind you, and the continued civilization of a race of beings hangs in the balance."

Jane spoke firmly. "Failure means death again for my family and, more importantly, countless years of suffering and death that can be prevented. No," she cried, "it stops here and now!"

"It has to," agreed Sally, "and to that end, here's what I have in mind."

Chapter 16

Completion

Alex and Steve had access to files on just about anyone and everyone, including Sally—especially Sally. Keeping Thomas Cunningham's heirs safe meant that they'd investigated anyone who came near them. Sally's dossier was very interesting. Test scores indicated she was in the 95th percentile or above in *everything*. A born problem solver and leader, Sally rose quickly through the ranks and became a CEO in a company engaged in the highly competitive business of consumer products.

They knew she was more than capable of coming up with an excellent plan. Her resume was replete with victories over some of the largest companies in the world. This was what Sally was born to do, so they avidly listened to her scheme.

Dave interrupted, "Sally, honey, I know your plan involves Tom going to Europe to have the neodymium magnets made, and I want you to know he's not going without me—period, *finÙ*, end of sentence. For all the reasons I shouldn't have to recite, I'm staying with Fatboy. We're a team. We've always been a team."

"Yes, I assumed that you'd go with him. I know you better than *you* know you.

"They are hoping that one or both of you will go overseas to obtain neodymium magnets. Both of you going will make a more enticing target. After all, we can't hide from them and be able to control their actions. Using you as bait gives us a good chance of controlling when and where they'll strike. I'm counting on the Company to keep you safe and provide a few major pieces of the puzzle I've put together.

"The basic premise of the plan is that we have to make them think that Tom and Dave are dead, or they won't stop until they really are," began Sally. "If we succeed, this would buy us time to finish the prototype and then safely make it public. Once it's done, we create a demonstration showing the motor can power a bank of lights without using any fuel or being hooked to any power source. Proof of what it can do, revealed for all to see and examine. Once that happens, we'll be free."

Sally told them she had contacted an attorney in Amsterdam, Holland who could be trusted. "In turn, he has located a research lab that has been set up by a manufacturer of wind turbines attempting to create a better generator. They have been unsuccessfully experimenting with fabricating a stronger magnet, so they are genuinely excited to work with Tom.

"As you know, the Netherlands has used natural movement from their constant sea breezes, captured and harvested by large windmills, to do everything from pumping water to generating electricity. This natural energy source has kept their country mostly free of big oil's clutches.

"Without that crushing and controlling monopoly, the Dutch were able to develop laws that place individual freedom and dignity above capitalism. Corporations are still free to do business, but in ways that make sense for everyone, and not just the few.

"Laws create the fabric on which our society is embroidered. They're the matrix, and if done well, they protect, nurture, and foster freedom, personal pride, and commercial growth. They protect us from the evil that is and flows from never-ending greed. They provide peace and predictability that sustains the soul and nurtures growth.

"Business organizations are created to make money and obtain power. By their very nature, they become greed-driven and must be regulated to prevent abuse of their employees, the environment, and the body politic.

"Dutch corporations pay fair wages and taxes. The government provides incentives for various employee benefits, innovation, and philanthropic endeavors. It imposes disincentives for unfair labor and trade practices.

"Good laws are not easy to draft, and it's even harder to keep them that way. It's an eternal game of cat and mouse with each side always reinventing new creatures. This process has an unfortunate tendency to result in laws born of the best intentions, but ultimately failing miserably in effectiveness and scope.

"Bad laws create unintended results and, often, injustice. They give rise to feelings of suspicion, distrust, and eventually a form of anarchy whereby any government action is viewed negatively. They are the greatest threat to the continued existence of a country. Great care and continual vigilance must be taken that no bad laws be written.

"Control over the government by the governed is the only way that good laws can be created and bad laws avoided. Laws should only be created that benefit *all* of the people—something that those with special interests are incapable of doing.

Their influence must not be allowed. Keeping it that way is the real trick, and not having to bow to an energy monopoly was a big help to the Dutch.

"The Dutch are doing what very few countries have accomplished, even for a brief period of time. They have laws that keep corporations in check while providing an environment for business growth and profit. Dutch companies are some of the oldest and strongest on the planet, yet their influence on their government is zealously prevented.

"The people elected to create and safeguard laws must have only one agenda—the best interest of the country. Once they stray from that, the process is tainted. Political parties, special interest lobbyists, and campaign donors expect influence that would remove the country's best interests from the equation.

"It begins with the election process. All candidates must have equal resources to run for office. This can only be accomplished if the government provides all campaign funding with no outside funds allowed. It's the only way elections can't be bought.

"The Dutch are very proud of their system of government and the body of laws it has enacted. They fiercely guard against any outside influence, so you can rest assured that United Oil will find no friends there. You should be safe there to do what we need to do. I think it's the perfect place!

"You four fly to Amsterdam to make the neodymium magnets. When they're ready, you won't be able to fly back with them, because no airline or air carrier will allow *that* dangerous package onboard. Aside from the magnetic fields' possible effect on the aircraft's sophisticated internal systems, the danger of it attracting another object is too great. Only a ship can safely bring the magnets across the Atlantic—a fact that they know and we can exploit.

"We'll need a small cargo ship to take from Holland to England and a 'leak' of information for this first leg of the journey home. It's important that they know Dave and Tom are on board that ship. It'll leave the Netherlands for Liverpool with you four and a crew of only Company people. In mid-channel, the boiler of the ship will explode and supposedly kill six, including you four. The balance of the crew will be picked up in lifeboats to regale the media with tales of your unfortunate demise. If we do this right, those miscreants at United Oil will think you guys bought the farm by accident."

Sally became increasingly animated. "We'll then have you and the magnets secreted into the country. You can't go through customs, for obvious reasons, so I'm thinking the Company could help us hire experts at such enterprises— like say, drug smugglers, for instance. Again, the magnets cannot travel by air, so once in-country, we will also hire them to arrange transportation home. What do you think, Alex? Can the Company help us acquire a ship to blow up and smugglers?"

"Hell, yes!" he cried. "That's a great plan! We can get help in Amsterdam—a ship to sink, smugglers to smuggle." *I've never written those two items on a list before,* he thought laughingly. He continued, "And end up with the magnets you need to change the world. In the meantime, it takes the focus off Jane and you, which is a wonderful thing. Most important, it'll cause them to back off, giving you a chance to complete your grandfather's work. Outstanding! I'll get right on it."

"Perfect! We can go over some more details later," she said.

Johnson appeared in Forsythe's outer office and quietly asked the receptionist if he could see her boss. Her eyebrows knitted, and she scanned the appointment calendar. "You don't have an appointment," she told him with finality.

"I know, but please tell Mr. Forsythe it's very important."

She turned and knocked on his door. After hearing "Yes," she entered and immediately re-emerged. "Please come in, Mr. Johnson."

"*Now* what?" asked Forsythe, dispensing with all formal greetings. He knew that, once again, it looked like bad news.

"We had another incident today, sir. It seemed a more aggressive action was attempted but, unfortunately, it resulted in some cleanup and no progress. I had to call in a few favors to keep the police out of it.

"We were expecting the brother that's the engineer to need some parts and eventually leave the compound to get them. That finally happened today when he went to a stainless steel distributor south of town. We followed him there, brought in assets, and executed a plan.

"Unfortunately, we underestimated the amount and quality of the protection around him. These guys are professional grade and equipped for anything. We lost one man and the rest are pretty banged up, but we did manage to get them released from police custody. I thought you should know."

"I didn't need to know what you may be doing behind my back, understand?"

"Yessir!"

"Then, take care of it! Good day."

Tom installed the new rods and bearings and reassembled the motor over the weekend. He also began work on the circuitry needed to provide the proper electricity to operate the motor from a generator powered by the motor, thus, forming a "loop." His concern was whether a neodymium magnet would have enough energy, or create enough torque, to operate at least a three kilowatt generator.

He thought, *If it does, it will clearly have enough electricity to operate the motor and a bank of lights.*

Monday arrived and so did the solid-state relays. Tom attached small LED lights to the outputs that would activate the electromagnets. This allowed him to visually confirm that the timing was correct and to fine tune the timing to enhance efficiency, increase torque, and control the motor's rpm. "That's it. I'm ready for the electromagnets," he proclaimed after working through the night.

Alex had made arrangements to have the electromagnets picked up from Ed, and they were set to arrive at the house around eight o'clock Tuesday evening. It seemed to Tom that it took days for those hours to pass. He constantly went back out to the prototype to lube this or tighten that. Finally, there was a knock at the back door.

"They're here!" Alex said jubilantly as Steve and he carried in a large box.

Tom ran over to open the box like it was his birthday. "One, two, three, four ...," he counted out loud, sifting through the package. "All here and ready to go!" He squealed as he took a magnet out and headed for the prototype. He was a man possessed and worked all through Tuesday night as well.

His behavior worried his loved ones.

In the morning, Tom sat at the kitchen table drinking yet another pot of coffee. Its rich aroma filled the room. He had a distant, dreamy look in his eyes.

"Alright? Really, Tom?" asked Jane, sitting down next to him at the table. "Another night without sleep—I'm beginning to see how your grandmother must have felt. You're so obsessed with this ... this *thing* that you're not yourself. You've lost yourself, and that's not healthy. Please, please take care not to go too far," she begged. Her face was sad, and her voice matched it. "You're really starting to freak me out. It's not just the obsession. It's more like a possession. The spirit of your grandfather can't be easily dismissed as the cause of your uncharacteristic behavior. Ever since you started working inside the house ... that's when it began!

"First the dream, then the file, then the prototype—with every discovery, you changed a little more. Now the obses sions and that distant look in your eyes ... you're never *here* anymore, even when you're here. Your mind has you somewhere else and has taken your eyes along for the ride. You need to stay in the moment. Stay with me!" she cried as she searched deep within his eyes. "Don't become your grandfather. Please, don't."

"I won't ... . Thank you, my love." Tom kissed her. "My love for you will always bring me back. You're my center, my ground zero. Nothing will ever change that. Hey, come and see what I've done!"

On their way to the safe room, Jane thought, *Well, that lasted about two seconds!*

He took her hand and led her to the garage.

There it was—completed—the first fully functional, albeit weak, magnetic motor. She did not think much about it yet, but Jane was witnessing history in the making. Tom strode over to the DC generator and pushed the *Start* button. He then went over to the computer control panel and touched a few points on the screen. It started.

At first, the pistons moved slowly, each in tandem going back and forth, turning the crankshaft as if by magic. They appeared to move by themselves, going back and forth completely on their own. Tom increased the speed of the generator, which he'd altered to increase the amps being fed to the motor. It instantly sped up. The faster he ran the generator, the faster the motor ran, in lockstep. Tom stopped increasing the speed when the rpm meter reached 600.

He left it running at that speed, and except for the generator, it made no noise! The motor itself was virtually silent. Tom reached in his pocket, pulled out a nickel, and said, "Check *this* out, Honey," as he balanced the coin on its edge on top of the crankshaft housing. The nickel stood with no sign of falling over. "This motor is *soooo* balanced, and so smooth, that the nickel will stay like that all day long. It's perfect! In fact, as old Colonel Potter would say, 'There aren't enough Os in smooth to describe it,'" he cried with a smile and a little dance she had never seen him do before.

"Nice, Sweetheart, great job. Now come in and let me make you some breakfast. Then, you need to get a little sleep."

"But ... ."

"No buts about it. You've done it—it's completed—now get some rest. I mean it!"

Sally and Dave came in, still in their robes and slippers, asking what all the commotion was about, and then they saw it running like a watch.

Tom said, "Watch this!" He took a two-by-four stud, braced one end of it under the end of the turning crankshaft and lifted the other end until the board was up against the crankshaft. Then, he lifted up on the board.

The board acted like a brake, slowing the crankshaft as Tom applied more force against it. The amount of force obviously being applied made it clear that the prototype, even with weak permanent magnets, had a significant amount of torque. "If the motor will run like this with a neodymium magnet a thousand times stronger, it'll run the WORLD! Off to Europe!" he cried.

"Excellent," said Sally, "I'll tell Alex it's a go."

Dave looked puzzled—still half asleep—and asked Tom, "So, what makes *this* motor better than other electric motors?"

"I don't think you quite understand," said Tom. "It's not even just some important invention. A new and limitless energy source is the invention that our species was tasked to create—or die. Energy is the lifeblood of civilization, and until now every civilization that ever existed on this planet used or uses an exhaustible energy source. All before us have died out.

"This means that the only way our civilization can continue is to discover an energy source that will not run out. All of our technology and all of our efforts to make life better will come to nothing if we deplete our only source of energy. It's happened every time in the past, and it will happen to us if we don't meet the challenge and find it. Well, here it is! It's the most important discovery ever made or that *will ever* be made.

"Unlike electric motors, this invention taps into and harvests energy from a little-understood, fundamental force of the universe—electromagnetism. This force demonstrates energy in all of its manifestations, especially in magnetic fields. But it's the same force that causes subatomic particles and planets to move. It is the "wheel work of the universe," as Tesla called it—the cardinal force that rules and motivates everything.

"It's not known where all of the energy comes from to accomplish these things. We know it takes energy to cause something to move or to cause it to stop moving. Yet, we don't consider that when we sense the force of, say, gravity at work, because we take the existence of this type of electromagnetic energy for granted. We watch it operate on an unseen and, ostensibly, an inexhaustible basis every day.

"Magnetic energy, or more precisely, the energy within magnetic fields, is another exhibition of electromagnetic energy that is unseen and, apparently, inexhaustible. The push and pull that magnets exhibit clearly takes energy to accomplish. Yet, its source remains a mystery. Ask anyone how gravity works, and you're likely to see their eyes glaze over before they begin mumbling a grade-school description of the force. Explaining the force and law of gravity is a tall order, because we don't understand what it is.

"Plainly, no matter where it comes from, electromagnetic energy exists, and Grandpa's invention is the first to harvest it for our use. It is the first to solve the riddle of how to make use of this source of energy.

"The ramifications of this discovery are impossible to over-state. It's the key to the future and our salvation. Limitless, low-cost energy is absolutely necessary for our civilization to continue. That's what this motor provides, and that's what makes it the most important discovery of all time.

"Simply put—for your benefit, Jackass—for the first time in human history, we have discovered an inexhaustible, pol-lution-free energy source that will allow our civilization to endure." Tom felt a strong *deja vu.*

"Cool," said Dave.

After dinner that evening, Alex and Sally met in the li-brary to complete the plan and discuss the details. The coop-eration of the Dutch government was essential, and Alex had the Company working on it. He also arranged a safe house, security vehicles, and personnel. Finally, he wanted to check out the attorney that Sally was contacting. The plan was tak-ing shape, but a dozen details remained.

The two worked tirelessly until the plan was formulated and ready to implement. Alex was amazed at Sally's ingenu-ity and attention to detail. She left nothing to chance and had backup plans just in case something went wrong. She was the consummate battlefield general in all her splendor.

Sally had a long list of tasks that only the Company could accomplish. She saw Alex make all of them happen and was confident.

"Well, Alex, our plan has to work. There won't be any second chances," she told him.

Chapter 17

Creation

Alex, head of *security extraordinaire*, knocked on the back door, and Sally opened it. The two had been working on her "plan" since Friday. "Hi, Alex, come in. What have you found?"

"The attorney in Amsterdam, a Mr. Ringer, checks out. Our Dutch members did a full background check and ... ."

"You have Dutch members?" she interrupted.

"Let's just say they are members living in the Netherlands. We have resources in every relevant country. Anyway, as I was saying, Mr. Ringer has everything set up with the Dutch research facility to make the magnets, and we have everything else ready. It's time. Every moment counts."

"How soon do you leave?"

"Friday. Tom, Dave, Steve, and I will leave Gerald R. Ford International Airport at 7:00 a.m. to catch a flight from Boston to Amsterdam. The Company has created new identities for Tom and Dave. Here are their packets. Each contains a driver's license, passport, credit cards, and normal items found in a wallet, which are embedded with tracking devices. We'll leave here at 6:00 a.m. Just one more thing, Sally. I know how hard this is on your families. And I want you to know how much I've come to admire you folks.

"You obviously don't need the money, and at this point in your lives, you should be enjoying retirement. You could've decided to put the file back in the floor and savor your lives. Instead, you all chose to try and help everyone else and to face down this evil head on. I want you to know that you four have earned the admiration of ... the Company, and we pledge to do everything we can to help you see it through." At this, Alex placed his hand on his heart and solemnly stated, "You have my oath. I will guard them with my life!"

His inflection was so sincerely genuine that Sally's eyes welled up with tears. She gave him a big hug. "If we play our cards just right, it won't come to that, Alex."

Tom woke and came down to the kitchen. "Hello, Alex. What have you two been conspiring about?"

Sally smiled and said, "Keeping your hides in one piece, that's what!"

"How's the prototype coming along, Tom?" asked Alex.

"Come see the future!" cried Tom, leading both of them into the safe room. "There it is—the answer the world has been seeking since the dawn of time—a sustainable and clean power source. Electromagnetic energy will be harvested by this and similar devices from now on, ushering us into a new age, the EM Age.

"I believe this motor is the key to unlocking potential discoveries in all fields of science. Imagine what we can do with unlimited and virtually free energy! Ancillary to scientific endeavors, we can do all the things that the price of energy made cost-prohibitive. Just think—desalinization plants and indoor farms could provide ample fresh water and nutritious foods for everyone regardless of location."

Tom explained how the device would generate electricity and its life-sustaining benefits, including water, light, heat, and refrigeration, available anywhere and everywhere on Earth. Every isolated location on the globe where people live and struggle to obtain life's necessities because they do not have electricity could now be transformed. No location would be too remote! He envisioned colonization of the ocean floors, and even the moon.

"Removing the high cost of transportation will have a drastic effect on the world economy. Think of all the jobs that'll be created. Workers will be needed to build these devices and to change appliances, vehicles, heaters, *everything* that uses fossil fuel as its power source over to electrical. Further, everything already electrical but using AC will be changed to DC. I can even envision a day when burning fossil fuels will be illegal!

"The environmental remediation that can now be done may be the greatest benefit of all, especially in the long run. The pursuit and use of fossil fuel energy has devastated the air, soil, and water. Using that same energy to attempt to clean our poisoned environment could never be the answer. Now, here, we have clean energy to power the filtration of the air and water. Free, clean, limitless energy makes all of these things—and much, much more—possible."

Sally agreed, and with a somewhat ethereal point of view said, "All of these advancements will result in the most magnificent achievement ever accomplished by our civilization: the end of the suffering caused by poverty.

"Limitless, free energy, and all of the life-sustaining effects that will flow from it, will provide housing, food, water, and medical care to all human beings. No one will be homeless, hungry, thirsty, or without medical care ever again! Can you even imagine that?

"Instead of focusing on just surviving, the entire human race can turn its attention to improving ourselves and our condition. The human spirit in all of us demands no less. We strive always to make things better for tomorrow than they are today, because it nurtures and satisfies the soul—not to mention, it's the right thing to do.

"Once freed of the rigors of daily survival, we can and will make the Earth a paradise. Unleashing the synergism of billions of people will catapult our civilization to places we cannot as yet conceive."

With all of that said, Tom fired up the motor and demonstrated it for them. It ran flawlessly. Alex was astounded by its balance and power.

"It's sadly lacking in torque due to the weak permanent magnets in the pistons," Tom divulged. "Frankly, I was surprised at how much power it has with Grandpa's old magnets. I can't wait to see what it can do with neodymium magnets!"

"Toward that end," replied Alex, "we leave for the Netherlands on Friday, and a company there is waiting to help you build them, Tom."

"Excellent." A wave of sadness washed over Tom when he realized that meant he'd be apart from Jane. But it had to be. He thought, *I have to swallow this hurt. It simply has to be done.*

The time between then and Friday morning was precious and brief for the brothers and their wives, especially Tom and Jane. Sally and Dave both had careers as busy executives and were used to often being apart. But not so with Jane and Tom. They'd met early in life, had always worked at the same school, and were inseparable. They thrived on being together, and this time apart would be torture for them.

Everyone knows, either consciously or somewhere deep inside, that there are different kinds of love. They're not different in type, like the love for a daughter versus the love for a spouse. Rather, they are different in depth and character. Love for a spouse can take an infinite number of shapes, but if it is true love, it is beautiful—regardless of what form it takes.

Like chocolate, be it inexpensive or made by the finest chocolatier, it is enjoyed. No one can judge one form to be over another, but some types of love are undeniably special—a type of love where two souls join for eternity. Make no mistake about it. Eternal love is rare. Few are willing to pledge their souls to each other. Jane and Tom shared this eternal love. Their devotion for each other was complete and infinite. All love is good, but some types of love are transcendental.

Tom believed that Jane was a God-sent angel. When she sang, it made him cry, because he thought he could hear the voice of the Lord in her perfectly resonating notes. They lived for and within each other. They shared a wonderful life, because it was filled with unconditional love—pure and abiding. Jane and Tom were lucky. And they knew it.

Thursday night, their last night together for awhile, was solemn and special. Tom lit lavender scented candles in their bedroom as he usually did on important occasions, like anniversaries and birthdays. Unbeknownst to Jane, he had a dozen yellow roses delivered. He arranged them in a vase on her night stand. She entered the bedroom and promptly wept softly. "Damn it, Tommy. I promised myself I wouldn't cry until you were gone. I'm sorry. I'm a real mood-buster," she said and then laughed through the tears. Jane called him *Tommy* only in the boudoir and always with wonderful results.

"Shhh, shhh. It's alright now." He wiped Jane's cheeks and softly kissed her. She responded immediately by ardently returning his kiss. Parting her lips, she fervently searched his waiting mouth with her tongue. They made love frantically, passionately, as if it was the first time. In the afterglow, Tom stroked her hair, lifted her chin from his chest, and with extra wide eyes said, "Wow, Honey. Maybe I should leave more often!"

"Maybe ... but that was nothing compared to when you get back," Jane purred. They stretched languorously and then spooned for the night's sleep. When they were first together they had slept in a small, double bed, adapting the spooning technique, as much to give them room in the tiny bed as it was to continue intimacy. Now, they did the same thing, even though they had plenty of space in the California king.

The alarm clock on Tom's cell went off at five o'clock that Friday morning. Tom awoke as the lone spoon in the drawer. Jane, as she often did, had gotten up before the dreadful cell buzz tone. He woke up and smelled the coffee, noticing a freshly brewed cup at his bedside. Carrying the mug down to the kitchen, he gave Jane a bear hug and loving kiss. "Good morning, my sweetheart."

Just then, Dave and Sally walked in holding hands, interrupting their quiet morning reverie. "Hey," they passed around to each other sleepily. Jane prepared an all-American breakfast of eggs-over-easy, bacon, hash browns, toast ... and more coffee. When they finished, Alex and Steve arrived.

"Any coffee left, Jane?" they asked in unison.

"For the two of you? Always." She poured each man a mug.

"Thanks again, Jane. Your coffee is the best," Steve praised and raised his cup toward her. Addressing the brothers, he said, "Everything is all set. You can call each other using these new phones. The other ones are still secure, but these are better for international calls. They can only call each other, plus Alex's and mine. Use the other phones for all other calls. Did you review your new identity?"

"Yes," answered Dave, "but aren't they going to simply follow us to the airport?"

"Nawww, we have a little *dog and pony show* for that! But it's true, the fake IDs aren't intended to keep them off our trail for long." Steve looked at his watch and said, "Check this out!" At that moment, the black suburban pulled out of the garage with escort cars on either side. As soon as *they* left, the linen service truck drove up to the garage.

"Time to go," ordered Alex. "We'll meet you in the linen van."

Tom turned to Jane. She lunged toward him and squeezed him as hard as she could. After a long, long kiss—the kind in a romance novel—he grabbed her shoulders and looked deep into her eyes. "I love you so much, my beautiful wife. We will get through this. Don't worry, I will see you soon!"

"I'll try not to. I love you *soooo* much. Be safe, my love."

The brothers hopped into the van and, just like that, they were gone. They drove downtown, and the driver pulled into the linen company's warehouse. All of them got out and emerged on the opposite side of the building in an enclosed parking lot. A van and two nondescript sedans were waiting for them. The four men got into the van and drove out onto a back street where anyone following them would be cut off.

"Looks like we're clear," the driver said to Alex.

"Cool. Let's get to the airport." Before long, they cleared security and boarded the plane. "Looks like our departure went unnoticed ... for now, anyway," Alex said.

They landed at Boston's Logan International. During their brief time there, they were joined by more Company men, while Alex and Steve briefly disappeared, leaving the brothers in the VIP lounge. Soon, Alex and Steve returned, and the troop boarded the flight. Altogether, they took up three rows of the side section that had four seats to a row. Dave and Tom sat in the middle row, with Steve and Alex on either side. At half past eleven, the direct flight left Logan and landed around 1:30 p.m. in the Netherlands at *Luchthaven Schiphol*, the largest airport in Amsterdam and one of the largest in Europe. Holland was six hours ahead of the eastern U.S.

"*Goededag,* ladies and gentlemen. *Welkom in Amsterdam*," announced their pilot.

They quickly cleared Customs, and within minutes, Alex and Steve whisked the brothers into vehicles and took them across town to the safe house. As bodyguards, the safety of Tom was assigned to Alex, and Steve was assigned to Dave. Neither were ever more than a few feet away from their charges.

"When do we see the facility?" Tom asked impatiently. He missed Jane already.

"How about now?" replied Alex. "It's across the street." He pointed out the car's front window to an old, but dignified, two-story building. The safe house was also two stories, divided into four apartments. Tom and Dave occupied one upstairs apartment, while Alex and Steve were in the other. Both downstairs apartments were stuffed with the Company's best security teams. It was a brick fortress with enough fire-power to stay an army.

The buildings were in an older part of the city that was slowly being converted from light industrial to residential. Young professionals were looking for reasonably priced apartments close to their downtown offices. Developers, seeing this trend, were buying the smaller, less successful businesses and converting the buildings into apartments.

Due to this influx of young professionals, technology companies and industry needing highly educated employees began to open shop there. The area was soon on its way to becoming Amsterdam's Silicon Valley. The research facility opened two years prior, and three of the four apartments of the safe house were occupied by technicians working there. They were all put up at the hotel of their choosing for the month or so that the Company would need their apartments, plus a per diem amount. They were quite pleased.

While it was an older part of the very old city, it was remodeled, modern, and as was the Dutch way, extremely clean. The roads and sidewalks were all redesigned to include the ubiquitous bicycle paths common in European cities and everywhere in Holland.

The four walked across the narrow street toward the building's front door. The brothers were amazed at how clean everything was, especially the air. The sky was bright blue—not the gunmetal gray they were used to in a city. The air smelled fresh and sweet, with a slight floral hint. Flowers grew in abundance everywhere.

They entered the building and were immediately greeted by a sharply dressed young man. He spoke surprisingly fluent

English. "Welcome to the Netherlands. It's an honor to meet you. Dr. Hoffmyer is anxious to see you. Please, if you will, right this way, gentlemen."

Along the way, Tom noticed a fully equipped lab adjacent to a complete machine shop. "This place looks *perfect*, Dave," said Tom as they walked through the facility.

They came to a group of offices and entered the last one. A middle-aged man rose from his desk and said something in Dutch. He fumbled around for the words, and finally said in English, "Forgive me. I am excited to know ... if we can help each other build strong neodymium magnet. I attended school in the west and am fairly proficient in your language, but was long time ago. Duz file you pozzezz contain your research? Sorry, I am Frederik Hoffmyer." He extended his hand.

"A pleasure to meet you, sir. Yes, well ... it's research our grandfather had," answered Tom as they exchanged a handshake.

"Your grandfather's! Iz zat zo? May I zee it, please?"

"Sure." He handed Dr. Hoffmyer the file. The scientist returned to his desk and thumbed through the information.

"Ja, ja ... hm ... yez, good! Fantastisch!" cried Dr. Hoffmyer as he looked up at Tom. "Your grootvader; I mean your opa? I mean grandfather? How old *iz* dis research?"

"It was done nearly one hundred years ago and has been hidden until now."

"That iz incredible, but you have come to right place. We should be able to build what we both need with thiz information. We believe we will build more productive generator with magnet." His English was quickly improving with use.

"You certainly can! And that's a perfect compliment to our motor."

Tom and Dr. Hoffmyer felt an instant bond, a scientific brotherhood created by their mutual quest to build that which had been suppressed for so long—too long. They shared the yearning to undo the wrongs perpetrated by fellow scientists.

Dr. Hoffmyer had garnered a reputation for thinking outside of the box, of coloring outside of the lines; in other words—he liked to go scientifically rouge. He explained to Tom that they were confident that they could create a more efficient generator if they had much stronger permanent magnets in it. Despite the naysayers, they recently began experimenting with different compounds using a variety of elements, but had little success. They suspected neodymium might have promise, but the published research showed it had no magnetic properties, and the extraction process was ineffective and could produce only an ore with a relatively low percentage of the element. Now they knew that was all one big lie.

United Oil's research showed that they produced a magnet that could pick up and hold a piece of steel many thousands of times the weight of the magnet itself. It also had all of the information as to how they extracted neodymium from ore and how they created the magnet by combining iron and boron.

"I believe we can do what they did, but better because of modern technology, particularly regarding purification of the element to close to ninety percent or better. They used double nitrate crystallization where we will use ion exchange."

Over the next few days, Tom and Frederik worked on purifying the neodymium, and they were very successful at achieving nearly ninety-nine percent purity. Next came the proper mix of iron and boron to create a compound resulting in the strongest possible magnet. Tom thought of his dream where his grandfather said how important this step is. Fortunately, United Oil's scientists did a great deal of testing in this area that saved much time.

Trial and error showed they could make the magnet only one inch thick, but that they could add three one-inch thick wafers together and triple the strength. This was perfect for the motor, because the pistons were designed to hold three-inch thick, round magnets. Making two of them would require that they make six of the one-inch wafers that for safety reasons would not be put together until they were ready to be mounted in the motor.

Tom and Frederik worked very well together and enjoyed making that which no one else had made—to their knowledge. After testing various compounds, their creation was complete. They found the right mixture and made the world's strongest permanent magnet. The neodymium magnet they produced was so strong that it was lethal. If a person got between it and steel, they would die, because there would be no way to pull it off of them and no way to stop it as it crushed its way to the attracting metal. The room they worked in had to be completely free of any metals that could become missiles if caught in a magnetic field.

The alloy proved to be brittle—like ceramic. They found this out the hard way when two small test pieces got loose and attracted each other. The resulting collision sent glasslike shards in every direction and two technicians to the hospital. If the full-sized wafers did that, no one nearby would survive!

They had to proceed very carefully and make sure that the wafers never got within ten feet of each other or anything metal. Shielded in one-inch thick aluminum, separated by stainless steel plates in a wooden box lined with stainless steel and filled with sawdust was the only way to transport them safely. Sally's plan would not work very well if the magnets killed them before they got home.

The next step was to manufacture the wafers for the prototype. Then, and only then, could the brothers and their group set Sally's plan in motion.

Just a few more days, thought Tom.

Work on the wafers went quickly and without incident. They did find it difficult to store the wafers far enough away from each other to feel safe. This tended to speed up the manufacturing of the other wafers, so the day they would all be removed would be sooner.

The prior incident with the small magnets really scared them, and they had not had any time to design safeguards and equipment to safely handle the wafers. Everyone at the facility was looking forward to the Americans taking away the magnets.

Chapter 18

Culmination

Tom and Dave had not been outside, except for brief walks between buildings, since they had arrived in Amsterdam. Oddly, it felt normal for them to stay indoors. On most days back home, it was too foul to venture out. Now that the neodymium magnet was designed and being built, they had some downtime and were anxious to explore the ancient and majestic city.

"We assume *they* realized at least a few days ago that you two are no longer stateside," mused Alex. "Consequently, they've been searching high and low for you guys. Our sources tell us they're sniffing around here. It's hard to not leave a footprint doing what we're doing. If they haven't found us by now, they will soon. The risk of leaving this secured area is too great. I'm sorry, but I aim to keep my promise to your wives."

"Understood," Dave replied glumly.

Tom nodded in agreement. "And thank you. Let's get those wafers built and get on with the rest of the plan."

That evening, after they had turned in, Alex and Steve burst into the apartment with guns drawn. In a hushed voice, Steve said, "It's time to get dressed, gentlemen. I think we have our answer about whether they've found us or not. Two men from downstairs dressed in battle gear and carrying assault rifles took up positions at the windows."

"Apparently, a breaking and entering was just attempted at the factory across the street. It seems they want to know what you guys are doing there," said Alex.

"Given the importance of this joint research effort, coupled with the fact that this type of research has been actively suppressed, the owner agreed that we place a couple of guards on the premises at night. They detected and subdued the would-be burglars, but we don't know if they have any other plans. We're investigating them as we speak. Once we're done, we'll call the police."

Sirens were soon heard, and the police arrived to take custody of the two men. While checking to be sure that the neighborhood was secure, Dave saw Alex speaking with what looked to be a high ranking police official. They shook hands, and Alex returned to the apartment. "The two men were hired to break in and were told what to look for—evidence of a neodymium magnet," Alex said. "They don't know who hired them, because it was all cash and strangers. But, clearly, we've been found. It's time to go. When will the magnets be ready?"

"It should take one more day to finish," said Tom. "Dave and I can make the aluminum containers for transporting them. We'll purchase a wooden box that must be lined with stainless steel to load them in."

Steve offered, "We can take care of that. Just tell me what size you need." Looking at Alex, he said, "I'm thinking maybe we should leave day after tomorrow, during midday. That would give us plenty of time to have our accident at sea happen that evening after dark so curious eyes and satellites won't reveal our ruse."

"That sounds good. I'll get everything ready to go. We leave Wednesday at high noon," said Alex.

Monday evening, Johnson waited for Mr. Forsythe to look up from the file he was reading. "Now what?" Forsythe asked with his head still bent.

"We found them in Amsterdam manufacturing neodymium magnets."

At this, Forsythe looked up at him. "Are you shitting me? It doesn't sound like you're making any progress, Mr. Johnson. What the hell?"

"They're well guarded and in a country where we have little influence. However, we found out that they'll be taking a small freighter to England, so I hope to have some good news for you soon."

Johnson immediately called a meeting of his lieutenants to discuss his plan. "I've learned they'll be leaving their safe house for Rotterdam on Wednesday. They intend to board a small freighter bound for Liverpool where they'll transfer to a trans-Atlantic ship.

"They finished the neodymium magnets and are headed back with them, gentlemen. They must NOT make it off the continent! We must strike when they leave the safe house.

"They have a lot of men with them, so we have to have more. I want at least a dozen men in two vans armed with RPGs and armor piercing bullets. At a predetermined location, the vans will intercept their vehicle, blow it apart with the grenades, and shoot the hell out of anything still moving.

"You will then briefly search for the magnets with a *gauss* meter and destroy anything you find. A nearby private airfield will have a plane waiting to get all of you out of there. Get what you need and get going—NOW!"

With the help of the facility's talented machinists, Tom and Dave prepared six, small, round sarcophagi, 3¼-inch by 1¼-inch each, made of one-inch thick aluminum to hold each of the neodymium magnet wafers. These in turn were loaded into the lined wooden box that was then packed with sawdust. The magnets were ready to go, and so were the brothers.

That evening dragged on relentlessly in anticipation of the next day's events. Dave kept peering out the window at the city they never got to see. "Someday ... I hope to visit this fair land when I can walk down the street and go where I please," he sighed. "It feels like that day is a long, long way off."

"One day at a time, O' Brother, one day at a time. Dreaming of the finish line only makes you feel overwhelmed." Tom patted Dave's shoulder and said to him, "In times like these, I always think about one of Dad's little riddles: *How do you eat an elephant? ... One bite at a time!*"

"Oh, but of course, it's always about food with you, isn't it? I don't know if you're the one to school me on patience, but your point is well taken. We have a number of things to accomplish and must fully focus on the task at hand. It's time for us to die, or at least look like we did."

On Wednesday at noon, the convoy headed southwest toward Rotterdam where the ship the Company purchased was berthed. The next step in Sally's plan was for them to sail to a predetermined point, disembark, and blow the boiler—sinking the ship. On that particular day, there was cloud cover in just the right area, and the weather was perfect for their plan.

Before long they boarded the boat that was moored in a very modern harbor on the New Waterway, a canal built to connect the Maas, or Meuse, River, one of the oldest navigated rivers in the world, to the North Sea. Rotterdam was a busy port, and it had been for over one thousand years. The group was surprised by the port's modernity and cleanliness. They headed to the galley while their luggage was stored in their staterooms.

Suddenly, Alex sat bolt upright, listened for a moment, and then spoke into his sleeve. "Roger that." To the group he said, "It seems we were being followed by some vans. The Dutch police detected them shadowing us and intercepted them with overwhelming force. And it's a good thing they did, because they detained a dozen heavily armed men. It was the Dutch counter terrorism unit, the *Unit Interventie Mariniers*, and they're very good at this sort of operation. The bad guys never stood a chance, and we won't be hearing from them any time soon."

Dave was incredulous. "Shit, shit, and shit ... that was close. How'd the Dutch police know what was going down?"

"Remember, boys, we have connections and friends everywhere," Alex replied confidently. "Sally and I figured they'd try to stop us as soon as we tried to leave for home with the magnets. We wanted to be sure they knew you boarded this vessel, and now we know that they know. Now, let's see if we can pull off the next phase. We're nearing culmination."

The ship they boarded was relatively small, a pre-WWII

cargo ship designed for freight delivery across the channel. Tom thought, *It has definitely seen better days, and that makes it perfect!*

They left the pier, headed down the New Waterway, or Nieuwe Waterweg, and out to the North Sea.

Fortune smiled upon them—the weather forecast called for cloudy skies and calm seas. Once it was dark and they were at the correct coordinates, the ship slowed to a stop and they were joined by a large, fast cigar boat that pulled up to a cargo net attached and deployed over the side of the ship. The four were joined by two Company men as they scrambled over the side and down the net to the waiting boat. The precious cargo—the magnet box—was lowered to them, and they pulled away.

As the cigar boat headed southwest, the remaining crew lowered a lifeboat over the side. Once they were all off the ship, they pulled away about two hundred yards and stopped.

The captain reached in his jacket and pulled out what looked like a small cell phone. He flipped back the lid and pushed the button inside. *Kaboom!!!!!* The boilers exploded in a massive conflagration.

The ensuing fireball in the night was enormous. Burning debris lit up the seas around the dying hulk. Fire on what was left of her wooden decks provided light that allowed the crew to watch her final moments.

It was a well-built vessel, and even with her starboard side blown off, she gallantly stayed afloat for a good ten minutes. Finally, she rolled over and disappeared below the dark sea, extinguishing her fires as she left. The captain then activated the distress signal and called for help. The British coast guard picked them up within an hour.

The entourage was taken down into the hull of the cigar boat where there were seats they could strap into if the going got rough. As soon as they were seated, the big engines throttled up. The boat violently sprung from the water and sped away. After an hour or so, it slowed to cruising speed. They noticed that the seas were more bumpy and assumed they were even further away from any coastline. After another hour passed, they slowed to a stop. The group filed their way to the upper deck.

It was dark out ... really dark—the kind of dark only those who have sailed far from shore have experienced, so black that the senses reel, searching for some point of focus. But low and behold, there it was! A faint green light to the rear appeared on their starboard side. Barely detectable at first, the light grew bigger and clearer. Suddenly, a searchlight flashed on and off in their direction. It was their rendezvous ship coming to a stop about a hundred yards away. The cigar boat slowly maneuvered to a door that swung inward to accept the weary passengers.

A light was turned on above the door and revealed the ship to be beautifully appointed—a sleek, shiny yacht. Its elegance was shocking.

"I didn't know anyone lived like this!" cried Tom as they were shown to their staterooms. "Hey, Jackass, I'll sleep like a baby now!"

"If by that you mean you'll wake up every two hours—hungry and crying—jeez, let's hope not, Fat Boy."

The yacht came about and headed for the east coast and the Port of Miami on Dodge Island, Florida. They'd reach port in approximately five days, having traveled nearly four thousand nautical miles.

While *en route* to Miami, they watched the media coverage of the ship's boiler explosion on satellite television. The BBC reported that six people were killed when a vintage vessel exploded and sank while traveling from the Netherlands to Liverpool. The report said there were a total of four American passengers and six crew members, including the captain, and that all four Americans and two crew members were instantly killed by the blast.

They watched an interview with the captain, who explained that after about five hours at sea, the boilers exploded, tearing off the starboard side of the ship and the cabins above the boiler room. The ship immediately listed and began to sink. The first mate and he were uninjured by the explosion and were able to search for other survivors.

The captain described how they found two dazed but uninjured crew members amidships, and they told him the remaining two crew members were with the Americans. They then searched the area of the ship near staterooms. He summoned up convincing tears and said, "It was clear there could be no survivors on that part of the ship. It began listing badly, so we got onto the lifeboat and abandoned ship. Immediately afterwards, it rolled over and sank. We searched around the floating debris hoping to find survivors, but found none. I'm afraid we lost six souls tonight, all four Americans and two Dutch seamen."

Dave said, "Well, that's the end of us! But because we were using fake IDs, we still live! Technically, we never left home. How strange!"

"That's right!" said Alex. "And at this moment, your wives are pretending to grieve without grieving publicly. How's that for strange? We want the bad guys to think the women are mourning and lamenting your passing, but they can't grieve publicly because the *rest* of the world still thinks you're alive. If the ladies pull this off, I'm predicting Academy and Emmy nominations!"

"What's next?" asked Dave.

"We get smuggled into the country, just like a load of Grade-A pot," answered Alex. "Remember, we're all dead, or at least our trip-assumed identities are. So, we can't use those documents any more. We certainly can't use our real names, so we can't go through regular Customs and neither can that box of magic magnets. We have to get into the country completely unnoticed.

"As you may guess, there are people in the business of avoiding the hassles of Customs. And as you also might guess, these are not very nice folks. They live completely outside the law—they're ruthless. They'll do anything you want, as long as you pay them enough money and convince them that they can't outrun retribution if their loyalty should falter."

"Bloody murderers," muttered Steve, "but it's the only way. We have to be extra careful!"

"It sounds a little funky," said Tom, "but I'm ready. How about you, Jackass?" he said sarcastically to Dave.

"Born that way, Bro. Long before you, by the way, Fat Boy ... Punk!"

Johnson was meeting with his lieutenants about the botched attack that ended in the arrest of their men in Holland. "What the hell do I tell him *this* time?" he cried to them. "He'll have my balls hanging from his desk when I leave!"

Just then, Johnson's secretary burst into the room and said, "You have a call from Liverpool." He picked up the receiver.

"Yes. Yes ... it what? Are you sure? What about ... ? How can we be sure? This sounds like bullshit. See what you can find out—now!" Johnson slammed the receiver back down in its cradle. "It seems the ship they left the Netherlands on exploded mid channel, allegedly killing the brothers and sinking, presumably, taking the magnets with it.

"Great news if it's real, but I smell a rat. Like the kind that leaves a sinking ship. They want us to *think* they're dead. It's too convenient! Start digging and looking for where they'd smuggle themselves into the country.

"Hit every piece of crap in the smuggling business you can. *Someone* must know *something, somewhere.* Florida seems likely. Don't stop until you find out!"

"Also, Mr. Forsythe wants to see you as soon as possible," his secretary added.

Johnson immediately reported to his boss's office to explain what had happened. Both men agreed that the supposed demise of the Craft brothers had to be confirmed.

The remaining days at sea seemed endless. They were longing for home and missed their wives terribly. Tom spent most of his time pouring over the designs of the various prototype parts to see if he could make any improvements. Dave worked tirelessly on the patent language with the help of his son on his secured phone line. Keeping themselves busy was the best way to make the time go by as quickly as possible.

The opulence of the yacht also helped, but they could

not help but wish that Jane and Sally were with them, especially when they were farther south and enjoying the tropical weather. But they also knew that the most dangerous part of Sally's plan was yet to unfold—and they took great comfort in knowing their wives were safe and sound at home. Soon, they were only about twenty-four hours from port.

Johnson's men also kept busy in a nonstop combing of the smuggling underworld looking for any information about whether the Craft brothers actually did perish at sea. They worked their way down the Florida coast as instructed by Johnson, but found nothing—until they hit Miami. Johnson knew that whoever was helping the brothers was top shelf, so he had his men focus on the high rent district of town.

Johnson's clandestine wing of the security department had low contacts in high places, and in many low places, just in case they might need such assistance. After going through most of them without finding anything, they finally got a hit. At a small, ritzy local bar on the south side of town, they talked to a guy who knew of a guy who might know something about a yacht circumventing Customs this week. Cash has a way of getting attention, and they were flinging it all over town.

The first guy called the second guy, and after awhile, he showed up. After a scotch and a couple of Benjamins, he told them that a big-time yacht was due in tomorrow night with four extremely wealthy men avoiding Customs and toting an unusual cargo. For two more Benjies, he would give them the name and address of the guy who worked on the piers and told him this little saga. "Tell him that 'Frankie' sent you."

Their lead took them to a dingy, bug-infested motel that rented rooms to those who wanted to remain unseen. They were directed to talk to a man known only as *Raymond in Room Number Twelve*. They got there as quickly as they could and knocked on the door with the number twelve poorly painted on it. The door swung open, a foul smell escaped the room, and a greasy yellow-haired, short guy stood before them with a .45 in his hand.

"Who the fuck are you?" he asked in a low but demanding tone.

"We were told you may have some information on some guys we're looking for. We were sent here by Frankie, and we'll pay two grand for solid information."

"Well, you look like cops to me, and I don't talk to cops, so fuck off and die." He then started to shut the door, but before he could, and in the blink of an eye, Johnson's men disarmed him and were on top of him. They were United Oil's henchmen, both with special forces backgrounds, very well-trained, and armed to the teeth. These guys were not about to fuck off, and little Raymond never stood a chance.

"Listen up good, you little asshole. If you want to live another moment you <u>will</u> tell us what you know. It's your choice. The two large can be in your pocket, or you can be in a landfill. What's it going to be?"

"Wait! Don't shoot. If Frankie sent you, then you can't be cops. What guys are you looking for?"

"There are four men who were supposedly killed in a boiler explosion at sea recently. We think they're still alive and that they're planning on entering the country without being noticed by Customs. They're arriving on a big, private yacht tomorrow night. Does any of this ring a bell in that nasty little head of yours?"

"As a matter of fact, yeah, it does," he squealed. "Let me up, and I'll tell you what I know."

"Of course you will, and if you lie to us, you'll wish we'd killed you now."

"I heard of a gig a couple of days ago where four men with, apparently, unlimited cash wanted to avoid Customs and have a guarded ride to Michigan. Does that sound like them?"

"Go on. We're all ears."

"They wanted a way into the country, a van with two armed guards, and an escort car with four more armed guards for the trip north. Unfortunately for me, they already had all the men they needed by the time I asked."

"That helps, but we need to know when and where they will be arriving here."

"All I know is that they'll be arriving here at an exclusive pier on Dodge Island sometime after dark tomorrow night."

"We need to know when! We need somebody there who won't spook them, but who can tell us when they arrive and what vehicle they're in."

"I know the guard working the gate there tomorrow night."

"I will give you another two grand for him, photos of the four men, and a phone number where he can call me, and you set it all up. Have him call me when they leave and tell me if it's our guys and what vehicle they're riding in. Got it?"

Raymond nodded.

"Okay. Here's the deal. We are going to trust you, but if anything fucks up, so will you. If you pull this off, we may have some very lucrative work for you in the future. If any-thing goes wrong, you won't have a future. We'll be parked outside the gate tomorrow night and will expect that call."

Raymond watched them get into the back of a big Cadillac and drive off. He was shaking and sweating, but he had four grand in his pocket for doing almost nothing. He thought, *I'm not sure if it's a good day or a bad day, but I'm sure it'll turn into a bad day if I don't get this right.*" He immediately contacted his friend, the guard, to set it all up, telling him he could earn a thousand dollars for information the next night.

Johnson got an update from his men and went to Forsythe's office to fill him in. "A boiler explosion—I thought it was too good to be true," he said to Forsythe.

"You've done a great job finding them. I'll leave the rest of it to your imagination, but don't screw this up. And clean up that mess you left in Holland!"

Johnson and his lieutenants immediately assembled to dis-cuss what had to be done. "I don't want any margin for error this time. I want confirmation as to which vehicle they're in, and I then want to blow them straight to hell. There should be nothing left but a smoking hole in the ground."

United Oil's vast connections and influence gave them some excellent options to plan the destruction of the vehicle. They quickly put their plans in place.

Tom and Dave arrived as planned, and the yacht eased into a restricted area reserved for wealthy, transoceanic arrivals. The combination of very light security, and a less-than-vigi-lant probing around by Customs, made it easy for the smug-glers to bribe their way onto the mainland from here and into the country's interior, with *whatever* was profitable.

A van drove up to the security gate. The guard let it in. The vehicle continued along a drive that went past the over-sized slips where the ships were moored, until it stopped in front of the yacht. "Time to go," said Alex as they calmly walked to the van and got in.

It was a large van, but was still a tight fit for six people—and a lot of guns. As they left the pier, the guard stopped the van and looked at each occupant. He then let them leave and without delay, called Johnson's men to describe the vehicle that the four men were in and its plate number. The van and the escort car headed north on the expressway.

Later that evening, when the van was north of Cincinnati where the Ohioan farm fields stretch for miles, an odd light shown on the horizon. A flash appeared from either side of the light, and the escort car drove away at high speed.

Two rockets slammed into the van—instantly shredding it and killing everyone inside. The occupants never stood a chance!

United Oil's political contacts had gotten the county sher-iff's department to block the northbound lane at an off-ramp just south of where the van was attacked. They created a de-tour that took the traffic back to the expressway a bit north of the van's location or at least what was left of it. They did the same for the southbound traffic.

A semi-trailer arrived on the scene and unloaded a fork-lift that put the pieces of the van into the trailer. The entire area was combed for parts of the ill-fated van and its occupants, which were also loaded into the trailer. In less than an hour, the wreckage was gone. A road repair crew then appeared, and before dawn they had the highway repaired and open for traffic.

Their examination of the wreckage revealed six badly mutilated corpses and a melted pile of aluminum with strong magnetic fields present in the cracks. Johnson knew that the brothers would have never parted with their precious magnets, so two of the bodies had to be theirs. Without DNA or dental information on the brothers, positive identification was not possible.

Chapter 19

Collaboration

Jane and Sally rarely left the house over the next month. They hung big, black wreaths on each gate. While the Company continued to watch over them, there were effectively no signs that United Oil was interested in the sisters-in-law.

"A job well done, Johnson," said Mr. Forsythe. "I don't think we'll be hearing from *that* family any longer. The Dutch facility that manufactured the magnets has been bought and summarily dismantled. It seems we've put this fire out—again—but who knows for how long?"

"Thank you, sir. What can I say? We got lucky after all. The ship blowing up was a nice try, but a little *too* convenient. Your hunch about them using a drug smuggling operation to sneak them into the country was spot on. We let the word out that information on when and where was worth big money.

"Eventually, we found out where and approximately when they were arriving at port. We then bribed the guard into observing what vehicle they were in and calling us when they left. We tailed them to Ohio where air surveillance took over using an attack helicopter that we borrowed from a nearby National Guard base.

"Using some of the local law enforcement, we were able to close off a predetermined location to attack and quickly clean up the vehicle. It was set up at night, and the public and everyone but our men could be kept far enough away. The plan came together.

"We already had confirmation that they'd gotten into the van in Miami, so the decision was made to take out the van in such a way that there could be no survivors.

"It was blown apart and pieces of six badly charred bodies were found among the debris. Identifying all of the bodies will be impossible, but we did find traces of neodymium in a melted pile of aluminum. That, coupled with the fact that they've not returned home and can't be located, leads me to the conclusion that they're dead."

"Well, then, that's *that*, at least for now. Your service will never be forgotten by me, Johnson, but this conversation never happened, right?"

"Yessir!"

Sally answered the knock at the back door. It was their driver, Ron. "We're ready when you are, madams."

Ron and Terry were the counterparts to Alex and Steve when it came to guarding Jane and Sally. The men went everywhere with them and coordinated the safety of the women. While Alex and Steve might outrank them, they could hardly be considered the second tier of security.

Like their comrades, Ron and Terry were descended from the Founding Fathers, and their training took a special path. Special forces training in the military was really only the beginning.

Advanced training in judo, tae kwon do, and boxing made them quite deadly in hand-to-hand combat.

To be on a security detail for the Company required world-class shooting skills in speed as well as accuracy. To pass the skills portion of the firearms training, an agent must draw his weapon and shoot a quarter. The difficult part is that the coin is suspended ten feet above the ground and thirty feet away. The agent cannot draw his gun until the quarter begins to fall, and the coin must be solidly shot before it hits the ground.

Finally, all members or agents must hold at least a bachelor's degree with a *juris doctor* or other advanced degree preferred. Simply being a descendant is not enough to be a member of this Company.

"Thank you, Ron. I'll go get Jane." The sisters-in-law got into the suburban and were driven to the airport. Naturally, Ron and Terry accompanied them on their flight, and after nine hours in the air, they landed in Amsterdam, Holland. The ladies were briskly VIP'd through the Customs Administration, or the *Douane*, and led to a waiting limousine parked in a restricted area.

Sally and Jane were ushered out a door that opened into a small parking garage. A stretch limousine with two escort cars awaited them. Ron opened the limousine door, and the women quickly settled into the back seat. In the facing seat sat Dave and Tom! Behind them, Alex and Steve were in the front seats.

This is quite the reunion, thought Alex. "Hello, ladies! So good to see you again," said Alex with a grin from ear to ear.

The two couples locked in a seemingly never-ending embrace. Clearly, their hugs and kisses would not be over soon. The vehicles exited the airport and were immediately joined by police escort. The foursome was driven to the presidential suite at the Waldorf Astoria Amsterdam, a hotel known for its classic luxury. Hotel security was world-class, especially with the Dutch *politie* on the job!

Once in the room, Tom brought Jane and Sally up to speed on the culmination of the rest of Sally's plan.

"The reach that the Company has into the underworld is deep and somewhat disconcerting. We knew everything that they knew, particularly that the pier guard was to tell them which vehicle we'd be in. Knowing that, we were able to use a huge, busy rest area in Georgia to switch with the four guys in the escort car without being seen.

"We paid them all two grand apiece to deliver the box of magnets to the house address while we followed in the escort vehicle. We told them we thought the change was for our safety and told them not to tell anyone about it until after the magnets were delivered in Michigan.

"At the next gas stop, we switched with four Company men who took over the escort car, again without being seen. We then drove to the nearest international airport where the Company had new ID packets for us and tickets *back* to Amsterdam.

"We knew at some point they'd attack the van—we just didn't know where or how, and that was nerve-racking. I was never so glad to get out of a vehicle!" Tom cried. "Our hope was that they'd destroy the van in such a way that identification of the bodies would be impossible. We knew that they'd find at least remnants of the neodymium magnets and that they'd assume Dave and I would never part with them."

"It all worked. They blew up the van, found traces of

the neodymium magnets, and took for granted that we were dead. That bought us enough time to return to Amsterdam and finish the prototype. Congratulations, Sally! Your plan played like a symphony orchestra. They bought it hook, line, and sinker!

"The final part of your plan—completion and publication of the prototype, including proving it's a new power source—also came together nicely. Using new passports and drivers' licenses, we flew back to Amsterdam to a different safe house and manufacturing facility that was already fabricating the parts for the prototype.

"The collaboration of the Dutch government, once convinced of what we could do, was astounding. They were helpful in finding us a secure safe house and facility. More important, they cherry-picked the best electrical and mechanical engineers from various research institutions. Talent in every relevant discipline was gathered into an all-star team. The team worked virtually around-the-clock and finished the prototype motor way ahead of schedule.

"Then came the hard part—creating the loop. The motor had to run itself first, and then we could see how much power was left over. The Dutch company developed a more powerful generator using neodymium magnets, so it was a perfect match. Circuitry had to be developed that would feed the correct amount of electricity to run the motor at the desired rpm or speed. That was a bit tricky, and took some doing, but we did it.

"Because the motor provides the power to run itself, we needed a way to start it, to get the loop going. One of our older engineers walked over, turned the switches on, grabbed the flywheel, and gave it an old-fashioned spin. The motor instantly came to life. 'Just like the old days,' he said, and with that we were done. Then, the Dutch Ministry of Science tested and verified that it is, in fact, a new energy source."

Tom was suddenly overcome with emotion. "An incredible team of individuals not blinded by science—willing to accept the 'unacceptable'—to dream the impossible, the forbidden, or the unknown. The day we flipped that switch and the generator hooked to the motor began running the motor ... well, that was the day the Earth stood still—it just didn't know it.

"Witnessing that moment—watching the motor do what the established scientific community said couldn't be done— was worth it all! The entire hundred year journey culminated in that one special moment. It works, and the rest is history— or it will be!

"The new Dutch generator puts out five thousand watts, and the motor can turn it at its optimal rpm while using only two thousand watts. That allows us to run a blinding amount of lights, indefinitely, or at least until the bulbs burn out." Tom paused to check his watch and said, "Holy moly, it's time. Do we have a demonstration for you!"

He sauntered over to the coffee table and clicked on the nearby television. "Hey, hey, hey, it's showtime, kiddies. We just told them to 'light it up,'" Tom announced to the room. "And I don't mean the type of lighting up one might do while in Amsterdam!" Everyone laughed at that. The television screen focused on a shiny, aluminum rectangle that was con- nected to a generator that was, in turn, hooked to a control panel and a very large bank of lights—like the kind you would see on a movie set.

The engineer manning the control panel flipped a switch and gave a flywheel a spin. The lights flickered, shone brightly, and then continued to do so. The demonstration was set up in the Amsterdam Science Park so that all could observe the lights and even inspect them if they chose. No noise came from it, except for the muffled *whirrrrrr* of moving machine parts.

The engineer announced to the growing crowd, "No power cord of any kind is connected to the motor, because it's a new power source—one that will never run out, emits no pollution, and comes from an easy-to-make magnetic motor."

News agency outlets across the globe instantly picked up on the story. Tom did his strange little dance again and cried, "Yahoo!!! We did it!!! Grandpa, we did it!!!"

Both couples busted moves when they heard that. Alex and Steve joined them, although, clearly, they could not cut a rug like the brothers and their wives. Dave reached for the bottle of *Perrier-Jouet* champagne, cooled to perfection in its bucket. *Pop!* The cork hit the television screen. They all doubled over with laughter.

"Grab a glass and line up. I have a toast. First, and foremost, here's to Grandpa Thomas. He gave up everything a man could ever want to try and make this day happen. So, this is for you, Grandpa, *and* Grandma Joanna, too. Congratulations!" cried Dave.

They clinked glasses and drank to the toast, "*Salud! Zazdarovje!*"

"Second, here's to our two saviors, Alex and Steve, and their wonderful Company. You've kept your sacred oaths and made your ancestors proud. Cheers! Here, here!"

Again, they clinked glasses and drank heartily.

After a refill all around, Dave continued, "And, finally, and most important, here's to humanity, here's to hope and rebirth, and here's to the future!" With that, he downed the delicious French libation and threw his glass into the fireplace.

Everyone else followed suit.

"Damn, I always wanted to do that! Hell, I've been *waiting* to do that," he laughed. "Let's get hammered and watch the world awaken to a brand new day. Man, I wish I could see the look on those pricks' faces at United Oil!"

"You go right ahead, Bro. That is the second thing I've been waiting to do. Right now, I've got other plans in mind," Tom said dreamily to Jane as he grabbed her hands and pulled her to her feet.

She giggled and said, "See you all in the morning."

Sally slipped her arms around Dave. "Hmm, on second thought, I can wait to see those looks. Yawn, yawn, stretch, stretch—I believe it's bed time."

Sally walked up to Alex, shook his hand, and said, "That was fun. But you know, we're not quite done yet."

"Indeed, yes, I look forward to seeing what you have planned for them next. We can show ourselves out. See all of you in the morning."

Love reunited is a beautiful thing. The reunion of long-separated soul mates causes angels to weep.

Jane whispered in Tom's ear, "Promise me that you'll never leave my side again."

"Never." Slowly, Tom slid his hands over her buttocks. Jane naturally thrust her pelvis into his. "I sure have missed this," he murmured sheepishly.

"I can tell!" Jane moaned, and they fell to the bed.

Early the next morning, the sun shone on Tom's face, awakening him. He stirred, reached out his hand, and *she was there*. Smiling, he briefly fell back to sleep.

Chapter 20

Conclusion

Johnson shuffled into Forsythe's office, concerned with the fate of his testicles. "Have a seat, Mike." It was the first time Forsythe had called him by his given name. Johnson desperately tried to explain.

"We did all we could, sir. They had world-class help, and … ."

"I don't want to know what you have been up to," Forsythe interrupted. "Neither United Oil nor I authorized you to do anything! We consider this matter concluded."

At that moment, Johnson understood why Forsythe was being so nice to him. *I'm their fall guy,* he thought. *These sons-of-bitches set me up from the day I was given the Watchdog file!*

"We know we can count on you to clean up your own messes while we figure out a way to survive what has happened. A lot depends on all of us doing our part to get through this crisis. You agree, don't you?" Forsythe glared at Johnson.

"Yes, yes, of course, sir," Johnson choked out of the back of his throat.

The look Forsythe gave him sent a shiver down his spine like he hadn't felt since childhood. Absolute power is not easily relinquished, and being around when it's happening could be fatal. Johnson, a modern-day mercenary, saw a glimpse of such power under siege, and he nearly wet himself. He knew he must do whatever they told him to do to stay alive, and if that meant going to jail—so be it.

News of the "Wonder of Amsterdam," as some were calling it, was spreading across the globe. Scientists from every corner were on their way to the Netherlands to see for themselves. Many were calling it a hoax and saying that it violated every known principle of physics.

Sally had anticipated that United Oil would use its considerable clout with research facilities and universities to disparage the motor and ridicule the presenters. She had asked for the Company's help getting the Dutch government to certify the test results of the motor. Later in the morning, the Dutch prime minister, on behalf of the Crown, and the chief scientists of the Netherlands Scientific Council held a press conference announcing that the ministry had participated in the testing of the invention and certified that it does generate more electricity than it uses to operate itself.

"In other words," the prime minister said, "this device is a new source of power generation that will change the world."

"That is our first salvo in our next battle, which will be their campaign to discredit, and then control, the motor," said Sally, but added grimly, "Now for *their* asses. I had our lawyers back in the states prepare lawsuits against United Oil; its board of directors; its president, Mr. Forsythe; and their head of security, Mr. Johnson. Also, the Company's friends in the FBI should be raiding the oil company's offices right about now. It seems they had an informant in the drug smuggling ring that tried to cash in on that reward. All in all, I think some of these guys will have their hands full for awhile, say forty to life."

"That takes care of some of the bad guys," said Alex, "but what about the motor? How does it get put into production, and what about a patent, Sally?"

She looked confidently at him. "All taken care of. We reached an agreement with the Dutch company that put the new prototype together. Our son created a company called the 'Cunningham Motor Company' that just filed patent applications in every industrialized country. We kept fifty-one percent of the new company, and in return for the other forty-nine percent, the Dutch company will license the patent to every relevant industry."

Sally was on a roll! "They'll also design and build research and manufacturing facilities to create generators and vehicles powered by the motor. They'll do all the work, and all we need to do is let them do it.

"In addition to electricity production and transportation, our company will be leading the way in researching and implementing environmental remediation and desalinization techniques. The possibilities are endless!

"The jobs that will be created by this technology are boundless. In addition to building millions, even billions, of electric generator units and vehicle drive trains, the world will convert to DC electricity.

"The simple truth is that we use AC because it can travel over many miles of electric wire without losing much of its energy. Conversely, DC loses energy quickly as it travels down wires to its destination. However, AC is deadly while DC generally is not.

"Thomas Edison pioneered DC electricity and created the first electric grid in New York City. It serviced a number of residences, including the Carnegie's and Vanderbilt's. While it was relatively safe from injury and fire, the infrastructure proved too expensive. Power substations had to be constructed in many places along its circuit, and this greatly increased the cost of the service.

"Nicola Tesla generated AC power from Niagara Falls and sent it on wires all the way to Buffalo, New York, to light the World's Fair. It was the death knell of DC power grids. AC could be generated at large power stations and sent wherever wires could stretch.

"A grid was created to send AC to every corner of our country. That infrastructure is now old and vulnerable. We've seen the catastrophic results when it fails. Being able to generate sufficient power on site is a complete game changer. It not only gets rid of the grid, it makes DC feasible for the first time ever.

"It won't happen overnight, but eventually every home, every building, will have its own DC generator providing power for all of its needs. That means that everything that uses AC will have to be remade into DC. That translates into millions of jobs for years to come.

"Last, but only marginally least, we should now be relatively safe! At least from those nasties at United Oil! The whole world knows about the motor, the patent applications have been filed, and a government-backed Dutch company is hell-bent on getting it manufactured in all of its many incarnations. Killing us now would have no effect whatsoever on any of what I've just mentioned. It cannot be stopped now. We are free!" cried Sally.

Alex whooped it up, and they all joined in, shouting, "Hip, hip, hooray; hip, hip, hooray; hip, hip, hooray!" in a form and cadence that paid homage to the Founders. It was most appropriate. "While it'll take a long time to scour their influence out of our government, *their* source of power is gone forever, and so, too, will they eventually be! Like our Founding Fathers, we will have ousted the tyrants and will have an opportunity to start anew," said Alex. "Their removal will create a power vacuum that we can fill with democracy and justice. The Grand Experiment goes on, and we must now try to ensure that power will never be wrestled away from the people again. "The Founders' use of the word 'experiment' conveys a sense of imperfection that often results when attempting the untried. This type of government was new, and they assumed that the framework creating it might prove to be wanting from time to time. After all, evil never sleeps and will constantly and forever try to undermine good in all its forms, including a just and appropriate government—one that protects, enhances, and preserves life and freedom for all people will always be under attack.

"Surely, this requires that the framework for such a government be flexible, so that it can prevent a subsequent occurrence of a nearly mortal attack. This is why the Founders encouraged amendments to the Constitution, as exemplified by our first ten, the Bill of Rights. We have an opportunity, a relatively small window of time, in which we can try to add constitutional protections against oligarchies and concentrations of power like corporations that would seek control. You have provided the means to make life better. Now, all of us must provide the framework to make that happen!"

Alex sat down, feeling a bit amazed and embarrassed by his unrehearsed diatribe. Tom began to clap his hands and slowly, the others joined in.

Sally stood and said, "There! Now *that's* the type of leadership we need in government. We need to talk about you running for office some day!"

They spent the remainder of that afternoon regaling each other with stories from each other's perspectives regarding the deployment of the plan.

Later, Jane and Tom enjoyed a romantic five-star meal in the spacious dining room. Fine dining had always been so much more than simply eating to them. The locale, the ambiance, the presentation, the intimacy of succor—eating was not just about sustenance to Jane and Tom— it was an experience to be savored, and not just with tastebuds.

Tom took her hand and said, "I'm so sorry for how I've been since finding that file. It's like I've been a man possessed by my grandfather's quest, or maybe by my grandfather *himself*. I felt like I was simply along for the ride. But now it's gone."

"It's alright, honey. It's alright."

"I knew you'd say that, my love. I had another dream last night—much like the one I had when this all began—ultra real, in HD, and startling! Grandpa Thomas walked up to the prototype running in the park, looked at the motor, and then looked up at me and smiled. Then, he turned, took Grandma Joanna by the hand, and disappeared into the crowd. I woke up feeling like myself again, and my overwhelming love for you was my very first thought. I'm back, and I'll never leave again."

They looked deeply into each other's eyes until the server brought a chocolate soufflé garnished with fresh raspberries, the specialty dessert of the house. At least that's what they *thought* he told them—his accent was very heavy. It certainly tasted like it was!

After they enjoyed its chocolatey goodness, Tom said, "There's something I've been waiting to do." Jane and he walked out the front door of the hotel and strolled down the sidewalk. "We're free to walk out in public, free to do what we want and, most important of all, free to rekindle our love for the rest of our lives!"

As they were walking down the sidewalk, a kid sauntered by with a boom box playing the beginning of a song that they simply could not believe they were hearing. They handed the kid a twenty and said, "Turn it up," which he gladly did.

Tom then took his wife by the arms and began dancing to Steely Dan's *Change of the Guard*. They twirled and boogied out into the street where passing cars yielded to their celebration. The conservative Dutch, being forced to stop their vehicles, protested at first, but succumbed to the beautiful spectacle of pure joy and love being exhibited in their presence. The protests were quickly replaced by cheers and applause for the love shining before them. Alex smiled and went back into the hotel.

Jane and Tom were free and together again—forever—dancing in the street.

The world began to celebrate a new day.

Chapter 21

2100

"One hundred years after Jane and Tom danced in the streets of Amsterdam, the world was renewed. Balance and purity were restored to the environment. The air, water, and soil were cleansed. Pollution was relegated to the history books—never to return," said Grandpa Andrew to the gathering of grandchildren and great-grandchildren.

"Limitless, free, and clean energy made every part of the globe habitable. Desalinization plants pumped potable water anywhere it was needed, making the deserts bloom. Large food plants were constructed in cold climates where floor after floor produced fresh fruits and vegetables year round.

"The motor was only the beginning of the advanced use of electromagnetic energy. It sparked research into its multitude of uses that included force fields as they used to be called. The invisible and impenetrable walls resulted in climate control, so that hurricanes, tornadoes, and all types of dangerous storms became a thing of the past. The same technology was also applied to eliminate earthquakes with the stabilization of the tectonic plates.

"Most impressive, from a purely scientific perspective, was the ability to neutralize gravity. This unleashed transportation, construction, and scientific innovations in compounds and alloys that were not possible except in a zero gravity lab. Additionally, ocean and space habitats were built that resulted in previously unknown elements being discovered and utilized to better the human condition."

"What happened to Tom and Jane after the motor was demonstrated in Amsterdam?" asked little Thomas. He was ten years old and exceptionally inquisitive.

"United Oil Company used its power to try and stop the new technology, and its power at that time was almost absolute," answered Grandpa Andrew. "It controlled the world's energy production and distribution. It owned almost all of the large companies that were involved in food production, construction, technology, and communications. It placed its people in governmental positions everywhere it could and, thereby, controlled the world's political machinery.

"All of United Oil's power came from, and was at that time still dependent upon, their monopoly over energy. Losing that meant the end of United Oil's grip upon the world, so it fought back with everything it had and in every way possible."

"How long did that work?"

"Not long, and it did get pretty nasty, but that is the subject of another story. Your ancestors and some very powerful allies, as we know, persevered. Scientists and engineers poured over the prototypes and the designs that were posted on what they then called the internet. Eventually, the scientific community had no choice but to admit it worked in order to avoid being a part of the backlash that arose from a ground swell of public consternation aimed at United Oil.

"Once it was revealed that they suppressed EM technology for a century, they were sued out of existence, and most of its principals were jailed. It was the first time corporate henchmen and those who controlled them were held criminally liable for corporate actions.

"This set a precedent that had nearly as great an effect as the motor itself. While it took awhile for the Supreme Court to dissolve the immunity corporations had enjoyed and abused for so long, public opinion demanded it.

"Justices, used to being above public pressure, were investigated and found to be bought and paid for by various big corporations. When a few judges were sent to jail, the power structure that buoyed corporations for decades crumbled like a stale cookie. Democracy slowly returned to the world and ignited a social and scientific revolution.

"The motor eventually brought these gangs of thugs to their knees, and the laws regarding corporations were dramatically changed. No longer could the ultrarich commit atrocities and be allowed to hide behind their corporate structures. Their ill-gotten gains were confiscated and used to rebuild the world's infrastructure, thus creating millions of jobs and lifting people out of poverty. This had a dramatic effect.

"Once the corporations and their iron grip were removed, everybody had a fair chance to succeed as opposed to only the well-connected few. This unleashed the hidden and suppressed talent that created the world you know today. The best and brightest in every area were allowed access to education and jobs again, as opposed to only the power holder's relatives.

"A society cannot advance if its most talented people are not allowed to participate and contribute. Once everybody had an opportunity to reach their potential, the world dramatically changed and advanced. Technology, medicine, social science, and the arts flourished like never before. Not exhausting our resources on energy and the greedy few resulted in the return of human dignity and justice. It was another Renaissance.

"While the motor solved all of our energy needs and related problems, its most enduring effect was its creation of a whole new mind-set for the human race. Essentially, the mantra of 'everybody for themselves' was replaced with 'all for one and one for all.' I believe that this made God smile upon us, and grace was returned. Advancements at that point were exponential.

"Cancer, heart disease, and viral and bacterial maladies were eradicated. These medical advancements in turn unleashed even more resources that bettered the human condition. The suffering that was endured for thousands of years has been swept from the planet.

"It may be hard for us to understand now how the greed of less than one percent was allowed to cause untold suffering for most of the remaining world's population, but that is what greed and power can do. Striking a balance between being rewarded for one's efforts and contributing to the betterment of all was not an easy task. But it was done, and the changes since then are immeasurable.

"No one goes hungry—no one goes without shelter from the elements. Equal opportunity and justice for all has resulted in the virtual elimination of crime. Wars ended because there was nothing left to fight over once the world shared in all of the benefits unleashed by these scientific and social changes. We live in paradise now—filled with goodwill and beauty, and it all began with solving the world's energy needs.

"You can be very proud of the fact that your predecessors played a part in bringing about the catalyst that caused all this to happen. Thomas Cunningham's sacrifice and the hard work of those who came after him changed the world, and they will never be forgotten."

THE END

CPSIA information can be obtained
at www.ICGtesting.com
Printed in the USA
FFOW04n0228230815
16249FF